Quin's gaze c̶ lips, and he was surprised by the flare of heat

The temptation to kiss her was so strong, it took all his willpower to resist. "There's a whole lot more to life—and cards—than luck. It takes skill to come out a winner. And sometimes the hand of fate."

Cassie felt the pull of his gaze and ran a tongue over lips that had gone dry. Sweet heaven, what would she do if he kissed her? The rush of heat left her trembling. But though she wanted to bolt, she stood her ground. "And do you always win, Mr. McAllister?"

"Not always, ma'am." With an effort, he opened his fingers, allowing the strands of hair to drift to her shoulder. Very deliberately, he lowered his hand to his side. "But I go into every game with the intention of winning...."

Dear Reader,

With nearly a dozen Harlequin Historical novels under her belt, Ruth Langan has proven time and time again to be one of our most popular authors. Described by *Romantic Times* as "a talented author who never disappoints," this mother of five has captured the hearts of our readers with stories that range from Texas to the Scottish Highlands. *Angel* is the story of a tumbleweed gambler who becomes the unlikely savior of a widow and her children one cold Montana Christmas.

Also this month, Harlequin Historicals is very pleased to present *Fire and Sword*, Theresa Michaels's first medieval romance, a classic tale of desire and revenge. Maura Seger has written the next book in her Belle Haven Saga, *The Tempting of Julia,* the story of a self-proclaimed spinster and the rogue who wins her heart. And, from Nina Beaumont, *Tapestry of Fate* is a passionate story set against the backdrop of a dangerous world.

We hope you'll keep a lookout for all four titles wherever Harlequin Historical books are sold.

Sincerely,

Tracy Farrell
Senior Editor

Please address questions and book requests to:
Harlequin Reader Service
U.S.: 3010 Walden Ave., P.O. Box 1325, Buffalo, NY 14269
Canadian: P.O. Box 609, Fort Erie, Ont. L2A 5X3

RUTH LANGAN

Angel

Harlequin Books

TORONTO • NEW YORK • LONDON
AMSTERDAM • PARIS • SYDNEY • HAMBURG
STOCKHOLM • ATHENS • TOKYO • MILAN
MADRID • WARSAW • BUDAPEST • AUCKLAND

ISBN 0-373-28845-X

ANGEL

Copyright © 1994 by Ruth Ryan Langan.

RUTH LANGAN

traces her ancestry to Scotland and Ireland. It is no surprise, then, that she feels a kinship with the characters in her historical novels.

Married to her childhood sweetheart, she has raised five children and lives in Michigan, the state where she was born and raised.

For my father, Jack Ryan, who is with the angels.
And watching out for us still.
And for Tom, lover, protector. My guardian angel.

Prologue

Ohio, 1864

The prison camp was little more than a shed surrounded by a makeshift fence. Union soldiers patrolled the perimeter. Inside, the captured Confederate soldiers shivered in the frigid night air. Even bone-chilling wind couldn't blow away the stench of rotting flesh mingled with the fetid odors of human waste. The darkness was punctuated with moans and the occasional whimper from a boy who had lost both legs.

A doctor came from a nearby town once a week, but could do little more than dispense a meager supply of painkilling powders. He would move among the prisoners, shaking his head, his eyes sad and haunted by what he was forced to witness. Then he would hurry away in his rig, eager to return to home and hearth, grateful to escape this glimpse of hell.

The door opened on a rush of freezing air, setting up a chorus of savage oaths, then was hurriedly shut. In the darkness, one moved among them, the glint of a coiled whip in his hand. Though they could not see his face, they knew him as the cruel, sadistic jailer who enjoyed tormenting them by inflicting random violence.

He paused, his head turning from side to side, feral eyes penetrating the darkness until he located his latest victim.

"You. Preacher." The whisper scraped across nerves already taut with terror.

The prisoner, who'd earned his name because he was stoic in defeat and urged his fellow prisoners to pray for deliverance, struggled to his feet, determined to face his assailant like a Southern gentleman. Weakened by his injuries and lack of food, he stumbled and nearly fell before he managed to regain his footing.

With an evil laugh the jailer uncoiled the whip. "Now we'll see if your prayers can save you, Reb."

As his arm swung in a wide arc, the cruel laughter suddenly died in his throat. He stiffened, then fell face-down, sending those in his path scurrying aside. Amid the stunned silence, a figure stepped from the shadows, bent over the dead man and pulled a small, gold-handled knife from his back.

"It's Gambler."

The whispers went up among the prisoners, along with an audible sigh of relief. No one else among them would have had the courage to do what this rogue did. They would not question how he came by the knife. Probably taken from a guard during a game of poker, which was how he'd earned his nickname. It was Gambler who secured food and blankets for his fellow prisoners. And Gambler who sometimes came up with whiskey to ease the pain and cold. No one would question his method of obtaining a forbidden weapon. It was enough to know that their tormentor was dead. Even the Union soldiers outside would offer little more than a cursory investigation, since the jailer was universally hated.

"Bastard," the gambler whispered as he stepped over the dead man and tucked the knife into his boot. Straightening, he caught his fellow prisoner before he could fall to his knees.

"Gambler, my name is Ethan Montgomery," the man said between shuddering breaths. "Tell me your real name."

"Quin McAllister."

"I am in your debt, Quin McAllister. And someday I shall repay you."

"You owe me nothing, Ethan Montgomery. In this place, we are all our brothers' keepers."

"Brother." Ethan offered a corner of his ragged blanket, and Quin sat beside him, sharing the warmth of his body. "My home is in Atlanta."

"As is mine."

"Would you like to hear about my family?"

Quin heard the warmth that crept into Ethan's voice. It was the only warmth he'd experienced in this hellish imprisonment. "If you'd like." He closed his eyes, his senses sharp to the sound of booted feet outside the encampment. "If it would help you pass the night."

"It is all that keeps me alive, my friend. The thought of my lovely wife, and the images of my beautiful daughters."

In the months that followed, these two very different men, the preacher and the gambler, formed a deep bond. And while the fabric of a nation was shredded by bloody civil war, they came to know each other better than brothers.

Chapter One

Montana Territory, 1867

"Cassie." The woman's voice was a high-pitched shriek of alarm as she raced across the open space that separated the house from the barn. Snowflakes swirled in on an icy gust of wind when she pushed open the barn door. "Looks like trouble coming. There's a rider heading this way." She had to stop and catch her breath before she added, "Don't recognize the horse. Better fetch your rifle, girl."

The young woman looked up from mucking the stall. The pitchfork dropped from her hands. Struggling into an oversized buckskin jacket, she picked up the rifle that stood beside the door. "Get back to the house, Ma." She turned to the startled girls who'd been helping her. "Jennifer. Rebecca. Go inside with your Gram. Ma, you'd better keep a rifle aimed through that crack in the door."

She waited until the others were safely inside the cabin before turning to watch the approach of the horse and rider across the northern slope. The horse, coal black against white snow, moved effortlessly through the knee-high drifts. The rider, who appeared to be dressed all in white, seemed to float like some sort of ethereal creature through the blinding snowflakes. When he drew closer Cassie realized that it wasn't his clothes that were white. The man's wide-brimmed hat was frosted with snow. A long cowhide duster was equally caked with snow and ice, giving him the appearance of a ghostly apparition.

He didn't speak until he drew alongside her.

Touching a hand to the brim of his hat, he drawled, "Ma'am. I'm looking for Ethan Montgomery."

In one glance she took in the expensive saddle and bridle, the shiny black boots hooked into silver stirrups. Whoever this stranger was, he didn't belong in this part of the wilderness. A handsome devil like this would look more at home in a glittery saloon, dealing cards and charming fancy painted ladies. "He isn't here."

"Have you heard of him?"

Her eyes narrowed. "Could be."

Seeing her rifle aimed at his heart, he kept his hands where she could see them. No sense spooking her. Especially since he'd spotted another rifle just inside the cabin. Montana homesteaders left nothing to chance. If he made any sudden moves, he'd be caught in the crossfire.

"Am I close to his place?"

"You're on it."

Surprise showed on his face before he quickly composed his features. Of course. In the few words she'd spoken, he'd detected the soft Georgia drawl. And beneath the hood of her jacket he could see wisps of fiery curls. But he would have never confused this tough wilderness creature with the gentle Atlanta beauty he had heard so much about. "Then you must be Cassie—Mrs. Montgomery."

"I am. Who are you, sir?"

"Ethan's friend. Ethan wrote and asked me to join him in Montana. Name's Quin McAllister."

"Quin..." He saw her look of astonishment. Lowering the rifle, she blinked against the swirling snowflakes. "Forgive me, Mr. McAllister. I don't usually welcome my husband's old friends in such a manner. You must be frozen. Please come inside and warm yourself."

He slid from the saddle and led his horse toward the cabin. The door opened and a middle-aged woman in a faded, shapeless gown stood just inside, still aiming her rifle at him.

"It's all right, Ma. This man is a friend."

The woman lowered her rifle and stepped aside. Just beyond her, Quin spotted two girls huddled together. The older one was trembling so violently even her red hair seemed to be shaking. The younger one, perhaps four or five, grasped her older sister's hand in both of hers. Despite her young age, she showed no fear, only avid interest in this stranger.

"You must be Jen and Becky," Quin said. "Becky, your daddy says you have a voice like an angel and sing in the church choir." He shook the snow from his hat before entering the cabin. "And look at you now. Why, you're practically a young lady. And Jen," he called to the younger one, "the last I heard of you, you were no bigger than a peanut."

"How'd you know all that?" The little girl's eyes opened wide, taking in the snow-covered figure, the white duster. Her mouth dropped open. "Are you one of Pa's angels?"

Her grandmother pointed her finger at the children's mother. "I warned you about such nonsense. Next the child will expect a heavenly host to help her with her chores."

Quin saw the flash of fire in the young woman's eyes before she turned away and made a great show of removing her parka and smoothing down her skirts. "This gentleman is Quin McAllister. Mr. McAllister, this is my mother, Luella Chalmers."

Quin knew how to pour on the charm. It came as easily to him as the richness of honey that softened his words. "I'm happy to meet you, ma'am."

The look she shot him let him know that she did not share his sentiments.

"You already know my children, Rebecca and Jennifer," Cassie added.

Quin smiled at the older girl and winked at the little one.

Jen looked crestfallen. "You aren't our guardian angel?"

"Sorry, Jen. I've been called a lot of things in my life, but never an angel. In fact, there are those who might say I'm more of a dev—"

"Rebecca and Jennifer," Cassie interrupted quickly, "you heard your father speak warmly of Mr. McAllister on many occasions. Isn't it nice that he came all this way to visit?"

"Actually," Quin said, crossing to the fire to warm himself, "I came here at the request of your husband, ma'am. He wrote about a big strike at his mine, and hoped I'd give him a hand with the operation."

He saw the looks exchanged between the older woman and her daughter before Cassie cleared her throat. "That was . . . is . . . my husband's dream, Mr.

McAllister. And perhaps, if all had gone well this past summer, he would have needed your services. But nature did not cooperate. We suffered through a drought and lost much of our crop. On top of that, Ethan wasn't able to work the mine as much as he'd hoped. So far, it has yielded nothing of value. He must have written that letter a long time ago, when things were looking hopeful."

Except for a slight narrowing of his eyes, Quin gave away none of his feelings. Whatever frustration he was experiencing was carefully banked. "I move around a lot. I suppose it took a long time for Ethan's letter to reach me." He glanced around the snug cabin. "Where is Ethan, ma'am?"

"He . . ." Cassie licked her lips and studied a puddle of water that was growing beneath his boots. "My husband is up on the high range with the herd."

"In this storm?"

"It came on suddenly. Now, I fear, he shall have to spend several weeks, or perhaps months, up there before he can return." She glanced up and met his puzzled look. "Ethan will be so sorry to learn that he's missed you, Mr. McAllister."

He felt his hackles rise. Her politely spoken words couldn't mask the fact that she was dismissing him. Without regard to the fact that he'd just traveled a thousand miles across primitive land. Dismissing him. As easily as if he'd just dropped by to say hello on his way through this god-awful wilderness. He wasn't going to let her off so easily. "I could ride up and find Ethan. Maybe give him a hand with that herd."

"No." She spoke the word a little too quickly and saw the way the others were watching her. "I mean, there's no sense in going out in this storm again, Mr. Mc-

Allister. Besides, you wouldn't get very far before you'd have to turn back. The drifts up in those hills will be higher than your horse's head." She set the rifle beside the door. "You'll stay to supper, Mr. McAllister, and spend the night before you go?"

Before you go. She was leaving nothing to chance. He was being told in no uncertain terms that he would be given food and a bed before being sent packing.

Quin nodded. "Thank you, ma'am. I'd like that. But first I need to see to my horse."

"I'll go with you." Jen began shrugging into her parka, but her mother put a hand on her shoulder to stop her.

"No, Jennifer." Her words, spoken softly, were commanding. "You and Rebecca can go over your sums before supper."

"But—"

"Mr. McAllister can find his way to the barn and back." She turned to Quin. "There's a rope that runs from the cabin to the barn, in case the snow gets too thick to find your way."

Jamming his hat onto his head, Quin let himself out of the cabin and led his horse to the barn. Inside he found an empty stall and removed the saddle and bridle, tossing them over a rail. Spotting the pitchfork that Cassie had dropped in her haste, he scattered hay and hauled a bucket of water from a nearby trough.

That done, he removed a bottle of whiskey from his saddlebag and uncorked it. Lifting it to his lips, he took a long pull and felt the warmth snake through his veins. Leaning against the stall, he stared around, taking in a wagon, a cow, a couple of aged horses, a cat curled up in the straw, and less than a dozen chickens already asleep on perches. Not exactly the prosperous farm he'd been expecting.

"What in hell is wrong here, Cutter?"

The horse, responding to the deep voice, lifted its head.

Quin took another pull on the bottle, deep in thought. "Why is Ethan's wife so eager to get rid of us, old boy? Not that I'm complaining, mind you. I can't think of a better place to be rid of than Montana Territory in the dead of winter. Especially on a hardscrabble farm like this. I'll be more than happy to make my way to San Francisco and find an interesting game, an elegant hotel and a beautiful woman to warm my bed."

The horse lowered its head and began to munch hay.

"Go ahead and eat," Quin said with a low chuckle. "I've got to go back inside that cabin and face down those icy looks from Ethan's wife and mother-in-law." He took a final swig and corked the bottle. As he stowed it in his saddlebag, he grinned. "Ah, well. We'll only have to put up with this until morning. Then we'll be on our way."

He ran a hand along the horse's flank, then closed the stall and made his way to the barn door. As he stepped outside he was assaulted by the full force of the storm. The snow was so thick that even the cabin, a mere hundred yards away, couldn't be seen. He found the rope attached to the barn door and he let it slide through his hand, guiding his way back.

When he opened the door to the cabin, the voices abruptly ceased. Though they appeared to have been having a vigorous discussion, they were now strangely silent. No one was willing to meet his eyes.

He leaned his weight against the door and forced it shut, then secured it against the howling wind.

Cassie, her face flushed, indicated a row of nails beside the door. "You can hang your hat and coat there, Mr. McAllister, and wash up." She pointed to a basin and pitcher of water. "Supper's ready."

"Thank you, ma'am."

He rolled his sleeves and washed, then ran his fingers through hair dampened by snowflakes. Across the room Cassie watched him, then turned away abruptly.

While Luella ladled beans into bowls, Cassie removed a batch of biscuits from the fire. The rich aroma of biscuits and coffee filled the little cabin, and Quin was reminded of the fact that he hadn't eaten since early morning.

Jen eagerly chose the seat beside the stranger, and Becky took the chair across from him, with their mother at the head of the table and their grandmother at the other end.

"Jennifer, you may lead the prayer tonight," Cassie said.

Quin was startled when they all clasped hands and lowered their heads. His big hand was caught by Jen's tiny, delicate fingers. His other hand was clasped by Cassie's. Her palm was small and warm. And callused. It would appear that this farm wife did a lot more than bake bread.

Shock rippled through Cassie as her hand was engulfed in Quin's. Her first impulse was to jerk her hand free. But pride and propriety would not permit it. Through veiled lashes she cast a sideways glance at this man who held her hand as gently as if it were fine porcelain. For all the softness of his touch, there was surprising strength. To her consternation she found that he was looking at her. She swallowed and ducked her head, but it was too late. She knew he had seen the direction of her gaze. She knew also that her cheeks were scarlet.

So this was the woman Ethan Montgomery had described in such perfect detail. Quin had been afraid she wouldn't live up to his expectations. If anything, she was even more beautiful than he'd pictured in his mind. Hair the color of autumn leaves, long and lush and curling softly around the face of an angel. Eyes more green than blue, hiding secrets in their depths. A figure that, though encased in a shapeless, tattered gown, was slender and womanly. He could imagine her in fine satin and jewels, descending a curving staircase in a lavishly appointed plantation, presiding over an elegant dinner for a hundred or more guests.

"Heavenly Father," little Jen said. Her eyes were closed. A sprinkling of freckles dusted her nose. A mop of unruly red curls fell across her forehead. It would appear that her blouse and britches had been made over from a faded Confederate uniform. Her father's, no doubt. Quin had spotted a matching faded Confederate cap on a peg by the door, still damp from the snow. It would seem that the little girl was very close to her father, and preferred his clothes to her mother's. "Bless this food and all of us who gather around your table. Especially bless my pa, out in the cold—"

Cassie's head came up sharply. "I've told you, Jennifer, your pa isn't cold. He is warm and safe from all harm." She glanced at Quin and then back to her daughter, adding, "Your pa has all the food and shelter he desires."

"Yes'm." As an afterthought, the little girl concluded, "And bless Mr. McAllister, even though he isn't our guardian angel."

The others mumbled a quick amen.

"Thank you, Jen." Quin shot her a grin. "That was a fine prayer." He broke apart a steamy biscuit and bit into it. "Mmm. And this is fine baking, ma'am."

Cassie flushed clear to her toes. "It's just a plain old biscuit."

"No, ma'am. I've eaten biscuits all over this country, and I've never tasted better."

Luella fixed him with a look and barked a challenge. "And what is it you do, Mr. McAllister, that has you traveling all over this country?"

"I guess I've done most everything it takes to survive. But mostly I play cards."

The older woman choked and was forced to take several sips of scalding coffee. When she could find her voice, she sputtered, "You're a gambler, Mr. McAllister?"

He gave her his most charming smile as he emptied his bowl. "Yes, ma'am."

At once Cassie filled his bowl with a second helping of beans. He couldn't recall when plain old beans and biscuits had tasted so wonderful. For the first time all day he felt warm and contented. Still, he thought it strange that this family had no meat. Why wouldn't Ethan provide them with some game before he left to fetch the herd?

"And what does your family think about your gambling?" Luella asked primly.

"The war took my family, ma'am. I'm the only one left. But in his day, my father took his share of risks. Of course," he quickly amended, "they weren't with cards. My father gambled on land. At one time he owned half of Atlanta. And my mother," he added with a wide smile, "took the biggest risk of all when she agreed to marry a hardheaded Scot.'' He polished off a second helping and sat back, draining his coffee.

"I must assume your father's risks did not pay off."

"Why do you say that?"

"If he had been as successful in land as you hint, you would be living on your inheritance by now, wouldn't you, Mr. McAllister?"

He set the cup down very carefully, aware that everyone was watching him. With considerable effort he kept his tone level. "By the time I got home from a prison camp, there were carpetbaggers living on my inheritance, ma'am. And all of the fine buildings had been torched." He turned to Cassie. "I thank you for that fine meal. Now if you don't mind, I think I'll go outside and enjoy a cigar."

Cassie placed a hand on his sleeve, then just as quickly withdrew it, as though shocked at having been so bold as to touch him. But she had done so instinctively, as much to offer comfort as to shield him from her mother's open hostility.

In a soft voice she said, "It isn't necessary to go outside to smoke, Mr. McAllister. Please stay and enjoy your cigar by the fire."

"Thank you, ma'am."

He pushed away from the table, walked to the fireplace and bent down. Removing a flaming stick, he held it to the tip of his cigar until a wreath of smoke curled over his head.

"I'd forgotten how much I miss the smell of a cigar," Cassie said, and sighed. Then, when she realized what she'd revealed, her eyes widened and she added, "Though Ethan's been gone but a few days, it seems like forever."

Quin said nothing as he took a seat in one of the rockers that flanked a bench in front of the fire. While the two women washed the dishes, the two girls sprawled on a rag rug on the floor, their faces flushed from the heat of the flames.

Jen, eyes downcast, did sums on a small slate. Every once in a while she would glance at the man who sat in her father's rocker.

Across the room, her mother did the same. Cassie thought about all the stories her husband had told her about Quin McAllister. If even half were true, he would have to be superhuman. Yet, from his outward appearance, he was nothing more than a rogue and a dandy.

"How many is two plus three?" Jen asked her sister.

"You're supposed to figure it out yourself," the older girl replied smugly.

The little one counted off her fingers, then said proudly, "I know. It's six."

"You don't know anything," her older sister snapped.

"Do too. It's six."

"It's five," Becky said.

The little girl looked crestfallen and began to count her fingers again.

"Maybe I can help." Quin took a deck of cards from his pocket and began to shuffle them. Walking to the table, he lay three cards facedown. In a second row he lay down two more.

Intrigued, the little girl got up and walked over to stand beside him.

"Now," Quin said, "how many are there?"

Jen counted. "Five."

"Right. That's because three and two," Quin said, pointing to the two rows, "are five. Now these two, when I turn them over, will make five, and so will these two."

"But how do you know that?" Jen touched the cards. "You can't even see them."

"That's right. But I know what every one of these cards is without turning them over."

"Nobody can know that," Jen said.

"Want to bet?"

"Mr. McAllister!" Luella cried in alarm. "We will not permit gambling in our home."

Cassie hurried over to drop an arm around her daughter. "My mother is right, Mr. McAllister."

"Sorry, ma'am." His eyes crinkled as he looked down into hers.

Cassie's frown deepened. He didn't look sorry. In fact, he looked downright pleased with himself.

He turned to the child. "How about if we wager good works, Jen?"

The little girl was intrigued. "What good works?"

Quin thought a minute. "If you're wrong, you'll have to muck my horse's stall in the morning."

"And if you're wrong?" she asked.

"The choice is yours."

After a moment's contemplation she said, "I know. You'll have to gather the eggs for breakfast."

"All right. But remember," he cautioned, "there's a rule all gamblers live by. A gentleman must always live up to the terms of his wager." He watched as the little girl considered the implications. Offering his hand, he asked, "Deal?"

"Deal," she said, and she shook his hand.

He flipped over the first two cards. "You see? A three and a two, for a total of five." He flipped over the next two to reveal a four and an ace.

"Another five," Jen said with a trace of awe.

"Right again. And this last one," Quin said, flipping over the card, "is the five of hearts. Which means that I won the bet, and you're going to have to start your chores early in the morning."

Rebecca, who had come up behind them, wore a puzzled frown. "How did you know what the cards were, Mr. McAllister?"

"A card player can't reveal all his secrets," he said with that same charming smile. He lifted the deck of cards and fanned them out. "Pick a card."

When she nervously backed away, he made the same offer to little Jen. She eagerly chose a card.

"Don't show me what it is. Just set it back in the deck and shuffle."

She took the deck of cards, fumbling several times as she tried to emulate him. When she had finished, she handed the deck back to him. He flipped up a card and showed it to her. She shook her head. He held up a second. Again she insisted that it wasn't the card she'd picked.

With mock concern he muttered, "I must be losing my touch. I've never been wrong before." He looked up, then gave them all a quick smile. "Ah. I see what went wrong. That slick old card got sidetracked by a pretty face." Stepping closer to Cassie, he touched a hand to her hair. Then he opened his hand and held out a card. "Is this yours, Jen?"

The little girl let out a squeal of excitement. "That's it. Ma. Gram. That's my card. But how did it get in Mama's hair?"

"Now that's a mystery," Quin said.

The softness of Cassie's hair had shocked him to his core. If he didn't know better, he'd swear his hand was trembling. But that was impossible. He had the steadiest hands of any gambler he knew.

"Can you teach me to do that, Mr. McAllister? Please?" the little girl begged.

"Me, too?" Becky asked, though more cautiously.

"Not in one simple lesson, I'm afraid. It took me years to learn this." Seeing their looks of disappointment, he added, "But if you promise to help your mother and grandmother with the dishes, I'll show you a few simple tricks."

Becky dropped her arm around her little sister's shoulders and said solemnly, "Come on, Jen. Let's not wait."

The two girls eagerly finished the dishes. As soon as the last one was dried, they hurried over to where Quin sat by the fire.

Cassie watched them with a mixture of fascination and affection. She couldn't remember the last time she had seen them so animated. With a few simple tricks this stranger had them agreeing to things they usually avoided.

She turned away and joined her mother at the table, preparing dough. Brushing her hair from her eyes, she glanced over to the bench where Quin McAllister sat, with Jen on one side and Becky on the other. Their laughter filled the little cabin with more warmth than the fire that burned in the fireplace.

A short time later, when her chores were finished, Luella called sternly, "Children. Time for bed."

"Oh, Gram," both children moaned in unison. "Just awhile longer. Please."

"You heard—"

She paused when Cassie dropped a hand on her shoulder. "Just awhile longer, Ma. I haven't heard them laugh like this in years."

"Card tricks and gambling." With a frown of displeasure the older woman turned away and picked up a basket of sewing. "Becky, come here and thread this needle, please."

"Gram," little Jen asked with all the innocence of childhood, "how come Mama says you can spot a chicken hawk when he's as high as the clouds, and you can't see to pull thread through a needle?"

"Jennifer," her mother cautioned.

"It's all right, girl," the older woman said. Turning to her granddaughter, she said, "It's an affliction of my age. If my arms were long enough to hold the needle across the room, I could easily thread it myself. But up close it's all a blur. But the Lord made up for it by giving Becky enough vision for both of us."

The girl did as she was told, easily threading the needle before handing it back to her grandmother.

Pulling her chair close to the fire, Luella tackled her mending while Becky returned to sit beside Quin.

Seeing Cassie watching him, Quin said, "Care to give it a try?"

She shook her head. "I've never handled cards, Mr. McAllister. I'm sure I'd be clumsy."

"You? You couldn't be clumsy if you tried, ma'am."

Across the room he saw the older woman's head come up sharply, and he quickly returned his attention to the children. But he was acutely aware of the woman who busied herself in the kitchen, kneading dough and covering it with a towel. In the warmth of the cabin little tendrils of fiery hair curled softly around her cheeks. Her gown, damp from chores, clung to her soft curves.

The apron clearly defined her waist. A waist so tiny his hands could easily span it.

It was a good thing he was leaving in the morning, he told himself sternly. He was thinking decidedly wicked thoughts about his best friend's wife.

Chapter Two

"Have you ever been to California, Mr. McAllister?" Becky asked.

"Yes, I have."

"What's it like?"

"Rough and wild."

Across the room, Cassie listened with interest to this man who had traveled so far and had seen so much.

"There are little towns springing up, filled with people from all over the world. There are valleys there with land so fertile they boast that they can grow melons as big as a man's head."

The children were suitably impressed.

"I want to hear about San Francisco," Becky coaxed.

"A fascinating city. The docks are teeming with people chattering in a dozen different languages. In one day you can have your shirt laundered by a Chinaman, your food cooked by a Frenchman, and a new suit made by an Englishman."

The children's eyes were wide with interest. The cards lay forgotten.

"Will you go back there?" Jen asked.

"I expect so."

"I sure would like to see it someday," Becky said wistfully.

"I'd just like to see Atlanta someday," Jen muttered.

"But you have seen it," Quin said gently. "That's where you were born."

"I know." Jen's tiny fingers fumbled with the deck of cards, and Quin picked up the ones that fell to the floor. "But I don't remember what it looks like. Mama said there were big sprawling houses, with green lawns and more flowers than you could name. But Gram said there's nothing left there. Everything is burned."

"I don't ever want to go back there." Becky shivered, and a fearful look came into her eyes.

"Atlanta will rise up from the ashes," Quin said softly. "And someday it will be even more beautiful than before. But it will take a long time."

"Speaking of time..." Cassie, who had been as caught up in Quin's narrative as her children, got to her feet. "It's time for bed, children."

This time Jen and Becky didn't argue. The truth was, despite the excitement generated by their visitor, their eyes had grown heavy.

They glanced at their grandmother, then shared a conspiratorial smile. She sat, eyes closed, her breathing soft and easy, her mending spilled across her lap.

Cassie gathered up the needle and thread and replaced the mending in the basket. Gently shaking her mother by the shoulder, she whispered, "Ma. Bedtime."

The older woman blinked, then got slowly to her feet. "Where is Mr. McAllister going to sleep, Cassie?"

"I'll sleep in the barn, ma'am," Quin said.

Luella looked relieved.

"No, Mr. McAllister." Cassie shook her head firmly. "It's much too cold in the barn. I'll make up a bed in the corner of the cabin, as soon as I've heard my children's prayers and tucked them in bed."

While the children and their mother retreated to a back room, their grandmother remained where she was, studying Quin in stony silence. It was plain that, though weary, she would keep an eye on this stranger until her daughter returned.

From the bedroom Quin could hear the softly murmured prayers of thanks and petition, then the lovingly whispered good-nights.

When Cassie returned and began gathering an armload of fur pelts and blankets, her mother watched as she prepared a bed for Quin.

"I'd like to do something to thank you, ma'am."

"Thanks are not necessary, Mr. McAllister. But I would be obliged if you would toss a log on the fire. One big enough to see us through the night."

"Yes, ma'am."

He bent to the pile of logs beside the fireplace. As he lifted one, she could see the ripple of muscles along his back and shoulders. For some unexplained reason she felt a dryness in her throat. Then, seeing her mother's stern gaze fixed on her, she turned away.

"Thank you, Mr. McAllister," she called softly. "I will bid you good-night."

"Good night, ma'am."

He watched as her mother entered the children's bedroom. Cassie carried a lantern into a second bedroom. Even after she lowered the blanket that served as a door, he could see the light from the lantern flickering as she moved about the room.

Stretching his feet toward the fire, he pulled a cigar from his pocket. As smoke curled upward he leaned back, deep in thought.

Ethan Montgomery was a modest, sensible man, not given to boastful ways. Why then had he described the mine as a successful, prosperous venture? The mine had yielded nothing of value, according to his wife.

His wife. Quin frowned. There was another puzzle. Ethan Montgomery had been a man deeply in love with his wife. Why had Ethan not confided in her that he'd sent for his old friend?

Her mother was easier to read. Luella Chalmers seemed as protective of Cassie as Cassie was of her children. Easy to understand, when a man as rock solid as Ethan Montgomery was trapped by a blizzard far from home.

But the one question that remained the most puzzling was, why had Ethan sent for him? As far as he could see, there was nothing here that required Quin's assistance.

Quin McAllister was a man who had always trusted his instincts. And right now his instincts told him that nothing was as it seemed.

Cassie lay in the big double bed her husband had made for her. Solid and sturdy. Like Ethan. She ran her hand over the embroidered pillowcases. She'd made them as a new bride. Not yet fifteen. Everything then had been shiny and new, like the gossamer gown, like the fine, translucent china. Like the lovely plantation they had built on one hundred prime acres of his father's land. Like the dreams they had for the future, before the country went mad.

She pressed a hand to her eyes, willing herself to sleep. After the day she had put in, she ought to be exhausted. But this unexpected turn of events had her too distraught to rest. Her thoughts were in turmoil.

Why had Quin McAllister come here now? What was he really after?

He said Ethan had sent for him. But that was impossible. Unless Ethan had known, all those months ago...

She rolled over, drawing the blankets up to her chin, and forced herself to relax. But the tension was there, like a coiled spring, tightening with every breath. When she considered all that she had been through, it was not surprising. What was surprising was that every morning, no matter how bad the night before had been, she managed to begin anew.

She sat up, shoving tangles of hair from her eyes. The nights were always like this. The days were filled with hard, mind-numbing work and the hundreds of dangers that had become their daily companion in this wilderness. But the nights seemed interminable, filled with nameless, faceless terrors that often kept her awake and trembling until dawn.

She slipped from bed and reached for a shawl, which she draped around her shoulders, then slid her feet into her boots. Moving soundlessly from the room, she glanced at the mound of fur in the corner of the cabin. Assured that their guest was asleep, she crossed to the door and let herself out.

The storm had blown over, leaving the countryside blanketed in white. The air was so sharp and cold it hurt to breathe it in. On a sigh Cassie lifted her head. The moon was a golden crescent in a black velvet sky sprinkled with a million glittering stars.

"Looks close enough to touch, doesn't it, ma'am?"

With a cry of alarm she twisted around and brought a hand to her throat. "Mr. McAllister. I...thought you were sleeping."

He was leaning against the porch railing, one booted foot crossed over the other. "Sorry. Didn't mean to startle you. I knew the storm was over. Thought I'd see how much snow it left behind." He didn't bother to add that he avoided sleep as much as possible. In sleep the demons came. As long as he remained awake, he could hold them at bay.

She watched as he pulled a cigar from his pocket and held a match to the tip. The flame illuminated the blackness and she saw his eyes, dark and mysterious, before he extinguished the flame. A moment later the rich aroma of tobacco stung the night air.

"I suppose you can't sleep thinking about your husband up there in those hills?"

She closed her eyes against the pain. "Yes."

"Maybe I ought to consider staying around until he returns."

Her eyes snapped open. "That...would not be fair to you, Mr. McAllister."

"I have no ties, ma'am. There's no place tugging on my sleeve." He smiled and she thought how dangerous he looked. Like a predator that had cornered its prey.

He was watching her too closely, as though trying to read her thoughts. "I had better get inside."

She started to walk past him, but his hand shot out, stilling her movements.

"Not just yet."

At the touch of his hand on her arm she stopped in midstride. Keeping her gaze averted, she whispered, "It's very late, Mr. McAllister."

"Yes, ma'am. But there are one or two things I'd like to ask you."

"Tomorrow."

She took a step, and his grasp tightened on her arm. Her head came up sharply. She found herself staring into dark, narrowed eyes. He was no longer smiling.

"If there's one thing a gambler needs in order to be successful, it's the ability to read his opponents. And I happen to be very good at what I do, ma'am." His tone was deceptively impersonal as he added, "That's why I'm so puzzled."

"Puzzled, Mr. McAllister?"

"By what I see in your eyes, ma'am."

She blinked. "I don't know what you mean. What could you possibly see in my eyes, Mr. McAllister?"

"Lies, ma'am."

She tried to pull free. When that failed, she went rigid with indignation and lifted her head in a haughty manner that would have wilted most men. But this man, she realized, was not like most. He continued staring at her with the same cool, challenging look.

"If my husband were here, sir, he would demand an apology immediately." Her words were as cold as the night air.

"I expect he would, ma'am." He saw the flash of fire in her eyes and felt an unexpected surge of admiration. By God, she had spunk. "But it is precisely because Ethan isn't here that we're having this discussion."

"I have explained to you. Ethan is—"

He brought a finger to her lips to silence her, and realized at once that it had been a dangerous miscalculation. The softness of her lips against his flesh aroused him as nothing he had ever before experienced.

He saw the look of alarm in her eyes and wondered if she had felt it, too. He lowered his hand to his side, clenching it into a fist. His voice was rougher than he intended. "Forgive me, Mrs. Montgomery. I have no right to accept your hospitality and then question your word. But I'd like to know—"

They both looked up at the sound of horses approaching.

"Ethan?" he asked.

She shook her head quickly and reached inside the door for her rifle.

"But how can you be sure?"

"Trust me, Mr. McAllister. It is not my husband."

Before he could question her further, three men on horseback drew near. In the darkness, they were no more than three silhouettes. Wide-brimmed hats, leather chaps, rifles cradled in the curve of their arms.

Instinctively Quin drew his pistol and stepped forward, sweeping her behind him in one smooth gesture.

"That you, Ethan Montgomery?" came a deep voice in the darkness.

"My husband isn't here." Cassie stepped from behind Quin, her rifle gripped so tightly in her hand the knuckles were white.

The leader of the three, whose horse, a massive red stallion, restlessly pawed the snow, had a voice tinged with heavy sarcasm. "I guess I expected as much. Where is he this time?"

"Got caught by this storm up in the hills."

"I don't believe you. Though your story changes, the message is always the same. I've always just missed your husband, it seems. I'm sure you won't mind if I take a look inside your cabin, Miz Montgomery—" he spoke her name in a deliberate imitation of a Southern drawl

that was insulting and sarcastic "—and see for myself."

As he began to slide from the saddle she lifted the rifle to her shoulder and took aim. Beside her, Quin was
amazed at the change in her. This soft-spoken woman
had another side to her. One that would brook no nonsense.

"I do mind, Mr. Stoner. My mother and children are
asleep inside. I will not have them disturbed."

His face was a mask of fury. "Don't threaten me, Miz
Montgomery, unless you mean it."

"The lady means it," Quin said in a dangerously soft
voice. "And so do I." He took up a stance, feet apart,
pistol cocked and aimed.

Stoner scrambled back into the saddle. "And who
might this be?"

"Name's Quin McAllister." Quin's voice remained
little more than a whisper, yet all three men seemed to
sit straighter in the saddle as they watched the man who
had the look and bearing of one accustomed to gun-
fights. "I'm a friend of Ethan's."

"McAllister, I'm Cyrus Stoner. Own most of the land
around these parts."

"But not this land," Cassie said.

"Not yet maybe. But soon I will. Your husband can't
keep refusing my offers forever." Cyrus asked cyni-
cally, "Just passing through, McAllister? Or have you
come to stay?"

Quin gave a negligible shrug of his shoulders.
"Haven't decided yet. Does it make a difference to
you?"

"No." The man laughed and glanced at his friends.
"But it might make a difference to you, McAllister. Or

I should say, it might make a big difference to your health."

The man threw back his head and roared, thoroughly enjoying his joke. The other two joined in the laughter.

A moment later there was no trace of humor in his tone as he said to Cassie, "You tell your husband I'm sick and tired of the way he's hiding behind your skirts. When he returns from the hills, or wherever he's hiding this time, I expect him to be man enough to come and see me."

"My husband has heard your proposal, Mr. Stoner. He is not interested in selling this land."

"I'll hear it from his lips, if you don't mind, Miz Montgomery. I think when he hears my latest offer, he'll be more than happy to accept it."

Again the men beside him laughed.

"There is no offer you can make that will entice him to sell to you."

"I wouldn't be so sure. Like I said, I'll hear that from his own lips, if you don't mind." He touched a hand to the rim of his hat, then tugged on his horse's reins. The other two followed, sending up a cloud of snowflakes.

Neither Cassie nor Quin moved until the horsemen disappeared below a snow-covered ridge. As she lowered her rifle, he heard the little sigh of relief that escaped her lips.

"Thank you, Mr. McAllister." She turned to face him and he thought, fleetingly, how incongruous the rifle seemed in the hands of one so small and delicate. Her hands were made for holding a fan, or perhaps a fluted glass of wine. "I regret that you were forced to be a party to this."

He gave her a roguish smile and, without thinking, lifted a fiery curl from her shoulder and watched the strands sift through his fingers. It was a purely sensual feeling that made his blood run hot. "Didn't Ethan tell you? I've always enjoyed a good fight, ma'am."

At his touch she felt the tingle deep inside and fought to ignore it. "But this isn't your fight, Mr. McAllister."

Though his smile remained in place, his voice took on a rough edge. "I've joined in a lot of fights that weren't mine."

"So Ethan has told me. Why?"

He looked into her eyes and felt the jolt clear to his toes. "It's the gambler in me." He shrugged and warmth returned to his tone. "I just like to even the odds."

Her words were sharp, to hide the feelings that curled along her spine. "Must everything be compared to a card game, Mr. McAllister?"

He twirled the strand of her hair around and around his finger, all the while staring into her eyes. "All of life's a gamble, ma'am. The way I look at it, we all have to play the cards that are dealt us."

She swallowed, hating the weakness that had spread to her limbs, leaving her unable to turn away from this man. "Then I suppose you think the outcome is purely luck."

"No, ma'am." His gaze centered on her lips and he was surprised by the flare of heat. The temptation to kiss her was so strong, it took all his willpower to resist. "There's a whole lot more to life, and cards, than luck. It takes skill to come out a winner. And sometimes the hand of fate."

She felt the pull of his gaze and ran her tongue over lips that had gone dry. Sweet heaven, what would she do if he kissed her? The rush of heat left her trembling. But though she wanted to bolt, she stood her ground. "And do you always win, Mr. McAllister?"

"Not always, ma'am." With an effort, he opened his fingers, allowing the strands of hair to drift to her shoulder. Very deliberately he lowered his hand to his side. "But I go into every game with the intention of winning."

She took a step back, then reached for the door. "I'll say good-night now, Mr. McAllister." When the door moved inward, she followed the movement, praying that her trembling legs wouldn't fail her.

"Good night, ma'am."

He waited until the door closed, then retrieved his cigar from the porch rail and held a match to the tip. His hands, he noted, were unsteady.

Damn the letter, he thought, that had dragged him away from the richest card game of his life and brought him to this godforsaken wilderness. And damn Ethan for not being here to explain what in hell was going on. And most of all, damn his best friend's wife for being so tempting.

Cassie Montgomery. She certainly wasn't the first woman he'd ever wanted. But she was the first who'd ever clouded his mind so that he couldn't recall a single word he'd spoken.

He blew out a stream of smoke and gave a slow shake of his head in admiration. The lady had done it all while managing to remain every inch the proper lady. And she'd managed to evade every one of his questions. She was still a complete mystery.

Chapter Three

Quin lay in the nest of furs and blankets, clinging to the last vestiges of sleep. Sleep that had, as always, been tormented. Morning sounds seeped into his consciousness so subtly he was hardly aware of them at first. The soft rustle of skirts. The sound of water being poured into a basin. Dough being kneaded and shaped on a board.

Now fully awake, he yawned then stretched, calling out a sleepy, "Good morning, ma'am."

Cassie swallowed. "Good morning, Mr. McAllister." To her own ears her voice sounded unusually strained. Though she'd tried, she'd been unable to keep her gaze from him as he'd slept. The sight of him, hair rumpled, chin darkened with stubble, had brought an unwelcome rush of feelings. "I hope you slept well."

"Very well, thank you." It was a lie, of course. He'd tossed and turned until nearly dawn, his mind struggling to sort out the pieces to this strange puzzle. But he would never admit that fact to her.

He rolled from his bed and unselfconsciously walked to the basin of water on a table by the door. From across the room Cassie's throat went dry at the sight of him, naked to the waist, wearing only tight black trousers that clung to his body like a second skin. As he washed and shaved, she studied the play of muscles along his back and shoulders, and stared in fascination as he pulled on a shirt and buttoned it before tucking it into the waistband of his pants.

She scolded herself for her wicked thoughts. After all, he was a friend of Ethan's. A good friend, who had once saved Ethan's life. Yet she felt so aware of this man. Aware of him in a way she had never before been aware of a man. That admission brought a flood of guilt.

When Quin glanced up he saw two bright spots of color on her cheeks before she turned away.

"It will be awhile before breakfast, Mr. McAllister." She set the pan of biscuits over the fire and placed the blackened coffeepot on a warming shelf of stone above the coals. Straightening, she moved back and forth across the cabin, setting the table, laying out the children's clothes on the hearth where they would be warmed by the fire. "I have a few morning chores to see to first."

"I'd like to help."

She glanced at the immaculate white shirt with its fancy cuff buttons, and the black boots polished to a high shine. "I don't think you're dressed for mucking out stalls or milking cows, Mr. McAllister."

Once again that roguish smile lifted the corners of his lips. "I was raised on a plantation, ma'am. I know my way around a barn. I'm sure Ethan has a parka I could borrow."

She seemed surprised by his offer. "Yes. I suppose I could find you something to wear." She withdrew to her bedroom, then returned carrying a fur parka over her arm. In her hand was a pair of mud-spattered boots.

Without a word Quin slipped them on while she pulled on an oversized buckskin jacket. When she stepped outside, he followed and pulled the cabin door shut behind him.

Cassie's gaze scanned the horizon. "More snow coming," she muttered.

He could feel it. In the bite of the North wind, in the dark clouds that billowed in a leaden sky.

"Was it difficult for a Southern lady to adjust to all this snow and cold?"

"It took some doing."

Such simple words. But to Quin they conveyed a depth of feeling.

They plodded through waist-high drifts to the barn. Once inside, Cassie broke through the thin layer of ice on the trough and carried buckets of water to the animals, while Quin picked up a pitchfork and began forking fresh hay into each stall. When all the animals had been fed and watered, Cassie lifted a bucket from a peg and called out a greeting to the cow, who raised its head to nuzzle her hand. She settled herself on the milking stool and pressed her cheek against the cow's warm side, losing herself in the familiar morning ritual.

Resting his hands on the pitchfork, Quin paused to drink in the sight of her as she worked. The gown, though faded and worn, fell in graceful folds to the floor, hiding the serviceable boots she wore. The mannish buckskin jacket was softened by her feminine curves. Fiery hair spilled in a riot of curls to her waist. A strand had fallen provocatively over one eye. The desire to reach out and brush it away had him clenching and unclenching his hand.

"Morning, Mr. McAllister." A child's voice shattered the silence.

Quin whirled, feeling a twinge of guilt at having been caught staring. "Good morning, Jen."

"Why are you mucking the stall?" the little girl asked innocently. "That's supposed to be my job, remember? I lost the bet last night."

"This is a pretty big job for one little girl."

Jen solemnly took the pitchfork from Quin's hands. "You said a gentleman must always live up to the terms of his agreement. Doesn't the same hold for a lady?"

Such a little lady, he thought. And so serious. "Indeed, it does. It looks like you were paying pretty close attention." He smiled. "I guess I can find something else to do." With a last glance at the girl's mother, Quin picked up an ax and walked from the barn.

A few minutes later the air was filled with the ringing of ax against wood as Quin began chopping firewood. Out of the corner of his eye he caught sight of Cassie walking slowly to the cabin, struggling under the weight of the heavy bucket of milk. Dropping the ax, he hurried over.

"I'll carry this, ma'am. It's too heavy for you."

When he reached for the bucket, she edged away. "I can manage, Mr. McAllister."

"I'm sure you can, but it'll make me feel better if you let me carry this."

As he took the bucket from her, their fingers brushed. Cassie was stunned by the rush of heat that danced along her chilled flesh. She chanced a quick glance at his face and found, to her dismay, that he was boldly studying her. Though she immediately looked away, she knew that her cheeks were flaming.

"Where does Ethan store your firewood?" There should have been several cords of wood to see them through the winter. Yet he had spotted none.

"He used to put it beside the cabin. But this year, with the mine and all…" she said lamely, "he never got to it."

"Never got…" Quin pressed his lips together to keep from saying anything more. Had Ethan let the thought of treasure cloud his mind? Didn't he know how important firewood was to survival in this wilderness?

Cassie opened the cabin door and turned, taking the bucket from Quin's hands. Again she was forced to endure his touch, along with his penetrating stare. "Thank you, Mr. McAllister. I can manage now."

He returned to the ax and log with a vengeance. Soon he had stripped off his parka and rolled the sleeves of his shirt. All the while he worked, he found himself wondering about Ethan Montgomery. What had happened to change his old friend? Why would an industrious, ambitious man like Ethan allow his farm to fall into such disrepair? If he no longer had an interest in the place, why not sell to Cyrus Stoner? The answer had to be the mine. Yet, Cassie Montgomery said the mine had yielded nothing of value.

Could Ethan have found a treasure without telling his wife? Wife. Quin brought the ax down hard, biting deep into the log. He would have to keep reminding himself that Cassie was Ethan's wife. He had no right to the thoughts he was entertaining. Thoughts as dark as the clouds that threatened another storm.

As she worked alongside her daughter and mother, Cassie was tormented by similar thoughts. She was grateful that Quin would be gone soon. It was wicked of her to permit such thoughts about Ethan's best friend.

When little Jen pushed open the cabin door, carrying a handful of eggs, Cassie caught sight of Quin stacking logs against the outer wall of the cabin. Muscles rippled beneath his beautifully tailored shirt. She stood very still, watching his every movement. Then, aware that her mother and daughter had glanced up, she quickly turned away.

"You may tell Mr. McAllister that breakfast is ready, Jennifer." She lifted the pan of biscuits from the fireplace.

A short time later, when the cabin door was blown open by a blast of frosty air, she forced herself not to turn around. But even with her back to him, she was entirely too aware of Quin as he hung the fur parka and pried off the snow-covered boots. Minutes later, when she approached the table, he turned away from the washbasin and ran a hand through his hair. It was beautiful hair, she mused. Slightly shaggy and dark as midnight, curling around the collar of his shirt. A lock of it tended to fall across his forehead. Probably quite a temptation for the painted women who frequented the saloons where he played his poker games. Cassie imagined such women often brushed it aside before wrapping their arms around his neck and lifting their faces for a kiss.

"Cassie," Luella Chalmers chided sharply. "You're burning the beans."

Startled out of her reverie, Cassie snatched the pot from the fire, only to drop it with a cry when she burned her hand.

"Lands, girl, where is your mind this morning?"

Pushing her aside, Luella wrapped a linen towel around her hand and took up the pot.

"You'd better let me see that, ma'am," Quin muttered, coming up beside her.

"No." Cassie pulled her hand behind her back like a reluctant child. "It's just a little burn."

He caught her hand and held it up. "That's a whole lot more than a little burn. Jen," he called, "I have some salve in my saddlebag that will help this. Want to fetch it?"

"Yes, sir." Jen jumped up and pulled on her parka. Within minutes she returned, clutching the saddlebag in her arms. From it she withdrew a small vial, along with a leather-bound book and a bottle of whiskey.

"Which one do you want, Mr. McAllister?" she asked, holding them up.

"Whiskey! Mr. McAllister," Luella cried in alarm. "We do not permit spirits in this house. We are good, God-fearing people."

"Yes, ma'am." He took the vial from the little girl's hand. To Cassie he muttered, "I'm afraid this is going to sting. You might want to consider a taste of my whiskey before I get started."

Squaring her shoulders, Cassie said, "I have no need of your artificial courage, Mr. McAllister. You may apply your salve."

"Yes, ma'am." He helped her into a chair in front of the fireplace. Dipping a finger into the sticky yellow substance, he began to spread it over her palm. Though she winced, she did not make a sound. The truth was, she found it hard to speak when he was so close to her.

His hands were so large, both of hers could fit in a single palm. Yet, for all their size, his touch was gentle.

For Quin, the nearness of Cassie brought a different kind of discomfort. When he knelt beside her, his face was level with hers. As he bent over her hand, he was aware of the faint fragrance of soap and water, and a lingering trace of lilac water. Working the ointment into her palm, he caught sight of the dark cleft between her breasts, and felt a rush of heat that had nothing to do with the cheery fire at his back.

Cassie sat very still while he ministered to her. After a few moments, the pain dissolved, to be replaced by a warm, stinging sensation. It matched the warmth that had spread low in her stomach.

"Where did you learn such things, Mr. McAllister?"

"During the war, ma'am. I saw many of our fine soldiers burned by cannon fire."

"Are you a doctor?"

"No. Just a jack-of-all-trades, I'm afraid."

Up close she smelled as clean and fresh as a new snowfall. There was a dusting of flour on her cheek and he ached to brush it away. Instead he took a fine linen handkerchief from his pocket and tied it carefully over the burn.

She stared at his hands as he worked. So strong and sure. He had unrolled his sleeves and buttoned the cuffs with jade buttons set in gold. While he worked over her, his shirt collar brushed her cheek and it was as fine and soft as the elegant clothes she remembered from another time, another place. Once, everything she owned had been fine and new and elegant.

"I'll leave the salve with you." He placed the vial on the mantel. "If you apply it for the next several days, the burn will heal without a scar."

"Thank you, Mr. McAllister. Now please eat your breakfast. I fear we've made far too much of this."

With his hand beneath her elbow he helped her up, then held her chair at the table. His gallantry was not lost on the others.

Cassie stared pointedly at the chipped plate and said, "Rebecca, you may lead the blessing."

Once again they grasped hands, and Cassie's bandaged hand was engulfed in Quin's.

"Father, bless this food and all who partake. And bless Pa—" the girl seemed momentarily speechless, then ended lamely "—and keep Mr. McAllister safe on his journey."

"Amen," the others intoned.

Luella quickly ladled beans and passed around the biscuits. Becky wrapped a towel around her hand and lifted the coffeepot from the fire.

"Coffee, Mr. McAllister?"

"Yes, thank you, Becky."

"The beans are burned." Luella made a face as she began to eat.

Quin took a bite and sighed. "They're just about perfect. Don't you agree, Jen?"

The little girl seemed surprised, then, following Quin's lead, tasted and smiled, enjoying the flush on her mother's cheeks. If a little flattery was all it would take to brighten her mother's day, Jen was more than willing to join in this game. "Yes, sir. My mama's the best cook in the whole world."

"I agree." Quin sipped hot black coffee and leaned back. "If you want to taste burned food, you ought to taste what I've had to cook for myself along the trail."

The children chuckled at his joke.

"I thought you could do just about everything, Mr. McAllister." Luella's tone was caustic as she fixed him with a challenging look.

"Just about."

"Do you not count cooking as one of your many talents?"

"Oh, I do admit that I can cook a bit. But after tasting your daughter's beans and biscuits, I'll be sorry to have to go back to eating my own cooking."

"Have another of Mama's biscuits," Jen urged.

"No, thanks. Three is enough." Quin drained his cup. "I think it's time I took my leave."

Luella breathed a sigh of relief.

"Would you show us another card trick first?" Jen pleaded. "Please?"

Ignoring Luella's frown of disapproval, Quin pulled the deck of cards from his pocket. "I suppose it's only fair, since you paid your bet. But I'll ask a favor of you first."

"What?" the little girl asked eagerly.

"I want you to help your mother with the farm chores. You should be especially helpful until her burned hand heals."

"Yes, sir," Jen said solemnly.

Across the room Cassie marveled at how easily this stranger managed to reach an accord with her youngest daughter. Jen needed no coaxing to agree to his terms.

"Now," Quin said, shuffling the cards, "pick a card. Any card."

Though Becky reluctantly hung back, she was soon caught up in the magic and joined her little sister's laughter. Quin regaled the children with card tricks, making cards disappear before their eyes, only to ap-

pear magically beneath the table or behind their
backs.

While she worked alongside her mother, Cassie was
warmed by the children's laughter. For a brief time, her
daughters had been lifted out of their bleak existence.
For that, she would be eternally grateful to Quin
McAllister.

When the dishes were done, Luella caught sight of the
book that Jen had retrieved from Quin's saddlebag.
Glancing at the title, she looked aghast. ''Shakespeare,
Mr. McAllister?''

''Yes, ma'am. When I'm on the trail, I take comfort
from the words.''

''I should think a man would find more comfort by
reading the holy Bible.''

''Some would, I suppose.'' He held out his hand and
the older woman returned the book to him. For a moment he studied it in silence. On his face was a look of
such intensity, it struck Cassie that he went to a lot of
trouble to hide his true feelings.

He glanced up, and the look was erased. ''It's time I
take my leave. Cutter has been waiting outside the door,
saddled and ready, for the past hour.''

''Not yet.'' Jen's voice was high-pitched, pleading.
''One more card trick. Please.''

''I'll tell you what, Jen.'' Quin placed the deck of
cards in the little girl's hands. ''I'll leave these cards
with you. You and your sister can practice card tricks
every night, as long as you promise to do your sums first
and help with the chores.''

Luella's voice was stern. ''Mr. McAllister, you know
how I feel about—''

Cassie dropped a hand on her mother's shoulder. The older woman shot her a glance, then clamped her mouth shut.

"Thank you, Mr. McAllister," Cassie said gently. "That is very kind of you, but I'm quite certain you will have need of those cards."

"No, ma'am. I have another deck in my saddlebag."

Seeing the pleading look in her daughter's eyes, she relented. "Very well, then, Mr. McAllister. I will permit her to accept your gift."

"Oh, thank you, Mama. And thank you, Mr. McAllister," Jen shouted.

"You're welcome." He hugged Jen and ruffled Becky's hair, then removed his cowhide duster from a peg by the door and slipped it on. "It's time I was on my way. But first," he said, "I'd like to thank all of you for your hospitality. Mrs. Chalmers." He took Luella's hand and felt the way she stiffened at his touch. It was all he could do to keep from laughing. "Thank you, ma'am. You have a daughter and grandchildren to be proud of. And you, Mrs. Montgomery..." he steeled himself before clasping Cassie's hands "...made this weary traveler feel welcome."

They both felt the sexual tug, and both struggled to show no emotion.

"Give my best to Ethan, ma'am. Tell him how sorry I am that we won't have time to catch up on the years."

Cassie knew her cheeks were burning. She could feel the stares from her mother and children. Avoiding Quin's eyes, she said softly, "Yes, Mr. McAllister. Safe journey."

He released her hands and turned. It seemed the most natural thing in the world to draw Becky and Jen close and hug them one last time.

When he pulled open the door, a gust of icy wind nearly tore it from his grasp. The storm had begun again, and snow fell like a gauzy curtain from the heavens.

Despite the cold, Cassie and her mother and the children gathered in the doorway and watched as Quin pulled himself into the saddle.

He touched a hand to the brim of his hat, then turned his horse into the wind and was gone in a cloud of snow.

For long minutes no one moved. No one spoke. And then, as Cassie closed the door against the cold, the cabin seemed somehow smaller, darker, bleaker. As though the light and warmth had gone out of it. And out of their lives.

Chapter Four

"Easy, Cutter." Quin reined in his mount and studied the tracks. Deer. Four or five doe and a big buck, from the size of the prints in the snow.

Quin turned to glance at the small cabin, barely visible through the curtain of snowflakes. It had been his intention to make it to the nearest town before dark. But the thought of finding a deer was too tempting. Cassie and her children had no meat. Didn't he owe them at least this much in return for their hospitality?

"Come on, boy." He urged his horse up the ridge and into the forest.

The tracks were easy to follow. A short time later he came upon the small herd in a thick stand of trees where they had taken shelter from the storm. He slid from the saddle and crept close. Knowing a rifle shot would scatter the herd, he slipped a small knife from his boot. When the buck was within range, he tossed the knife and watched as the animal stiffened, then dropped silently to the ground. The herd, skittish now, milled about in confusion, then bolted when Quin approached.

"Sorry, Cutter. You've quite a load to carry," he murmured as he finished tying the deer to the horse's back and began to lead him through the tall drifts.

The time spent skinning and gutting the deer back at the barn would set him back several hours, he realized, leaving him no time to reach town before dark. The thought of camping out in this blizzard held no appeal, but at least the Montgomery family would have some meat until Ethan returned.

Quin huddled deeper into his duster and chuckled. "I'd better hope this good deed offers a measure of warmth tonight when I'm lying in my bedroll, buried in snow."

He lifted his head. Had there been a sound? If so, it had been muffled by the sound of his own voice. He walked several paces in silence, straining to listen. When he heard nothing more, he shook his head. It must have been the sighing of the wind in the trees.

He had gone only a short distance when he heard it again, louder. Not the wind. A sound like...a child, or possibly a woman, crying.

Dropping the reins, he left the horse in a grove of trees and moved forward. At the edge of the forest he saw Cassie Montgomery kneeling in a snowdrift.

He swore savagely. Was she in distress? Had she fallen or hurt herself? He plowed ahead, eager to aid her in whatever way he could.

Inching closer, he could hear bits and pieces of words she was uttering.

"...afraid to take him into my confidence. I dare not trust anyone. Oh, Ethan, what am I to do?"

Ethan? Confused, Quin stopped in his tracks. And then he saw it. What he had thought to be a snowdrift was really a mound of earth covered with snow. A crude wooden cross was dusted with snow, making it almost invisible.

God in heaven. Here at the edge of the forest, hidden from view of all but the woodland creatures, Cassie Montgomery was kneeling beside her husband's grave.

Seeing the figure looming out of the snow, Cassie's eyes went wide with fear. Tears blinded her. Picking up her rifle, she took aim. But a hand swept out and knocked it away. She started to struggle, but rough hands caught her, pinning her to the ground. She fought frantically, kicking, biting, but the hands were too strong. Despite her struggles, she could not break free. At last her arms were held roughly over her head. Her legs were pinned beneath hard, muscled thighs.

"Release me at once. Please. You must not..." She blinked once, twice. Her breath came out in a long rush of air. "Mr. McAllister?"

He felt a little breathless himself. But he couldn't tell if it was because of their struggle, or because he found himself lying on top of her. Despite their heavy coats, he was shockingly aware of the softness of the body beneath his.

His voice was gruff. "I believe you owe me an explanation."

The fire returned to her eyes. "I owe you nothing. Release me at once."

"When you tell me what this is all about."

"How did you find me here?" Her tone became indignant. "Have you been following me?"

"Of course not."

"Then how do you explain this? Just what are you doing here, Mr. McAllister? You ought to be miles from here by now."

He felt his temper rising. Once again, she was turning the tables and asking questions instead of answering them. But not this time. This time, by God, she was going to explain everything to his satisfaction.

"I want answers, Mrs. Montgomery. And I want them now."

She felt the sting of his hot breath against her cheek, felt the heat of his touch as his strong hands continued to grip her wrists. But she resolutely held her silence.

"All right," Quin said softly, "I'll make it easy for you. One question at a time. To begin with, how long has Ethan been dead?"

"It's been . . . almost six months."

"Six months." His eyes narrowed, calculating. No wonder the farm had fallen into such disrepair. It was a wonder they had survived this long. "But Ethan's letter . . ." How many towns had he been in in the past months? How many saloons? How had Ethan's letter ever managed to find him? That wasn't important now. Instead he asked, "How did he die?"

"A fever of some kind. He was never robust after he returned from the war. But he pushed himself to the limit. He refused to give in until his body . . . simply failed him."

"And nobody knows about his death?"

She shook her head. "Only my mother and the children. Please release me, Mr. McAllister. You're hurting me."

Quin rolled to one side, then helped her to sit up in the snow. For long silent moments they both stared at the grave. Then, dusting himself off, he got to his feet and helped her to stand.

"Why do you feel you have to keep Ethan's death a secret?"

"That was his dying wish. He told me that Cyrus Stoner would take advantage of the fact if he knew. And so I've been forced to live a lie all these long months."

"I don't understand." She was too close, and the touch of her had him reeling. "Why not sell to Stoner and be done with this place?"

"Cyrus Stoner." Her tone frosted over. "The man is unscrupulous."

"In what way?"

"There have been accidents. Nothing I can prove. But I suspect Cyrus Stoner is behind them."

He was suddenly alert. "What sort of accidents?"

"Our small herd of cattle, one by one, wandered off or was found dead in the hills. A foul-smelling substance in our well. And our dog, who always barked a warning when anyone approached, was found dead. Cyrus insisted it was the work of Indians. But I suspect him. He has long coveted our land."

"Then I ask you again. Why not sell to Stoner and be done with this place?"

"This place, as you call it, is our home, Mr. McAllister."

"Look at you," he said with a trace of anger. "A gently bred Southern lady. You no more belong here than I do. Do you ever stop to think what this land will do to you?"

"What this land does to me is of no consequence, Mr. McAllister. The important thing is what it can do for my children. Ethan believed in the mine. He was convinced that it would produce a fortune."

"What has it produced so far?"

There was a slight pause. "Nothing."

"And what if it never produces a single thing?"

"Then we will survive."

"Survive." He gave a scornful laugh. "And what if this place sucks all the life out of you? Or worse, kills all of you?"

She drew herself up to her full height and met his gaze squarely. "You think we are soft. You see us as displaced plantation owners who do not know how to work for ourselves. But you don't understand, Mr. McAllister. While our men were off fighting and dying, we were also at war. We watched our land destroyed, our buildings burned, and everything we owned reduced to ashes. Before our very eyes the place we knew as home became an inferno." Tears threatened and her lips trembled, but she forced herself to go on. "Once you have walked through hell, Mr. McAllister, you no longer fear anything, even death."

Her words touched a chord deep inside him. Hadn't he said those very things when he'd been released from the hellish prisoner-of-war camp?

Without thinking, he reached out and drew her close. She was so small and brave and angry and frightened. And for all his glib talk, he could think of nothing at all to say that would offer her comfort.

She thought about fighting the arms that held her. But it had been so long. So long. And for just a moment she wanted to forget the endless work and worry of their impossibly hard existence and just give in to the need to be held. Like a woman. Like a lover.

"I'm sorry about Ethan," he murmured. His hands were in her hair, though he had no recollection of lifting them there. "And I'm sorry about your home in Atlanta. And the war. And the unfairness of it all."

His voice washed over her, cleansing, soothing. It wasn't so much what he said as the way he said it. Softly, as though he were whispering a prayer. A little gruffly, as though wrenched from his heart. Fiercely, as though he meant every word of it.

She found it impossible to say anything over the lump that was forming in her throat.

"And I'm sorry—"

"Shh. No more." She touched a finger to his mouth to still his words. At once she realized her mistake.

He caught her hand and continued holding it against his mouth.

Glancing up, she found herself mesmerized by his lips as they pressed a kiss to each finger, and then her palm, and then her wrist.

A tiny thrill raced along her spine, followed by a trail of heat that left her weak.

"Please don't."

"Shh." Now it was his turn to silence her by pressing a finger to her lips. For long moments he stared at her mouth, and she felt the heat as surely as if he had already touched his lips to hers.

He lifted both her hands and kissed them, all the while staring into her eyes with a hunger that left her trembling.

She could sense that he wanted to kiss her. And the truth was, she wanted him to. Yet she was afraid. Afraid of the feelings that pulsed through her, igniting sparks along her spine. Afraid of the hunger that suddenly gnawed deep inside.

"You must leave now, Mr. McAllister." She could hear the panic in her voice, and hated herself for it. But her only salvation was sending him away. Quickly.

"Ma'am, I—" They both looked up when his horse ambled into the clearing. Spotting the deer across its back, Cassie suddenly understood.

"You weren't following me."

"I wanted to repay you for your hospitality." This was a safe topic, one with which they were both more comfortable. He released her hands and caught the reins of his horse.

Though he no longer held her, she could still feel the heat of his touch. She shivered uncontrollably.

"My family will be grateful for the meat, Mr. McAllister."

They walked side by side through the drifts, taking great care to see that they did not touch each other in any way. When they reached the cabin, the door burst open and Jen let out a whoop.

"Gram. Becky. Mr. McAllister is back."

Her older sister poked her head around the door. "Are you going to stay, Mr. McAllister?"

"I guess I can stay long enough to skin and clean this deer."

He saw the frown that wrinkled Luella's brow and couldn't help adding, "Of course, darkness comes early this time of year. I may have to put off leaving until tomorrow." That would give the old woman something to chew on. With a teasing smile he called, "Come on, Jen and Becky. Want to help me?"

Becky was repulsed at the thought of the bloody task. "No. I can't watch." She hurried to the bedroom she shared with her sister and grandmother, and lowered the blanket in the doorway for privacy.

"I will." Little Jen danced out the door, pulling on her parka as she followed Quin into the barn.

Cassie watched until they disappeared inside, then turned to find her mother studying her.

Carefully schooling her features, she said, "Mr. McAllister wanted to repay us for our hospitality. If we're careful, we'll have enough meat to last us through the winter."

"He's bound to find out about Ethan if he stays around long enough."

"He knows." Cassie saw her mother's frown deepen. "He happened upon me at the grave. I...had to tell him the truth."

Her mother's eyes narrowed. "Do you intend to allow him to stay the night?"

Cassie shrugged. "I don't see how I can ask him to go when he's just provided us with the first meat we've had in months."

"It isn't fitting for an unmarried woman to allow a man to sleep under her roof."

Cassie lowered her voice so her daughter wouldn't overhear. "He was Ethan's friend, Ma. He can be ours, too."

"And what if it isn't friendship he's looking for?"

The two women studied each other for long, silent moments.

"You're playing with fire, girl." With a sigh, Luella Chalmers turned away.

Lifting her skirts above the snow, Cassie made her way to the barn to assist in cutting the meat.

Dinner was a festive affair. The little cabin was perfumed with the aroma of meat roasting slowly over the fire. A huge blackened pot had simmered all afternoon with bones and innards. Its contents were then strained to make a rich broth, to which Cassie added chunks of meat and cut up vegetables from their precious supply. On top of it all she placed biscuit dough, which formed mouth-watering dumplings. Added to that was the rich aroma of coffee bubbling on the hot coals.

"I would like to lead the blessing tonight," Cassie said as they took their places around the table.

When her hand was engulfed in Quin's, she had to fight a tremor that rippled through her. Bowing her head, she began. "We thank Thee for the gift of this meat, and for our good friend, Mr. McAllister, who provided it. We ask Your blessings on all who are gathered here. And we ask You, Father, to remember the one who can no longer be with us. Look kindly on your servant, Ethan, who lies in his grave these long months."

The children's eyes widened, and they glanced from their mother to Quin, who kept his gaze focused on the table.

"And we ask Thee for the strength to see us through this winter."

After a chorus of amens, Becky asked timidly, "You told him, Mama?"

"Mr. McAllister discovered your father's grave this morning."

"Did Mama tell you how long our Pa's been dead?" Jen asked.

"Yes, Jen. Your mother told me everything."

The children seemed relieved to have this burden of lies lifted from their shoulders. Suddenly their conversation became animated as they talked openly of their father. It was as though a floodgate had been opened.

"Mama says Pa's in heaven with the angels." Jen lifted solemn eyes to Quin. "Mama says he doesn't feel any pain anymore. But I worry that he's cold at night."

"I wouldn't worry, Jen. That's why they call it paradise. It wouldn't be a happy place to be if the people there suffered any discomfort, would it?"

The little girl thought about that for a moment, then nodded, obviously relieved. "Do you think Pa knows what we're doing, and saying, and thinking?"

"I think your father wouldn't consider it heaven if he couldn't watch his daughters grow into fine women."

"Then you think he still looks out for us?"

"I'm sure of it. Even though he's gone, he's still your father."

His words were reassuring to two frightened, confused children. With each of Quin's responses, they seemed to relax a little more.

"Pa tracked a mountain lion once. Have you ever killed a mountain lion, Mr. McAllister?"

"No, Jen. But I once had to shoot a fox in the henhouse."

"Is a fox as mean as a mountain lion?"

"He is to the chickens." Quin winked at her, and the girl broke into spasms of giggles.

"Aw, you're teasing me, aren't you, Mr. McAllister?"

He nodded, then, seeing how withdrawn Becky was, he attempted to pull her into the conversation. "What about you, Becky? What do you remember about your father?"

"Papa loved my hair," Becky said with a flush.

"I can see why," Quin said. "It reminded him of your mother's beautiful hair."

Across the table, Cassie felt the heat of a blush begin at her throat and move upward.

"Papa used to tug on my curls, didn't he, Mama?"

Cassie nodded and felt Quin's gaze linger as though mentally tugging on her hair, making her cheeks even redder.

"He told me that you could sing like an angel." Quin studied the young girl, so like her mother. "And he vowed that one day you would study at the Conservatory of Music in Savannah just as your grandmother did."

Becky's smile fled. Her tone grew flat. "Pa was wrong. That was just a silly dream. I'm never going back to the South." She pushed back her chair and said, "I'd like to be excused."

Cassie nodded and the girl fled to her bedroom. When she was gone, Cassie explained, "Rebecca hasn't sung a note since her father died."

"I'm sorry, ma'am. I didn't realize."

For a minute they were all silent. Then Jen's enthusiasm returned. "My papa could do anything," she announced proudly. "Gram said Pa was a hero. Did you know that?"

"Yes." Quin sipped his coffee.

"He stood up to those Yankees," Jen said. "Even when he was in a Yankee prison, he never lost faith that he would make it home to us. And when he returned and found everything burned, he promised that we could all start over in a better place. Isn't that right, Gram?"

"Yes, indeed." Luella bit into another dumpling.

"You knew our pa when he was in prison, didn't you?" Jen asked.

"Yes, I did." Quin didn't like where this was leading. The subject was still too raw and painful.

"Then you knew he was a hero?" Jen turned big trusting eyes on Quin.

"Every man **who fought** for his country was a hero, Jen."

"Not the Yankees," she insisted.

"Even the Yankees. I met a lot of brave men who fought on different sides."

"But Gram said—"

"The war is over," Quin said gently. "And we have to learn to let it be over in our minds and hearts, as well."

In the awkward silence, Luella scraped back her chair and began to gather up the dishes.

Quin glanced over at Cassie. "I believe that was one of the finest meals I've ever eaten, ma'am."

"Thank you, Mr. McAllister. We have you to thank for the lovely meal."

"No, ma'am. You can thank the deer that happened to cross my path."

Jen chuckled at his joke. "Will you show me some more card tricks tonight?"

"I don't see why not. As long as your chores are finished and you work on your sums first."

Without a word of protest she skipped happily to the fireplace where she retrieved her slate. A short time later, when Cassie had checked Jen's sums and given approval of the work she'd done, Jen settled down beside Quin, prepared once again to be entertained. At the sound of her laughter, she was soon joined by Becky, who shyly took a seat beside Quin.

Late into the night the little cabin rang with their laughter.

* * *

The cabin was dark. The log in the fireplace had long ago burned to glowing embers.

Quin sat in the rocker, deep in thought, occasionally drawing on his cigar. His mood was somber.

If he had any sense at all, he'd be out of here at first light. After all, the last place he wanted to be was Montana in the dead of winter. By war's end he'd had his fill of snow. He'd vowed to never again be cold or hungry.

He was good at what he did. He made, and spent, great quantities of money. A man's man, he attracted the kind of gamblers with sizable fortunes, who lost with grace and humor. He'd rarely had to resort to a gun to settle a dispute. But when he did, he knew he was fast enough to come out a winner.

The life of a gambler suited him. He lived by his wit and charm. He loved a good cigar, fine whiskey, the company of men bent on a little fun, and an occasional perfumed woman to warm his bed.

So what was he doing here? It was one thing when he'd thought to share the adventure of searching for treasure with his old friend. But Ethan was dead. Dead. He shook his head in disbelief, then drew deeply on his cigar.

Despite their differences, he had loved Ethan like a brother. Through Ethan's words, Quin had come to know Jen and Becky as though they were his own. And Cassie. Quin frowned in the darkness. No woman could live up to the praise heaped upon her by her adoring husband. Maybe that was why he'd been persuaded to come. To see for himself if the woman and children were all that Ethan had boasted of.

And what now? He stood and tossed the remains of his cigar into the embers, watching as sparks leapt for a moment, then died. He had come; he had seen. Now it was time to move on. Before he found himself hopelessly entangled in their lives, and they in his.

Chapter Five

Cassie knew she was taking more time than usual as she washed, pouring a few drops of her precious lilac water into the basin. But, she consoled herself, it wasn't often that they entertained a visitor. In fact, Quin McAllister was the first one they'd had since their arrival in Montana. It wasn't only her children who were excited. Her own heartbeat was none too steady.

Her choice of dresses was limited to three, and all three were worn and faded. But she kept them in good repair, and they were clean. She chose a faded yellow, which had once been the color of golden buttercups. Because she had lost weight, the dress was too big, but she compensated by tying a clean apron around her middle. She ran a brush through her waist-length hair, then tied it back from her face with yellow ribbons. The boots she wore were old and scuffed, but, thankfully, only the toes were visible.

Moving aside the blanket that served as a door to her bedroom, she stepped into the main room of the cabin. At once her glance took in the empty bed in the corner. The furs and blankets were neatly folded. A fresh log blazed and crackled. Coffee bubbled on the fire. An empty cup rested on the table. Quin's cowhide duster was missing from the peg by the door.

He was gone. Gone without a word. She felt a wave of bitter disappointment.

As she moved mechanically around the kitchen, preparing breakfast for her family, she was surprised by how deeply wounded she felt. But what had she expected? He was a friend of Ethan's, brought to this wilderness under false pretenses. He had more than repaid their hospitality by providing them with enough meat to last the winter if they were frugal. Now he had to get on with his life.

She laid out the children's clothes on the hearth to warm, and prepared a pan of biscuits, then pulled on her buckskin jacket and headed to the barn for her morning chores.

A brittle morning sun nearly blinded her, reflected off a fresh snowfall that had obliterated the path to the barn. As she shoved open the door, she caught sight of Quin mucking a stall.

"Good morning," he called. "I thought I'd get an early start on the chores."

"Good morning." Her eyes danced with unconcealed delight. "I thought..."

"Thought what?" He leaned the pitchfork against the stall and walked closer. Comprehension dawned. "You thought that I'd left?"

She nodded, suddenly shy.

"Without saying goodbye?" The truth was, he had considered the idea but had instantly rejected it. "How could I leave without first lending a hand with the chores?"

"I'm glad. I wanted the chance to return this to you." From her pocket she removed his elegant, monogrammed handkerchief, freshly washed and ironed. "It was kind of you to lend it to me, but I know you'll be needing it."

As he accepted it from her hands he asked, "How is your burn?"

"It's healed. Thanks to you." She felt a little breathless and chided herself for it. "I'm so glad I had a chance to thank you one more time before you took leave of us."

He brought his hands to the collar of her jacket and surprised her by lifting her hair from beneath, where it had been trapped. "I'd be a fool to leave without one more sample of your fine home cooking."

At his touch her blood heated. The cold barn was suddenly too warm.

On a sigh she whispered, "The children would have been so disappointed if they couldn't say goodbye to you."

He chuckled. "Not to mention your mother."

Cassie couldn't help grinning. "Don't fault Ma. She's had so many disappointments, she's begun to expect the worst from life."

"I've seen it happen to a lot of people." He ran his knuckles along her cheek and felt the jolt run up his spine. Without realizing it, his tone lowered to a seductive whisper. "I'm glad to see it hasn't rubbed off on you."

"Oh. There are days." Her voice, too, had lowered. "But for the sake of the children, I have to remain hopeful."

He brushed snowflakes from her hair and thought about plunging his hands deep into the tangles. "They're beautiful children. Ethan used to love to talk about them."

She knew she needed to put some distance between them, but with his hand on her hair, she was frozen to the spot. "He spoke often about you, too."

He said nothing, merely stared into eyes so green they made him think about cool summer ponds in his native Georgia.

"He said you were the unsung hero in the prison camp. Without your skill with cards, it seems, there would have been no spare blankets, nor enough food to survive. I can't tell you how many nights he lay awake talking about how Gambler had saved his life."

Quin's voice deepened with feeling. "I'm no hero. I was just like everyone else who was trying to survive." With his big hands framing her face, he murmured, "And right now, I'm trying to do the right thing. But what I really want to do is..."

He lowered his face and brushed her lips with his. He'd meant it to be the merest touch of lips to lips. But the instant his mouth was on hers, his good intentions fled.

Fire. It engulfed him. His blood heated, slowing his movements, clouding his mind.

"No." She started to back up, but his hands were already at her shoulders, holding her still when she would have bolted.

And then, without any plan or design, her arms were around his waist and she was clinging to him, offering her lips for more.

With a muffled oath his arms came around her, dragging her against him until her breasts were flattened against his chest. He heard her sigh as he took the kiss deeper. And then he was lost. Lost in a kiss that was both sweet and bold. He tasted her hunger. It fed his own. With a sort of desperation he plunged his hands into her hair and rained kisses across her eyelids, her cheek, her jaw, then back to her lips. She smelled of soap and water, and faintly of summer lilacs. Her lips were the sweetest he'd ever tasted. Clean, fresh, like new-fallen snow. She felt so good in his arms. So right.

Cassie clung to him, feeling more alive than she could ever remember. All her senses were heightened by the nearness of this man. The taste of him, dark and mysterious. The carefully controlled strength in the arms that held her, the powerful thighs pressed to hers. She knew she had no right to such feelings. But she could no more resist his kisses than she could stop the snow from falling. With a sigh she gave herself up to the pleasure.

Quin could almost taste the loneliness, the longing that flowed from her. He knew he had to stop, but the need was too great. He wanted one more drugging kiss, one more moment to hold her just so, feeling her heartbeat keeping time with his own.

"Mama. Mr. McAllister. You in there?" At the sound of Jen's voice, followed by the opening of the barn door, their heads snapped up. They stepped apart seconds before the little girl rushed in and peered about in the gloom.

"Am I in time to help muck out the stalls?" she asked innocently.

"You sure are." Quin spun around, drawing attention away from Cassie, and handed the little girl a pitchfork.

"Haven't you milked the cow yet, Mama?"

Cassie ran sweating palms along her skirt, smoothing it down. On trembling legs she crossed to where the pail hung on a peg. "I was just going to get to it, Jennifer."

She dropped weakly to the stool, leaning her cheek against the solid, steady bulk of the cow, and took deep breaths to calm herself.

Across the barn, Quin busied himself with his horse. But his gaze kept straying to the woman whose mere touch set him on fire. His hands, he noted, weren't steady. And it would be a long time before his pulse returned to normal. Even his horse seemed to notice the change in him, dancing skittishly as he ran the brush over the sleek coat.

From her vantage point, Cassie watched as Quin groomed his horse. She found herself trembling with each movement as she imagined those same hands touching her.

Breakfast was as festive as supper had been the night before. Strips of venison snapped and sizzled in a pan over the fire. The wonderful aroma permeated the small cabin. They feasted on leftover stew, mopping up the gravy with fresh biscuits. The children drank milk warm from the cow, while the adults sipped scalding coffee.

Even Luella, fortified by such good food, seemed in high spirits. But Quin suspected that his imminent departure might have something to do with her good humor.

"Do you expect to make it to Prospect by day's end, Mr. McAllister?" Luella asked during a lull in the conversation.

At once, Quin saw the way the children's heads came up. He'd hoped not to cast a pall over the pleasant meal.

"That would be the town nearest here? Yes, ma'am. That was my intention yesterday until I was distracted by a herd of deer."

Out of the corner of his eye he saw Cassie watching him. He deliberately kept his gaze averted. Leaving was going to be harder than he'd thought.

"Quite a push for your horse, I'd say." Luella realized that the children had grown too quiet, and regretted her question. But they may as well get used to the idea of this man walking out of their lives as brusquely as he'd walked in. Cassie, too, for that matter. And if the lesson was hard, all the more reason to face it now rather than later. After all, life would deal many a harsh lesson.

"Cutter is used to the trail. He and I have crossed the entire country and back."

"I expect a gambler never stays in one place very long." Luella sipped her coffee and glanced around at the others to drive home her point.

Quin knew the game being played. But though it hurt, the older woman was right. There was no sense in any of them getting comfortable with the idea of having him around. "That's right, ma'am." He glanced at Cassie, then away. "The last thing a gambler needs is roots."

"But you just came back." Jen pushed away from the table and sprang to her feet. Her eyes had grown huge and tear-filled. "Why can't you stay with us awhile longer?"

"Young lady," Luella called sharply, "did you ask to be excused from the table?"

"Ma." Cassie placed a hand over her mother's to still her reprimand, then turned to her little daughter and said gently, "Come back to the table, Jennifer."

"No." Tears streamed down her cheeks. Embarrassed, she lifted clenched fists and swiped at them, then tore open the door and ran outside.

"I'll go after her, Mama," Becky said.

"No, Rebecca." Cassie pushed away from the table. "I'll go."

But before she could reach the door, it was thrown open, and Cyrus Stoner stepped over the threshold, carrying the kicking, flailing little girl in his arms.

"Look what I just found thrashing around in the snow."

At once Quin was on his feet, his pistol in his hand. But Stoner's men pushed their way across the room, aiming their guns at the women.

Tucking Jen under his arm, Stoner called, "I'd drop that, McAllister, unless you want to see these good people dead."

Quin let the pistol drop to the floor.

"That's better," Stoner snarled. "Now, Miz Montgomery, I'll ask you again about that husband of yours."

"He's still in the hills—" she began, but he cut her off with a string of savage oaths that had Luella drawing Becky close and covering her ears with her gnarled hands.

"And I thought you were such a virtuous lady," Stoner said with a sly smile. "Why, Miz Montgomery, don't you know it's a sin to lie?"

"I don't know what you—"

"Enough," he thundered.

The little girl in his arms whimpered, but he continued to hold her under one arm like a sack of grain.

"My men happened upon something interesting near the forest." Stoner smiled at the stunned look on Cassie's face. "They were following McAllister's trail, Miz Montgomery, and what do you think they stumbled on?"

When she held her silence he hissed, "A grave, that's what. And do you have any idea whose grave it is?"

"Please give me my little girl, Mr. Stoner." Her voice was little more than a whisper. But the fear vibrated.

"I intend to do that, just as soon as we come to some terms, Miz Montgomery."

"I will not discuss terms with—"

"You have no choice," he interrupted. "Now that I know your husband is dead. He is dead, isn't he?"

She said nothing, and he went on, as casually as though he were discussing the weather. "That's what I thought. How long have you been keeping that fact from me?"

She lifted her head a fraction but held her silence.

"No matter. I guess you're the one I need to deal with now. Isn't that right, Miz Montgomery?"

She swallowed and nodded.

"All right." Satisfied at this minor concession, he said, "You just listen. I'll do the talking. The deal is this." His voice was low, reasonable. "I'll pay you five hundred dollars for your land. My men will be here tomorrow with a couple of wagons to help you move your belongings to Prospect. From there the stage will take you to wherever you want to go."

"Pack up and leave? Just like that?" Her tone was incredulous. "You don't really expect me to accept that offer, Mr. Stoner."

"And why not? That's a dollar an acre. For useless wilderness land. Nobody with any sense would offer you that much, Miz Montgomery. My offer is more than generous."

"This is our home, Mr. Stoner. We can't just leave and settle somewhere else."

"I've learned, Miz Montgomery, that with enough money, a person can do anything he pleases."

"Maybe. But I have no intention of selling, to you or to anyone."

He lifted Jen up and turned the little girl around so that Cassie could see her eyes wide with fear.

"Take a good look, Miz Montgomery. If you value her safety, and that of your other daughter, you'll think twice about what I've offered."

"Are you threatening this family?" Quin asked. It was the first time he'd spoken, and the barely controlled fury was evident in his tone.

The two men turned and lifted their pistols until they were pointed directly at his temple. Becky whimpered. Luella's lips moved in prayer. But Quin didn't flinch.

"Threatening?" Cyrus Stoner turned to Quin with a cool look. "McAllister, I don't make threats. I make predictions." He hoisted Jen over his head, where the little girl thrashed about ineffectively. "And I predict that, unless the lady packs up and leaves, bad things are going to start happening around here. Maybe this time they won't just happen to farm animals. You know those Indians up in the hills? They're savages." He laughed. "I don't think these proper ladies would care to hear what savages do to women and children."

He let go the struggling girl, and for a moment it looked as though he would let Jen fall to the floor. Everyone caught their breaths. Becky let out a scream.

At the last second, Stoner caught the child and set her down. "You see? Be glad I'm not one of those savages," he said with a sneer.

On trembling legs the little girl rushed into her mother's arms.

"Tomorrow," Cyrus Stoner said as he spun on his heel and started out the door. "My men and I will be by with the cash, Miz Montgomery. Be packed up and ready to leave." He tipped his hat and signaled to his men, who backed from the cabin, their guns still aimed at Quin until the door closed.

Cassie dropped to her knees and gathered Jen into a fierce embrace. Luella and Becky drew close and wrapped their arms around the girl and her mother, forming a protective circle.

Across the room, Quin stood very still, watching the scene with eyes that had gone as cold as ice.

"Looks like I'll be staying awhile," he said flatly.

Everyone turned to look at him as he bent and picked up his gun. Twirling the chamber, he checked the bullets, then jammed it back into his holster.

In that moment, Cassie realized, he had changed. The roguish glint in his eyes was gone, along with the charming, teasing manner. The man who stood before them was a tough, hardened gunfighter. In the blink of an eye, he had become once more the shadowy figure Ethan had boasted about, who had patrolled the prison camp, keeping his fellow prisoners alive despite impossible odds.

"I guess," he muttered as he made his way out the door to unsaddle his horse, "some wars are never over."

Chapter Six

Cassie should have been elated to learn that Quin was staying. So why, she asked herself, was she so troubled? While she went through the motions of completing her daily chores, her mind worked feverishly. A part of her desperately wanted him to stay. She had seen the transformation in him when Stoner had made his threats. She had no doubt that his gun could make a difference if she decided to hold out against Stoner and his men. And, though she tried, she could hardly deny her attraction to this man. But the feelings he aroused in her worried and frightened her. The last thing she needed in her life was to lose her heart to a rogue gambler.

Perhaps she should send him away. Yet, even while her mind formed the thought, she rejected it. His staying meant that she was not alone in this fight. She would not have to accept Cyrus Stoner's ultimatum.

Still, the truth was, she wasn't at all certain that she was doing the right thing. Maybe she ought to take the money. For five hundred dollars she could relocate her family to a warmer, more hospitable climate. For all her brave talk in front of Quin, this harsh land terrified her. She was here for only one reason—to keep a promise.

She thought again about Ethan's emotional plea while he lay dying.

"Promise me, Cassie, that you won't give up on this land."

"But how will we survive without you, Ethan? How can you ask us to stay here, alone, miles from our nearest neighbor?"

"You won't be alone. I beg you, Cassie. Trust me on this. For your sake, and that of the children, please don't allow yourself to give up. Promise me."

And so she had given her solemn promise to her dying husband. But when she had given her word to follow his dream, she hadn't known the price that would be exacted. How could she sacrifice her children for a dead man's dream?

"Becky, do you know how to use this rifle?" Quin asked.

At once the girl let out a cry.

Cassie, looking up from the dough she was kneading, was abruptly yanked from her troublesome thoughts. Rushing to her daughter's side, she said gently, "Rebecca, it's all right. You may go to your room."

When the girl was out of earshot, Cassie explained, "The war has left her terrified of guns and violence, Mr. McAllister. By the time we fled Atlanta, Rebecca was unable to even hear the sound of gunfire without weeping and trembling."

"I'm not afraid," little Jen announced. "Will you teach me how to handle my pa's rifle, Mr. McAllister?"

"No, Jen." He touched a hand to her mop of curls. "I don't think that's necessary. But I don't ever want to see you or your sister leave this house without one of us accompanying you. Understand?"

"Yes, sir."

Luella looked horrified. "Then you believe that man will carry out his threats?"

"I don't know what to believe, ma'am. But I tend to take all threats seriously."

"Do you really think we are strong enough to be able to defend ourselves against those evil men?"

"A gun is the only thing they respect. At least they'll think twice about attacking us if they see that we're armed. Without our weapons, we don't stand a chance. From now on we don't leave this cabin without protection. Not even for an armload of firewood." He turned to Luella. "Mrs. Chalmers, do you know how to fire a gun?"

The older woman drew herself up very straight. "I once held off a passel of Yankees for two days when they tried to raid my barn and run off my best sow."

The corners of Quin's lips turned up, and he swallowed his smile as he handed her a rifle, cleaned and oiled, along with a sack of ammunition. "I expect you to keep this by your side, even when you're sleeping."

She took the rifle and examined it closely, pleased that it was in good condition. Her gray head bent as she loaded the rifle, before placing the rest of the bullets in the pocket of her faded gown. When she lifted her head she gave him a stern, appraising look. "My father used to say that a man who keeps his weapons sharp, keeps his mind in the same order, Mr. McAllister."

He crossed the room to Cassie. "Did Ethan keep a pistol?"

"Yes." Wiping her hands on a towel, she walked into her bedroom and emerged carrying her husband's holster and pistol.

Quin examined it closely. Assured that the pistol was in good working order, he handed it back to her. "You won't need the holster. But keep the pistol on your person, whether awake or asleep."

She swallowed and dropped it into the pocket of her gown, but not before he saw the fear in her eyes. "Are we to be prisoners in our own home now, Mr. Mc-Allister?"

He wished he could offer her some measure of comfort. To keep from touching her he strode across the room and pulled on the heavy fur parka. "I think this might be a good time to chop more wood."

"You mean we can go about our chores?" Jen called.

"I don't see why not, as long as we're careful."

All afternoon, while the fragrance of freshly baking bread wafted on the air, the silence of the frozen wilderness rang with the sound of an ax biting into logs. And by evening, Quin had piled enough wood beside the fireplace to last them a week or more.

"That was a fine supper, ma'am."

"Thank you, Mr. McAllister."

"Think I'll take a walk around the barn. Maybe enjoy a cigar while I walk."

"Can I go with you, Mr. McAllister?" Jen asked.

"May I, Jennifer," Cassie said softly. "Not can I."

"Yes, Mama. May I, Mr. McAllister?"

"Sure, Jen. I'd like the company." He glanced at Becky, who had been quiet and withdrawn all day. "Would you like to come, too, Becky?"

She shrugged, but it was plain that she was happy to be included. "I suppose." She pulled on her parka and followed Quin and Jen outside.

When they were gone, Luella frowned. "You shouldn't have let them go, girl. It isn't safe out there."

"I know, Ma. But I can't keep them cooped up inside forever. Besides, there's something about Mr. McAllister. I feel like—" Cassie shrugged "—like he'd risk his life for theirs."

"Don't go making him into something he isn't, girl. He told you himself. He's a gambler. Plain and simple. And gamblers aren't the kind of men you trust with your valuables or your life."

Deep in thought, Cassie cleared the table and began to wash the dishes. Her mother worked alongside her, giving voice to her worries.

"I know that Mr. McAllister's gun will be useful against Cyrus Stoner. But I still feel that it is unwise to permit him to stay beneath our roof. Perhaps he could sleep in the barn...."

"No, Ma." Cassie set down a clean plate and reached for another. "He will sleep in the cabin."

"He is a strong, virile man, with a man's appetites."

"I don't want to argue with you, Ma, but Mr. McAllister is not going to sleep in the cold barn."

"I just want to warn you, girl, that you are inviting scandal upon your family if you should succumb to that gambler's charms."

Dishes clattered in the soapy water. Cassie's eyes flashed fire. "That gambler, as you call him, is risking his life for us."

"Maybe," Luella said with a trace of suspicion. "And then again..."

"What?" Cassie whirled on her mother.

"Maybe this gambler sees a fortune for the taking."

"What fortune?"

"The fortune that Ethan said was to be found in the mine."

"I told you, Ma," Cassie struggled to hold on to her last thread of patience. "That fortune was in Ethan's mind. He never found a trace of any treasure."

Luella shrugged. "Maybe. But it appears that Ethan didn't tell you everything. There were some things he kept to himself."

"And what is that supposed to mean?"

The two women eyed each other for long, silent moments.

Finally Luella spoke. "You had no idea that he'd even written to Quin McAllister."

Defeated, Cassie looked away. She had nothing left to say. The question rankled. Why had Ethan not told her about his letter to Quin McAllister?

While she finished the last of her kitchen chores, her mother picked up a basket of mending and settled herself in front of the fire.

"I need Becky," the old woman complained, "to thread my needle."

Without a word Cassie took the needle and thread from her mother's hands, looped thread through the eye and returned it to her mother's fingers. Deeply troubled, she then immersed herself in work.

"Have you ever played poker with any famous men, Mr. McAllister?" Jen asked.

The two children were seated on either side of Quin while he, over Luella's protestations, taught them the basics of poker. Cassie had argued that it would help them pass the time. And, although she refused to join them, she couldn't help glancing over from time to time while she prepared dough for the morning biscuits.

"A few."

"Who?" Jen asked with sudden interest.

"James Butler Hickok, for one."

The children seemed disinterested until he added, "I'm sure you've heard of him. Wild Bill Hickok."

"Wild Bill!" Jen's eyes were as wide as saucers. "You met Wild Bill? Where?"

"In Deadwood."

"And you played poker with him?"

Quin nodded.

Luella looked up. "Isn't he a respected lawman?"

Quin showed his familiar grin. "Some would say. But the truth is, law is just a diversion for Wild Bill. His first love is gambling."

"Did you beat him?" Jen asked.

"That I did. And handsomely. Needless to say, I didn't linger too long in Deadwood, for fear the marshal would find some way to get his money back."

"You mean you thought he'd beat you in another game?"

"No, Becky. I figured if I stayed around, he'd find some reason to put me behind bars."

"Have you ever broken the law?" Jen asked.

Aware that Luella's needle and thread had gone slack, Quin answered carefully. "Some laws are meant to be broken."

"What laws?" Becky handed the cards over to Quin and watched as his long fingers easily manipulated them.

"Any law that favors the strong and powerful over the weak and defenseless."

"Do you set yourself above the law, Mr. Mc-Allister?" Luella's voice rang with challenge.

"No, ma'am. But I'm not above fighting to change what ought to be changed."

"And breaking the law if you can't change it?"

Quin gave her a lazy smile. "Yes, ma'am. I guess that's so."

"My daughter is raising her children to abide by the law. All the laws." For emphasis, the old woman brought the needle angrily through the cloth with such force she pricked her finger. With a hiss of pain she returned her attention to her sewing.

"An admirable thing. My mother did the same." Quin dealt the hand and the two children picked up their cards. "But my father was always a bit of a rebel. He taught me to ask why."

Something in his tone had changed. Though his voice was still low, with little inflection, there was an edge of steel to it.

The two children looked up from their cards. Across the room, Cassie watched and listened.

"And sometimes," Quin said softly, "just by asking, you discover that nobody knows the why of things. They'll tell you it's the way things have always been done. But that's really no answer. In this life we have to challenge, to ask. And when we see an injustice, we have to act to correct it. Even if it means we will have to pay the ultimate price."

"What is the—" Jen struggled with this new, unfamiliar word "—ultimate price, Mr. McAllister?"

"Its meaning is found in the Bible." Cassie's voice had them all turning to stare at her. "Greater love hath no man than that he would lay down his life for another." She crossed the room and lowered her hand to

the little girl's shoulder, but her gaze remained steady
on Quin. "The ultimate price, Jennifer, is to risk your
life for a cause that is noble, even if that cause should
prove to be unpopular with others."

Glancing up, Becky saw the look that passed between her mother and Quin McAllister.

From her position before the fire, Luella saw it as
well. Her mouth tightened into a grim, tight line.

"Time for bed, children." Cassie had allowed them
to linger over their card game in order to soothe the
tensions of this difficult day.

"Good night, Mr. McAllister," they called in unison
as they followed their mother to the bedroom.

A few minutes later he could hear their voices muffled in prayer. Through the doorway he saw Cassie
standing between them, head bent, one hand on each
shoulder as they recited a litany of blessings on those
they loved. They prayed for their father, their mother
and grandmother, and for deliverance from Cyrus
Stoner's guns.

"She is very beautiful, isn't she?"

Quin looked up to find Luella watching him closely.
When he made no comment she went on, "You are a
very worldly man, Mr. McAllister. My daughter has
never met anyone quite like you before."

He set the cards aside and waited. It was obvious that
the words had been building up inside her and needed
to find expression.

"Cassie has been alone now for some time." Luella
set aside her mending and eased herself out of the chair,
pressing a hand to the small of her back. "With the war,
and then Ethan's long illness, she was forced to handle
more than most young women."

"She seems to be doing fine."

Luella frowned. "This is not the life I'd hoped for my daughter."

"The war changed a lot of lives."

"Some more than others." She cast a quick glance at her daughter and grandchildren, then said, "Cassie is unaware of how her beauty affects men. Even as a young woman in Atlanta there were several who were beginning to pay too much attention. But Ethan came from one of the finest families in Georgia. I knew that Cassie, at not yet fifteen, wasn't ready for marriage, but an opportunity like that does not present itself often. And so, when Ethan pressed for her hand, her father and I agreed, knowing she would be a good and dutiful wife." For a moment Luella's eyes glowed, and Quin could see that she was remembering happier times. "He built her the finest house, staffed with the finest servants. The furnishings were brought from Europe. Belgian lace, Irish crystal. Oh, the lavish balls. It was a life fit for a queen. All my friends were so envious."

Quin wondered if she knew how much she had revealed in that last statement. "It must be quite a disappointment to live your days in a rough cabin, and see your daughter fighting to save this little plot of ground in the middle of a wilderness. I can see why you would be protective of her."

Luella's head came up. "She is still my daughter, Mr. McAllister. Though I question the wisdom of her actions, I will support her in whatever way I can." She turned and, seeing Cassie tucking the children into bed, added quickly, "I just want you to understand something. Despite her once lavish life-style, my daughter has little sophistication. A woman of her background just might confuse loneliness and gratitude with love. Have I made myself clear, Mr. McAllister?"

"Perfectly clear, Mrs. Chalmers."

She turned away and whispered furiously, "A woman like Cassie has no defense against a man like you."

As she made her way to the bedroom she shared with her grandchildren, her words echoed in Quin's mind. *A man like you.*

Deep in thought, he lifted a parka from a peg and walked outside.

A few minutes later, when Cassie emerged from the children's bedroom, she glanced around, expecting to find Quin in front of the fire. Instead the cabin was empty.

Out on the porch she saw a sudden flare of light as he held a match to his cigar. She had hoped to spend a few quiet moments with him, talking about what laws he thought were unfair, and how he hoped to change them. But from the angry frown on his face, she decided the time wasn't right.

She made up his bed in the corner of the room, then snuffed out the candles, leaving the cabin dark except for the light from the fire.

This was when the loneliness became the most difficult to bear. In the quiet of the night, she missed the easy camaraderie, the long, intimate conversations, the sharing of ideas. She shivered. The mating of two minds, Ethan had called it. Though he had been a man of few passions, he had understood and respected hers. Her deepest and most abiding passion had been her family. And her education at the hands of an order of French nuns at the Convent of Notre Dame du Lac had opened her eyes to the world and its ills. But being a dutiful daughter and wife, she had kept her thoughts locked away in silence, devoting herself to those things that took precedence. At first, those things had been a social life that would have rivaled that of royalty. During and after the war, her every thought had been the survival of her family. But now, when Quin had spoken out so passionately, he had touched a chord deep inside her.

"I thought you would be asleep."

She had been so deep in thought, she hadn't heard Quin come in. Her hand flew to her throat as she whirled to face him. "Once again you have managed to startle me, Mr. McAllister."

In the firelight, her hair gleamed like flame. He thought about touching a hand to it, but her mother's words still rankled. "And once again I find you lost in thought. Care to share?"

She saw the teasing smile that always seemed to play at the corners of his mouth, the light that always danced in those dark, mysterious eyes. How could she have believed that he was a man of deep passions? Her mother's words came back to taunt her. He was a gambler, whose only real passion lay in winning.

"It's late, Mr. McAllister. I'll say good-night."

"Good night, ma'am." He carefully curled his hand into a fist as she moved past him, to keep from reaching out to stop her.

At the door to her bedroom she turned. "I am most grateful to you for staying to see us through this battle."

His tone was rougher than he'd intended. "I don't want your gratitude, Mrs. Montgomery."

He turned away and stared into the flickering flames of the fire. Her mother's words echoed in his mind. Was Cassie a woman who might confuse gratitude with love?

With a savage oath he tossed the remains of his cigar into the fire.

Chapter Seven

Darkness shrouded the room. Cassie shifted beneath the covers. For hours she had fought the dreams that tormented her. In her sleep Ethan had come to her, reminding her about her promise to him. But the image of her dead husband faded, to be replaced by the figure of Cyrus Stoner, holding a gun to her little daughter's heart. Her plea for mercy had been met with cruel, chilling laughter. She awoke with a start, her night shift damp, her heart pounding.

Though it would be some time until dawn, she couldn't stay in bed any longer. She had a need to do something, anything, to keep from thinking about Cyrus Stoner's threat.

Did he really believe that she would be packed and ready to leave her home just because he'd ordered it? She shivered, anticipating the confrontation. Despite her family's attempt at bravado, their guns would be ineffective against a man like Stoner. How many men would ride with him? How much force would he use?

She had thought, after surviving the fiery siege of Atlanta, that nothing else would ever have the power to bring her to the edge of terror. But right now, as the hour hovered between darkness and dawn, she felt all the old fears rising within her. What if Stoner made good his threats? What if her stubborn determination to stay here caused harm to one of her loved ones? Once again she fretted over the wisdom of her action. Did she have the right to place her mother, her innocent children in danger?

Throwing aside the covers, she slipped from bed and padded barefoot across the room. As she poured icy water from a pitcher into a basin and began to wash herself, she shivered violently. It wasn't merely the cold, she knew. It was nerves strung as tautly as the strings of her grandfather's violin.

With hurried movements she pulled on long woolen hose, chemise and petticoats. From a hook beside the door she lifted down a pale ivory wool gown, with long sleeves and a high, modest neckline. After running a brush through her hair, and pulling it back with white ribbons, she draped a shawl over her shoulders.

The simple act of making up the bed gave her a sense of normalcy. How could there be danger pending when she had the luxury of household chores?

Within minutes the bedroom was tidied, and she lifted aside the blanket that hung at the doorway.

She was startled to see Quin standing at the small window, a rifle in his hand. His straight razor lay beside a basin of water. Droplets still glistened in his dark hair.

"Have you been awake all night?" she asked softly.

He turned, and caught his breath at the sight of her. Dressed all in white, she could have been some ethereal creature, had it not been for the blaze of hair that spilled down her back in a riot of curls. Damp tendrils still kissed her cheeks, cheeks as red as holly berries from her icy ablutions.

"I slept some. But I thought Stoner and his men might try to surprise us with an early morning visit."

She walked up beside him and glanced out the window. "Any sign of him?"

"None." He breathed in the clean, fresh scent of her and felt the stirring of feelings he'd thought long buried.

"Do you think it's safe for me to go to the barn? I'd really like to milk the cow."

He nodded. "I'll go with you."

They pulled on their parkas and stepped out into the frigid predawn darkness. Starlight reflected off the frozen crust that had formed on the snow. The moon was a pale sliver in a darkened sky. Snow crunched beneath their feet. The air was sharp and pure, and carried the tang of evergreen from the nearby forest.

Inside the barn, they breathed in the mingled scents of fresh hay, earth and dung. The chickens, awakened by their early visitors, clustered around their feet, eager for grain. When Cassie tossed some into the hay, they scratched and pecked. The cow lowed softly in her stall, while Cutter tossed his head and nuzzled Quin's hand.

Cassie and Quin worked in companionable silence, mucking stalls, gathering eggs, milking the cow. The hard physical work offered a release from the tensions that were building. Tensions brought on by the knowledge that this day they could face a confrontation with an enemy bent on destroying them.

It was Quin who broke the silence. "I've been thinking that maybe you and your mother ought to take the children and hide."

She looked up from milking the cow. His suggestion took her by surprise. "And if I hide, what would prevent Cyrus Stoner from simply taking over my house and barn and property?"

"I'll see to Stoner."

She got to her feet so quickly she knocked over the milking stool. "I have no intention of abandoning my home."

"I'm not suggesting you abandon it." He watched as she righted the stool and lifted the heavy pail of milk. "Just . . . stay out of sight until he leaves."

She placed the pail by the door and turned, pulling on the parka, which she'd shed while doing her chores. "So, you think I should hide like a coward, while you stay and face Cyrus Stoner and his men alone?"

"I've faced worse."

With her hands on her hips she crossed the space that separated them. "This is my home, Mr. McAllister. And my problem. I won't be persuaded to run away while someone else fights my battles."

Giving in to anger and frustration, he caught her by the front of the parka and dragged her close. "Then at least make plans to get the children out of the line of fire, in the event there's a gunfight." He saw the flash of fear that came into her eyes and cursed his clumsiness. Why was it, in time of grave peril, when the need for comfort was greatest, there was so little time for it? In a softer tone he asked, "Is there someplace we can hide them?"

She swallowed, touched by his attempt at gentleness. "In the mine shaft."

"Is it far from here?"

She smiled. "Come on, Mr. McAllister. It's time I showed you."

With his rifle in one hand and the pail of milk in the other, he followed her from the barn.

When she retraced her steps to the cabin, he hesitated. "I thought we were going to the mine."

"We are." She held open the door to the cabin. Inside, she crossed the room and moved aside a small handmade rug to reveal a portion of the floor that could be lifted up. "The entrance to the mine is under here."

When he lifted the door, Cassie handed him a lantern and he climbed down a rough-hewn ladder. Cassie followed.

Quin found himself in a dark, narrow tunnel. As he inched forward he whispered, "Why did Ethan build the cabin over the mine?"

Cassie's voice was close behind him. "He didn't. The mine is actually on the other side of a series of large hills. He dug a separate shaft leading to the mine, so that he could come and go, day or night, without being observed."

"Then he had to believe in this mine."

"He did," she said softly. "He never gave up hope of finding a treasure."

The tunnel suddenly split into two passageways. Lifting the lantern, Quin asked, "Which way?"

Cassie shrugged. "Ethan left no map. But the last place he worked, before the illness overtook him, was this way."

He followed her lead and found himself in a labyrinth of tunnels.

"Did Ethan dig all these?" Quin asked.

Cassie shook her head. "Most of these were already here. When Ethan discovered them, he became convinced that this was the mine he had heard about when he was a boy. An old man who had befriended his father had boasted of it on his deathbed, and had left behind a faded map. Ethan and his father often talked about searching for treasure, but..." She shrugged. "The time was never right. Montana Territory sounded, to a Georgia farm boy, like the end of the earth."

Quin gave a low whistle of appreciation as he set the lantern on a shelf of rock. "I'm impressed."

"That would please Ethan." At his arched brow, Cassie explained, "Ethan credited the war, and his friendship with you, for bringing him here. He claimed that, once our home was destroyed, he was forced to turn his back on all that he knew and loved. And you had convinced him that a man must be willing to risk everything for what he believes in. He swore that without you, he never would have found the courage to chase his dream. As you well know, it was not in Ethan's nature to take risks."

Quin chuckled. "For a man who didn't like to take risks, he managed to finally do it in grand style." He turned to study her. "But what about you? Didn't you have anything to say about traveling all the way to Montana Territory and settling in this godforsaken wilderness?"

She blushed and looked away. "I suppose I could have dissuaded Ethan. But it was his dream, and I felt I had no right to trample on it. Besides," she added softly, "all my life I've had to do the right thing, the sensible thing. I was always the good daughter, then the good wife and mother. And I suppose there was, deep inside me, a yearning to do something completely unexpected."

Her admission caught him by surprise. He felt a sudden kinship with this woman.

Tugging on a lock of her hair, he said, "Couldn't you have chosen something a little less dangerous, until you got it out of your system? Like flirting with the preacher? Or sipping some of Ethan's whiskey?''

She laughed, a rich, golden sound that seemed to trickle over his senses like warm honey. He found himself wishing he could always bring that light of amusement to her eyes with such ease.

''I did try Ethan's whiskey.''

''Why Mrs. Montgomery. How bold of you.''

She grinned. ''I discovered I didn't like it. As for the preacher back in Georgia, he had lost his front teeth, and had a face that resembled a mule. In fact, I would rather flirt with a mule than with Reverend Poindexter.''

Quin threw back his head and roared. Then, leaning his forehead against hers, he whispered, ''I believe, Mrs. Montgomery, that you are the most delightful creature I have ever had the good fortune to meet.''

She joined in the laughter, but her smile faded when he suddenly framed her face with his hands and lifted it for his inspection.

''And the most beautiful,'' he breathed.

His gaze centered on her mouth and she felt her throat go dry. ''Don't...'' she started, but the word was swallowed by his kiss.

The rest of the words died in her throat. Her thoughts scrambled and fled in a wild rush, leaving her feeling strangely disoriented.

His lips were warm and firm and practiced as they moved seductively over hers. Her lips trembled slightly when she struggled to absorb the first shock.

He lifted his head and stared down into her eyes. His hands still framed her face, but his thumbs now moved slowly, tracing the outline of her lips, sending strange, curling sensations along her spine.

She saw the fire smoldering in his eyes and thought fleetingly about stepping back from it. But though his touch was gentle, she was held as surely as if she'd been ensnared by a steel trap. She found it impossible to move away from the flame that poured from him into her, heating her blood, searing her flesh.

"Mr. McAllister—"

"It's Quin," he muttered thickly. His thumb traced her full lower lip, while his eyes held hers when she tried to look away. "I think the time for formality is over, Cassie."

He lowered his head and brushed his lips over hers. His arms came around her, dragging her roughly against him.

Fear jolted through her. Fear of the tightly controlled passion she could feel pulsing through him like waves of heat. Fear of her own response to such passion. But as quickly as she recognized it, the fear was replaced by something even stronger. Needs. Needs she hadn't even recognized until now. Needs so potent they left her trembling. At his touch, his kiss, she felt the awakening of long-slumbering passions that struggled for expression.

With her hands against his shoulders, she pushed away. "We can't—"

"The hell we can't." His hands tangled in her hair as he kissed her with a thoroughness, a savageness that left them both breathless.

Her protest was forgotten. Everything was forgotten except this man, this moment. Her arms twined around his neck. Her body pressed tightly against his. With a sigh she gave herself up to the pleasure of his kiss.

His mouth moved on hers. Lingering over her lips, he drew out every exquisite taste, like a starving man.

In that instant before their lips met, he'd seen a flash of something in her eyes. Something dark and liquid and fathomless. Fear or passion. Or perhaps both.

"Cassie." Her name was wrenched from him as he took the kiss deeper.

She forgot to breathe. Her heart forgot to beat.

Quin had an almost savage need to take her here, now. The thought brought a fierce, shocking arousal that had him clutching her so tightly she cried out. At once his touch softened, while his lips continued to plunder.

"Open your eyes," he muttered against her mouth.

Her heavy lids fluttered, then opened. In her eyes he could read the newly awakened passion, which only excited him more.

"I want to see you while I kiss you. I want you to see me."

His mouth crushed hers, ruthless, savage. He could feel her heartbeat, ragged, racing, keeping time with his as he took the kiss deeper. With a little moan her lips parted for him. His tongue probed all her sweetness, unlocking hidden mysterious tastes. Tastes that sharpened his appetite to feast until his hunger was satisfied, to take until he was sated.

Cassie felt desire claw at her. Wants, needs, warred within her, struggling to be set free. It would be so easy to put aside everything except the pleasure he could bring her. Into her harsh, frigid world, this gambler's kisses offered the treasures of summer, a garden of sensual delights. Still, though all her senses had been assaulted, a tiny voice of reason found its way to her consciousness.

"No. Quin, no."

He lifted his head but kept his hands on her shoulders, as much to steady himself as her. Even as she tried to back away, he brushed kisses across her forehead, her cheek, the tip of her nose. But before he could take her lips again she stopped him.

"We must get back," she whispered. But she made no move to turn away.

He waited until his erratic heartbeat slowed, then dropped his hands to his sides and took a step back.

"I'll lead the way."

He picked up the lantern, held it high and began to retrace his steps. He noted idly that his hand trembled, and blamed it on the crude footpath. But there was no denying the need for her that still pulsed. Or the taste of her that was still on his lips.

Chapter Eight

Luella and her grandchildren were gathered around the fireplace. Jen and Becky had shrugged into their clothes, which their mother had laid out to warm on the hearth. All heads came up when Cassie and Quin emerged from the mine shaft.

While Cassie blew out the lantern, Quin met the questioning looks of the others.

"What were you doing in the mine?" Luella asked.

At her mother's sharp words, Cassie felt her cheeks flame.

It was Quin who answered. "I wanted to see if it might offer a safe haven for the children."

Immediately Luella's attitude softened. "You expect a gunfight, do you?"

Quin shrugged. "With a man like Cyrus Stoner, I don't know what to expect. It's always wise to plan for the worst."

"I'm not surprised." Luella wrapped a towel around her hand and lifted the coffeepot from the fire. "Sit. I'll fix breakfast. We'll want to fortify ourselves for the day. I expect we'll be...entertaining company before very long."

Cassie found herself drawing strength from her mother's stoic acceptance of danger. As she took a seat, she glanced around at her daughters, and wished again that she could spare them this confrontation.

"Ma," she said softly, "would you like to lead the blessing?"

As they joined hands the older woman's voice rang out like a preacher. "Bless this food, Lord. And bless Your humble servants. This day, as we face the enemy, we ask for the wisdom of Solomon, and the strength of David, who smote the mighty Goliath."

To a chorus of amens, they began to pass around biscuits and coddled eggs and thick slabs of venison.

They were clearing the table a short time later when they heard the sound of hoofbeats. Following Quin's lead, the two women took up their weapons.

"Jennifer and Rebecca," Cassie called softly. "I want you to climb down to the mine shaft."

"But Mama—" Jen began.

"There's no time to argue. Hurry."

Quin led the way, handing them a lantern and blanket.

As they started down the ladder, Cassie bent and kissed each of them tenderly. "No matter what you hear, you must not show yourselves," she whispered. "If I don't summon you, remain below."

"For how long, Mama?" Becky's voice trembled, betraying her fear.

"Until darkness, Rebecca. Then take the horse and the two of you ride to town."

"But—"

"Go now," Cassie said firmly.

"Yes, Mama."

Quin waited until they had descended before lowering the trapdoor and replacing the rug.

"Mrs. Chalmers," he said softly, "you might want to stand away from that window. Here." He tipped the kitchen table on end and motioned for her to take up a position behind it.

"Miz Montgomery." The sound of Cyrus Stoner's voice came from outside the cabin. "Are you ready to leave?"

Quin opened the cabin door a fraction, then shielded Cassie's body with his and whispered, "I don't see his men. They might be surrounding the cabin right now."

"Where are your men, Mr. Stoner?" she called.

"I told my men to stay back by that line of trees until you invited them to come closer."

Surprised, Cassie shot a suspicious glance at Quin. "Do you believe him?"

Quin shrugged. "I haven't figured out his game yet, but he could be telling the truth."

"I've brought you five hundred dollars," called Stoner. "Are you ready to accept my offer, Miz Montgomery?"

As she started forward Quin clamped a hand around her arm. "Don't show yourself," he whispered. "Just give him your answer."

"I'm sorry, Mr. Stoner." Cassie was amazed at how calm her voice sounded. There was no trace of the fear that bubbled just below the surface. Perhaps it was the presence of Quin beside her, silent and steady, or the touch of his hand on her arm, strong, sure. "I've decided not to accept your offer. My family and I are happy here. We'd like to stay in the cabin my husband built for us."

"I don't think you understand," replied Stoner, his voice reasonable, persuasive. Slipping from the saddle, he boldly walked to the cabin door. He kicked it open. Seeing the guns aimed at him, he held up his hands and gave a broad smile. "Now that isn't very neighborly. I didn't come here to fight, Miz Montgomery. I came here to make you wealthy." He reached into his breast pocket, retrieved a handful of bills, and held them out to her. "There's enough money here to build a fine house in Prospect, where your children can go to school, and your poor mother can walk to Sunday services and chat with her neighbors."

Cassie wondered if Stoner knew that he'd just described paradise. Putting aside such thoughts, she said, "We like it here, Mr. Stoner."

He glanced around the bleak surroundings, his smile widening. His words were as smooth as honey. "And who wouldn't? A snug, sturdy cabin. Of course," he added, "it seems a bit crowded, with all these bodies. But then I'm sure a man like Quin McAllister won't be staying around these parts very long."

He could see he'd touched a nerve. Cassie glanced uncertainly toward Quin, then looked away. There was fear in her eyes, along with indecision. She was quite certain that if Quin and his guns had not been here, they would not even be having this discussion. Stoner and his men would have simply forced her out as soon as they'd discovered Ethan's grave. Now Stoner was trying persuasion.

"Still," Cyrus went on in that same friendly tone, "any fool can see there's room to grow out here, with all this land around you. As long," he added slyly, "as you're willing to hold off Indian attacks, chop down forests, and survive the ever-changing whims of nature." He fixed Cassie with a look. "Is that what you want for yourself and an old woman and two helpless children, Miz Montgomery?"

Cassie swallowed. "How can I resist, now that you've made it sound so inviting?"

"Maybe you feel you need a little more money." He reached into his breast pocket and pulled out more bills. "I'll add another two hundred, just so you'll understand that I'm a fair and generous man."

He saw Cassie's gaze fasten on the money and he thrust it toward her. He'd had enough business dealings to recognize the signs of hunger, of desperation. If he could get her to take the money into her own hands, to hold it, feel it, her resolve would weaken. "Go ahead now, Miz Montgomery. You take this money and count it yourself."

For the space of several seconds she studied the bills in his hand. Suddenly lifting her chin in a defiant gesture, she stiffened her spine and took a step back. "No, Mr. Stoner. This land is not for sale. At any price."

Quin, standing beside her, felt a rush of admiration and wondered how many others would have been able to resist such an offer.

Cyrus Stoner's hands fisted in sudden fury before he composed himself. He'd hoped they could conclude this offer in a civilized manner. Now the lady had just forced him to resort to his second plan.

With an exaggerated shrug of his shoulders, he returned the money to his pocket. Tipping his hat, he murmured, "That was my last offer, Miz Montgomery. I won't be bothering you again."

Puzzled by his bland reaction, Cassie watched as he turned and made his way back to his horse. She'd expected blazing temper, threats, even a gunfight.

As he pulled himself into the saddle, he gave her a chilling smile. "By the way. My men and I happened upon a cow out behind your barn. I sure hope it wasn't yours."

"Out behind..." She took a step forward. "What do you mean?"

He thought of his men, awaiting his signal, and his smile was smug. "It was dead, ma'am. All mangled and bloody." He looked up, as though suddenly seized with a new thought. "Would you care to have my men drag it up here for your inspection?"

Before she could reply, he aimed his pistol into the air and fired two quick shots in succession. The sound of the gunshots echoed and reechoed across the hills. Long minutes later two men emerged from the edge of the forest and rode slowly toward the cabin, their ropes dragging a heavy burden between them. When they drew closer, Cassie recognized the cow as hers. With a cry she rushed out into the snow. Quin darted out behind her, followed by her mother.

Quin dropped to one knee and examined the cow. It was plain that the animal had been freshly slaughtered, probably as soon as the men had heard Stoner's gunshots. Blood still spurted from the deep cuts across its throat and stomach.

"Looks like it might have got itself tangled up with a wolf, poor thing," Cyrus muttered sarcastically.

Quin stood. "I've never seen a wolf slit an animal's throat with the precision of a knife."

"Besides," Cassie said through clenched teeth, "I milked that cow not an hour ago. Before I left, she was safely locked in her stall."

"Maybe an Indian sneaked into your barn and stole your cow. I've heard those Crow are thieving savages."

"And slit its throat?" Quin asked in ominously quiet tones.

"Looks like."

"No Indian would waste something as precious as a cow. They know the importance of its milk and meat. They would never leave it for scavengers."

Ignoring Quin, Cyrus turned to Cassie. "Between the wolves and the Indians, Miz Montgomery, I'd say you're going to have your hands full." He tipped his hat and gave an exaggerated bow. "I hope you won't find our Montana Territory winters too harsh, ma'am. Good day now."

He urged his horse several paces, then turned. His voice was a low purr of satisfaction. "Let me know if you change your mind and decide to leave, Miz Montgomery. Of course, the price will be much less than I offered today, but I might be able to take this land off your hands." As an afterthought he added, "I hear you're a gambler, McAllister. I'm a fair card player myself. If you'd ever like to enjoy a friendly game, ride on over to my place. You'll recognize it. It's the biggest spread in these parts."

He and his men rode smartly away, leaving Cassie and her mother staring with shock and horror at the remains of their only cow.

For a minute tears stung Cassie's eyes as she thought about how much milk she could have bought with Cyrus Stoner's money. Then she thought about her promise to Ethan and she blinked away the tears.

Lifting her skirts, she headed toward the cabin. "I'll summon the children from the mine shaft and return with some knives. We'll have to work fast if we're going to butcher this cow before it freezes."

Quin watched her with growing admiration. Cassie Montgomery was stronger than she looked. It was going to take a lot more than threats and intimidation to drive her from this land. Still, the cow was just the beginning. How much more would she have to sacrifice, in order to follow Ethan's dream?

"How much milk is left, Mama?" Becky asked as they cleared away the supper dishes.

"Enough for a day or two."

"Then what?"

Cassie avoided her daughter's eyes. "I don't know."

"Growing children need milk." Luella's voice held a hint of disapproval.

"I know, Ma." Cassie struggled with impatience as she immersed her hands in the dishpan. "But we still have eggs. And plenty of meat. We'll manage."

While she dried the dishes, Luella fixed Quin with a curious look. "How did Cyrus Stoner know that you are a gambler, Mr. McAllister?"

Quin looked up from the harness he was mending. From the looks of the farm implements in the barn, Ethan's health had been much poorer than he'd let on. Everything from plow to wagon had fallen into disrepair. "I've been wondering about that myself. It would seem Stoner made it his business to find out all he could about me."

"Why?"

"A gunman likes to know his adversaries. My guess is he's been learning all he can about all of you, as well, looking for a weakness."

Luella appeared indignant. "I don't think I like that at all, Mr. McAllister. Why, the very idea of a man poking into my business—"

"It doesn't matter, Ma," Cassie said gently. "The only thing Cyrus Stoner needs to know is that I'm not giving up this land."

"Maybe…" Luella paused, as if choosing her words carefully. Glancing at Jen and Becky, who were lying in front of the fire, she lowered her voice "…you ought to give some thought to his offer." Seeing her daughter's shocked expression, she explained, "You ought to know, Cassie, that men who would butcher our only cow, might not be above resorting to other forms of bloodshed." She shivered, seeing in her mind the crimson stains in the snow outside their cabin.

"I do know that, Ma." Cassie felt the lump that formed in her throat and quickly swallowed it back. "But I won't be driven from my home again. I've run as far as I can."

Hearing the emotions that clogged her daughter's voice, Luella softened her tone. "I know, Cassie." She placed a hand on her shoulder. "We've both run as far as we can. I just want you to consider the consequences of your actions." She turned away, and in a brighter voice called, "Children, it's been a long day. I think it's time for bed."

Jen and Becky, made drowsy by the warmth of the fire, offered no protest as they followed their grandmother into the bedroom, calling out a sleepy goodnight to Quin as they did.

Quin bent to his work while, in the other room, the children murmured their prayers before climbing into bed.

When Cassie emerged from their bedroom, she poured a cup of coffee and handed it to Quin. "There was one cup left in the pot."

"Thank you." He sipped, then handed it back to her. "We'll share."

Surprised and pleased, she took several swallows of coffee before returning it to him. Then she turned toward the fire and stood, deep in thought.

After hanging the mended harness on a peg by the door, Quin set the empty cup on the table, then turned and studied her for long, silent minutes.

"Cassie, you need to have a plan."

"A plan." The sound she made could have been a laugh or a cry. "My only plan is to stay on my land and try to survive the winter."

"When spring comes, will everything be suddenly right?"

She drew her arms around herself, feeling chilled despite the warmth of the fire. "Maybe in the spring I can plant a garden and raise enough crops to trade for another cow. And then..." Her voice faded as the enormity of her situation dawned.

"And then what? Weather another winter? And another?" Quin's tone was low, angry. "Do you think that's what Ethan wanted when he exacted your promise to remain on this land?"

"I don't know." She rubbed her temples, feeling a welling of despair. "I don't know anything anymore. All I know is, we survived another day." With eyes downcast she turned away from the fire and headed toward her room. "Right now I need to rest, to sleep."

He caught her roughly by the arm as she passed him. "Damn it, woman. You need to think, to plan."

His words brought her head up sharply. "In this house we do not swear, Mr. McAllister."

At another time he would have laughed at her injured tone. But worry over her had his temper close to the surface. "The way you're going, there may not be any house. Is that what you want?"

"Take your hand off me."

He brought his face so close she could feel the heat of his breath. "Not until you listen. This is a game with Cyrus Stoner. A deadly game in which you're allowing him to make all the rules."

She pushed his hand away and took a step back. "I was never very good at games, Mr. McAllister."

"Then it's time you learned."

"And I suppose you'd like to be my teacher."

He studied the way she looked, head high, eyes challenging. Oh, the things he could teach her. He struggled to keep from reaching out to her. He dared not touch her again. Not when the cabin was so quiet and temper still heated his blood.

"The lessons will begin in the morning. I suggest you get a good night's sleep, ma'am."

He pulled on a parka and picked up the harness before opening the door. Sparks danced in the fireplace when the door slammed behind him. She listened to the sound of snow crunching beneath his boots, and the creak of the barn door. Then there was only the silence of the cabin, punctuated by the occasional sighing of the wind.

Chapter Nine

The morning sky was gray, with the promise of more snow. Already a fine dusting frosted the snow's crust, obliterating the blood that marked the spot where the cow had been butchered.

Cassie emerged from her bedroom to find the children dressing in front of the fire. Luella set a blackened coffeepot on the fire. Within minutes it was bubbling, filling the cabin with its wonderful aroma.

In the corner of the room, Quin's bedding had been carefully folded. Fresh logs had been placed beside the fireplace.

"Where is Mr. McAllister?" Jen asked.

Cassie shrugged. "In the barn, I expect."

"Is it safe for us to go out there?" Becky peered through the snow-frosted window.

Cassie nodded and picked up a rifle. "Come on. Rebecca, you can gather eggs while Jennifer and I muck the stalls."

"Fresh hoofprints," Jen exclaimed as they crossed to the barn. "Looks like Mr. McAllister is out riding Cutter. Where do you think he went, Mama?"

"I don't know." Cassie's gaze took in the wide expanse of white that stretched as far as the eye could see.

"Maybe he left," Becky suggested.

Jen's eyes widened. "Mr. McAllister wouldn't leave without saying goodbye, would he, Mama?"

Cassie shivered as she pulled open the barn door. "No, Jennifer. I don't think he would do such a thing."

"How do you know?" Becky asked. "He's a gambler. And Gram said gamblers can't be depended upon to stay in one place for very long. Gram said gamblers need the excitement of taking risks." There was contempt in her voice. "How much excitement can there be around here?"

"There's lots of excitement," Jen cried. "Mr. McAllister can teach us card tricks. That's exciting. And don't forget Mr. Stoner and his gunmen. They're exciting."

"You don't know anything," Becky taunted. "You don't even know enough to be afraid."

"Mr. McAllister isn't afraid of Cyrus Stoner or anyone. And neither is Mama," the little girl added with all the confidence of the very young.

"See what I mean? You don't know anything," Becky said.

"Do too," Jen announced with pride. "Mr. McAllister said I would have been proud of my mama if I'd seen the way she stood up to Cyrus Stoner yesterday."

"Really?" Surprised by the rare compliment, Cassie smiled as she leaned her weight against the barn door to shut out the cold. "What else did Mr. McAllister say?"

"Nothing. Except that you're pretty."

Jen turned away and began to gather eggs from the hay. But Becky caught the flush that touched her mother's cheeks before she turned away.

While she worked, Cassie's thoughts were on Quin and the things her mother had said about him. She couldn't fault her mother for her opinion. Even so, Cassie's opinion of him was changing. Though Quin gave the appearance of a self-centered, easygoing gambler whose only concern was the next card game, his actions belied such a misleading reputation. A man concerned only with himself would not have paused to hunt deer to replenish the larder of strangers. Nor would he have stayed to face possible death at the hands of Cyrus Stoner.

She thought about the things Ethan had told her after the war. The man called Gambler had become a legend among the soldiers held in the prison camp. According to Ethan, Quin had been a loner who kept his own counsel. A man of mystery who always managed to provide food or medicine or blankets for those who most needed them. A ruthless man, not above killing. Some thought he was a spy, sent to the camp to learn military secrets. Some thought him a traitor for engaging in poker games with their jailers. Yet, according to Ethan, Quin McAllister had never done anything to make his own life easier. Everything he had done had been for the benefit of the other, less fortunate, prisoners.

And now he was here in Montana Territory. Probably against his will. Certainly against his better judgment. But for now, he was here, and his presence had been the deciding factor in yesterday's confrontation with Cyrus Stoner.

Hearing the sound of hoofbeats, Cassie reached for the rifle and peered through a crack in the door. Relief flooded through her at the sight of Quin astride his horse. Amid a flurry of snowflakes he reined in and dismounted.

She pulled open the barn door and was surprised to see two more deer tied behind his saddle. "Did you think one butchered cow and deer weren't enough to keep you in meat?"

As he led his mount inside the barn, he was relieved to see that her good nature had returned. Her eyes were less shadowed, the strain around her mouth less pronounced. For a minute he just wanted to drink in the sight of her, with her hair all shiny and combed, her skin still flushed from morning chores. He smiled, and she thought again how handsome he was. "Maybe I just woke up hungry, ma'am."

"Then you'll be happy to know that there is beef roasting over the fire, and biscuits warming on the hearth. My mother and I fixed enough food for half a dozen hungry men."

"You do know how to please a man."

He turned away, missing the color that flooded her cheeks.

After untying the deer, he hung them from a rafter of the barn, then followed her and the children to the cabin. Shaking the snow from his wide-brimmed hat, he stepped inside and hung his hat and parka by the door. While the food was carried to the table he paused by a basin and washed, then took a seat at the table.

After a brief prayer, Cassie turned to her mother. "Mr. McAllister has brought us two more deer."

"Well, ma'am, they're not exactly for you," he said, helping himself to a thick slab of beef and several eggs. Hunting before dawn had given him a ravenous appetite.

"I don't understand."

He eyed her over the rim of his cup and took several gulps of scalding coffee. "Your first lesson, ma'am. When engaging the enemy, know your friends."

"Friends, Mr. McAllister?"

"Yes, ma'am. Allies. Neighbors. People you can count on to come to your aid in the event of a fight."

"But we have no neighbors," Luella protested.

"If you believe that, ma'am, then you haven't been looking around."

The food forgotten, everyone watched as he tucked into his breakfast, sighing over the biscuits, devouring the meat and eggs. When he was finished, he accepted a second cup of coffee and leaned back. "Now that was a meal fit for a king. I couldn't have had better if I were staying in the finest hotel in Boston, ma'am."

He glanced at Cassie's food, as yet untasted. "Aren't you going to eat?"

"In a minute, Mr. McAllister. I'd like you to explain about our neighbors."

"Actually, it was something that Cyrus Stoner said that made me realize just how many friends you have." He reached for a cigar, thought better of it and drank his coffee instead.

"We have no—"

"Indians," he interrupted. "Crow. There are hundreds of them here in Montana Territory."

"If you think the Indians are our friends—"

"Not yet, maybe. But they are your nearest neighbors. And if you treat them kindly, I'm willing to bet they'll be your friends."

"But how—?"

He held up a hand to silence her questions. "I saw their markings and knew that they'd been hunting on your land." To the others he explained, "Crow ponies are unshod. It's easy to distinguish them from a party of white men, especially with snow on the ground." He turned to Cassie. "I thought, since I knew where a herd of deer had taken shelter, that I'd just hunt a couple. I sent a message to the leader of the Crow asking him to come by your cabin."

"A message to the Crow! How?"

He smiled. "It was easy. I called out to two braves who had concealed themselves in the woods. Asked them to take a message to their chief."

"But why?"

"So that you can present the deer as a gift of friend-ship."

"But Mr. McAllister, I've never spoken to an Indian. I don't even know how to speak their language."

"That's all right. The missionaries were here before you. The Crow speak our language, ma'am."

"You mean they are civilized, Mr. McAllister?" Luella was clearly intrigued.

He swallowed his smile. A woman like Mrs. Chalmers set great store by manners and customs. "They consider us the uncivilized people, ma'am."

"We must make them welcome." She started toward the fireplace. "Would they care for coddled eggs and beef, Mr. McAllister?"

"I wouldn't bother, Mrs. Chalmers. They don't care much for white man's cooking."

"Oh." She appeared deflated, then brightened. "Will they be bringing any women and children?"

"I'm afraid not. Just their chief and a couple of warriors."

"How will we welcome them?" Cassie asked.

"The same way you'd welcome any neighbor. Invite them—" He looked up at the sound of hoofbeats.

"Looks like they're here." He snatched up the rifles and set them out of sight in Cassie's bedroom. "Wouldn't want them to think we brought them here for a shooting match."

He gave a final glance around the cabin and at the others. "Ready?"

Cassie nodded and walked to the door of the cabin. When she opened it, a party of six Crow sat astride their ponies. She struggled to show no fear as she studied their stern countenances, all peering at her in stony silence.

"Welcome to our home. Please come in."

Clearly puzzled, the braves slid from their ponies and strode to the porch. As they stepped inside, they stared around, fascinated by what they saw. Except for a few abandoned cabins, they had little chance to see how the white men lived.

"You must be cold," Cassie said. "Please warm yourselves by the fire."

Following the chief's lead, the braves moved closer to the fire, all the while keeping their hands on the knives they carried at their waists. One of them bumped into the rocking chair, setting it into motion. At once they gathered around, touching it, watching as it rocked back and forth.

"Maybe the chief would like to sit," Quin suggested.

The chief took a seat, clearly enchanted with the movement.

Plucking a cigar from his pocket, Quin offered it to the chief, then held a flaming stick to the tip. The chief took several puffs. A smile of pure delight crossed his face. When he offered it back, Quin shook his head and withdrew a second cigar, which he lit. The two men puffed contentedly.

"Coffee?" Cassie asked.

Luella and Cassie filled cups with coffee, sweetened with sugar, and passed them among the braves. At Cassie's whispered command, Becky offered a plate of biscuits. Stuffing the biscuits into their mouths, the braves choked them down, then drank the coffee without even seeming to taste it. When one of them burned his tongue, he spat a mouthful into the fire.

Luella looked appalled at their lack of manners. The children, who had never been close to an Indian before, merely stared in fascination at the long hair, braided with feathers and beads, and the buckskin leggings and fringed winter shirts.

The younger men were lean and muscular, and carried themselves with the assurance of royalty.

The chief, who waited until the others had eaten, followed suit, managing to swallow his coffee without incident. Then he returned his attention to the cigar.

"I think it's time to present your gift," Quin muttered, afraid that at any moment Luella might order them out of the cabin.

The women draped shawls around their shoulders and led the way to the barn, with Quin and the Crow following.

Inside, Cassie indicated the deer. "We would like to present this to you, as a token of our friendship."

The chief showed no emotion, though several of his younger braves showed surprise at such a generous offer.

Ignoring Cassie, the chief spoke to Quin. "Why do you desire our friendship?"

Quin chose his words carefully. "As you can see, we are few. And we live far from our own people. There are those who would harm us."

"The People have never brought harm to you."

"We know this. We do not accuse the People. But some of our own people have tried to drive us from this land. All we desire is the chance to live in peace. But as the chief knows, it is sometimes necessary to do battle with those who would harm us, before we can live in peace."

"Do you ask the People to join your battle?"

"No."

"Then what do you ask of the People?"

"We ask only that you warn us if you see strangers on our land."

The chief digested this, then said, "In the name of the People I accept this gift." He turned to his braves and uttered a command.

The deer were cut down and placed on the backs of their ponies.

When he had pulled himself onto his pony's back, the chief studied Cassie for long moments, then addressed Quin. "Your woman?"

Out of the corner of his eye, Quin saw Cassie's mouth open to protest.

"Yes," he said quickly.

"And the old one?"

"Also mine."

"Ah." The chief turned toward Becky, seeing, beneath the faded gown and ragged shawl, the beginnings of womanhood. "The young one. Daughter?"

Quin nodded.

"I have a son—" he indicated a handsome brave who was staring boldly at Becky's flaming hair and green eyes "—in need of a woman."

The three women froze, too startled to react. Even little Jen seemed to understand the significance of what was being said.

Quin was careful to keep his steady gaze fixed on the chief. "She is too young to leave her mother."

The chief had seen the look of interest in the eyes of his son. The boy was special to him, being his first-born, who would one day be chief. As for the girl, she was young and a bit thin for his taste. But if the interest continued . . .

He nodded in understanding. "We will talk again when the snows are gone and the land is green. She will make a fine squaw."

At a signal, the braves moved out and the chief raised his hand in a symbol of friendship. Quin did the same.

"The People will remember the kindness of those who dwell in this place."

Without a glance at the others, he urged his horse into a trot.

As soon as they were out of earshot, Luella's barely controlled temper erupted.

"You lied to that man. You told him that Cassie and I were your . . . women." She spoke the word as though it were an obscenity.

"It was the only way to keep him from taking you."

"This would have kept him from taking us," Cassie said, pulling the pistol from her pocket.

"Yes, ma'am. And those braves would have worn my scalp on their belts tonight while they feasted on your deer, which you and your mother and daughters would have served in their camp."

"Are you saying that those heathens would have stolen us?"

"They don't consider it stealing. They see it as their right, and even their duty, to take any women who have no men to protect them."

"And what about poor little Rebecca," Cassie said, drawing her daughter close. "He actually suggested that he would be back in the spring to take her for his son."

"The chief considered that a supreme compliment," Quin said patiently.

"Compliment?" Luella was so agitated her voice was little more than a squeak.

"Yes, ma'am. To be part of the chief's family is an honor that any Crow maiden would relish."

"Oh, Cassie," Luella wailed, "what have we done? By listening to this wicked man, we have invited those savages into our home, and we have exposed our innocent children to even more danger than that which was threatened by Cyrus Stoner."

Becky, who had been strangely silent, suddenly blurted, "I didn't think they were savages, Gram. Different, maybe. But..." she shrugged "...they seemed..." her voice took on a dreamy tone "...not savage like Cyrus Stoner."

Cassie watched as her daughter turned and walked back to the cabin. Becky lifted her head a fraction. Her walk slowed, her hips began to sway in that unmistakable way of a woman.

Though she tried to tell herself that nothing had changed, Cassie was achingly aware that everything had changed. The Crow considered Quin McAllister the head of this household. And what was far worse, in the space of a heartbeat, her little girl had seen herself reflected in a man's eyes, not as a child, but as a woman.

Her heart ached at the realization that some part of her daughter's childhood had just slipped away forever.

Chapter Ten

Quin sighed in his sleep, then sat bolt upright, listening. His hand went automatically to the gun beneath his pillow.

What had awakened him?

Outside, the wind picked up speed, hurling sleet and snow against the northern walls of the cabin. On a gust of wind, sparks danced in the fireplace.

Beyond the wind, he could distinguish nothing that would have roused him. Yet the prickly feeling persisted. Something, or someone, was out there.

Trusting his instincts, he slid silently from his bed and pulled on his boots. Moving with the stealth of a cat, he listened at the door, then peered through the window.

At first he couldn't distinguish the darkened forms from the trees in the forest. But as he continued watching, several shadows separated themselves from the woods and moved ever so slightly. Though he tried to count them, a cloud passed over the moon, making it impossible to see.

He swore and strode across the room to Cassie's bedroom.

"Cassie. Wake the others."

"What? Why...?" Even as the questions formed, she slipped from her bed and was racing to the other room.

"Men," Quin whispered. "Creeping toward the cabin."

"Ma." Cassie shook her mother, then moved to the small bunks where her daughters slept. "Rebecca, Jennifer. Hide yourselves."

Without a word of protest Luella flew to a rear window, while little Jen took up a position peering through a chink in the cabin wall. Becky sat huddled in the corner of the cabin, her hands over her ears, her eyes squeezed tightly shut, reliving the horrors of the war that had ravaged her beloved home.

Cassie hurried to Quin's side, holding the pistol in her hand. "I don't see them."

"There." He pointed.

She peered into the darkness. Two of the figures had crept closer until they were between the barn and the cabin. Several others separated and began to slink around to the far side.

"What do you think they're planning?"

"What would you do, if you wanted to drive people from their home against their will?" At the thought, his blood seemed to freeze.

Cassie's eyes widened at the sudden blaze of light. "Oh. Dear heaven, Quin. Fire."

It was what he had most feared.

Cassie could see the men clearly now, holding aloft flaming torches as they ran toward the cabin.

"There are more back here," Luella shouted from the back of the cabin. "And all of them are carrying torches."

"I'll help, Ma." Cassie raced to her mother's side.

"Stay low," Quin shouted as he took aim with his rifle.

He felt sweat bead his forehead. He knew he could take out these two. But how many more men were coming at them from all sides? It would be next to impossible to get all of them in time. Already the figures were close enough to reach the cabin by merely tossing the torches as they fell.

In quick succession he fired several shots, stopping the two men in his line of fire. Then he rushed to the rear of the cabin, ready to join the women in another gunfight. Instead, he was surprised to see the torches in the snow, sputtering uselessly, while several men lay sprawled in a semicircle.

"You managed to stop all of them?" he asked.

Luella and Cassie seemed as surprised as he was.

"I don't understand it. They dropped before we could fire a shot," Cassie said incredulously.

Just then their heads came up at the sound of thundering hoofbeats. As they took aim once more they found themselves staring at a cluster of Indians, led by the chief and his son.

Several of the Crow slid from their ponies and examined the dead men, before nodding to their chief.

"I ordered my braves to see that these men did not use the fire sticks against you," the chief called out loudly.

"You killed them?" Cassie looked from the chief to his son, then back. "But they are not your enemies. This is not your fight."

"Once a warrior of the People gives his hand in friendship, the enemies of his friends become his enemies, as well."

"We're grateful," Quin said. "I hate to think what would have happened to us if you hadn't been here."

The chief lifted a hand. "Such words are never necessary between friends."

He wheeled his mount and his braves followed suit. All except his son, who continued staring at Becky. In a pristine white night shift, she stood several paces behind her mother, her skin still pale from the shock of the gunfight, her eyes still wide with fear. For long moments he continued to study her. Then, without a word, he followed the others.

"Mama! Gram!" Jen's high-pitched shrieks as she raced from the barn to the cabin had everyone looking up. "Mr. McAllister saw the Indians coming."

Cassie wiped her hands on a towel. Luella looked longingly at the rifle propped up beside the door, then, remembering how these strangers had intervened in their behalf, opted instead for a small kitchen knife, which she tucked beneath the folds of her apron. For a woman like Luella, who had been through so much grief in her life, trust did not come easily.

Keeping the children behind them, the two women opened the door just as Quin reached the porch.

There were more than a dozen Crow, riding in single file, with their chief at the head of the column. Beside him, in a place of honor, rode his son. Though their expressions were unreadable, the chief's voice rang out with pride as he addressed Quin.

"My braves saw more white men."

Quin was instantly alert. "Where?"

"Here on your land."

"When?"

"While the sun was at rest and the moon and stars filled the sky."

Dear heaven, Cassie thought. Would they now be robbed of all sleep? Day and night, their safety was being threatened.

"What were these white men doing?" Quin asked.

The chief turned to his son, who took up the narrative in a deep, strangely cultured voice. "They carried fire sticks toward your barn."

"Not again." Quin swore savagely. "I'll have to sleep in the barn from now on."

The chief's face showed no emotion when he said, "These men will visit your land no more."

"What do you mean?"

"My son ordered my braves to stop these men from doing harm to your animals. We left their bodies where other men will see and understand. If they are wise, they will leave you in peace."

At his signal one of the braves nudged his horse forward. In his hand was a rope from which trailed a cow. The warrior handed the rope to the chief's son, who in turn handed it to Cassie.

"You gave the People food," the chief said. "Now the People return the favor."

For a moment Cassie was speechless. Fighting tears she whispered, "I can't tell you how grateful we are."

"As I have said, words are not necessary between friends." With that same fierce expression, the chief turned his mount and rode between the column of horsemen. His son remained behind for several moments, his gaze holding Becky's. When he turned away, the braves followed his lead.

No one spoke, no one moved, until the Crow disappeared over a rise. While her mother and children re-

turned to the cabin, Cassie led the cow toward the barn.
Inside, after a thorough examination, she lifted her
head to find Quin watching her.

"Where do you think they got this cow?"

With an amused expression he shrugged his shoulders. "Stole it, most likely."

"Stole it?" She was horrified. Her outrage grew when
she saw the grin on his face. "And I suppose you think
that's funny."

"No, ma'am. But it does seem like some kind of justice if that cow came from Cyrus Stoner's herd. You did
say he owned most of the land around these parts."

With a trace of impatience she muttered, "Now what
am I supposed to do with a stolen cow?"

He picked up a pitchfork and said with a deadpan
expression, "First thing you'd better do is milk it. After that I'd give it some hay."

"Mama," Jen shouted, "there's a horseman coming."

Grabbing up the rifle, Cassie stepped onto the porch
just as Quin walked from the barn holding his pistol.
Both of them watched as a horse and rider crested a
ridge.

When the rider drew near, Cassie smiled and set aside
the rifle. "It's all right," she said with a sigh of relief.
"That's Jedediah Taylor. He lives in Prospect and stops
by a couple of times a year. Good morning, Jedediah," she called.

"Mornin', Miss Cassie." The words were muttered
around a pipe clenched between his teeth, several of
which were missing. In a courtly gesture, he snatched
his hat from his head and held it in one leathery hand.
His hair was the color of ripe cotton, as was the beard
that flowed down the front of his bearskin parka.

"Jedediah Taylor, meet Quin McAllister."

The two men nodded. Despite the white hair and wrinkles, the eyes looking into Quin's were as sparkling and lively as a child's.

"Will you come inside?"

"Thank you, I will." He slid from the saddle and followed Cassie. From the pronounced limp, it was obvious that he favored his left leg.

Inside, he greeted Luella and the children, and took a seat in front of the fire. Reaching into his pocket, he pulled out several pieces of rock candy and held them out to the girls. "You know I wouldn't come all this way without bringing you some of your favorite candy, now, would I?"

"Thank you, Jedediah." With giggles, the two girls accepted his offering and eagerly popped them into their mouths.

"Coffee, Jedediah?"

"Thank you." He blew into the steaming mug before drinking, and accepted a plate of venison stew and biscuits, which he downed in a few hungry bites. Cassie refilled the plate and handed it back to him. He ate the second serving as quickly as he'd eaten the first.

When he had mopped up every drop of gravy with his biscuit, he glanced at Quin, considering his words carefully before saying to Cassie, "There's been some talk in town."

"About what?"

"Cyrus Stoner said he found Ethan's grave. That right?"

Reluctantly Cassie nodded.

"How long's he been dead?"

"Almost six months."

"Six months." He seemed to be calculating. "You should have told me, Miss Cassie. That's a long time for women and children to survive alone out here."

"Thank you for your concern, Jedediah, but we've managed."

He tamped a bit of precious tobacco into his pipe. "Last time I saw Ethan, I thought he was looking pale."

"When was that?"

"'Bout six months ago. He asked me to take a pouch to the assayer's office for him. I recall thinking that what he needed was—"

Quin saw the look of surprise on Cassie's face. "Pouch?"

The old man pulled himself back from his ramblings. "Yes'm. Ethan didn't tell you?"

She shook her head. "What was the assayer's report?"

"Can't say." Jedediah shrugged. "It was in a sealed envelope I gave to Ethan."

"Did he read the report?"

"Yes'm."

There was a sense of barely contained excitement in her voice. "Did he seem happy or sad after he read the report?"

Jedediah thought a minute. "Can't say as he was either. He looked...grim. Like a man about to go to war."

Cassie's face fell. She'd hoped...

"I recollect," Jedediah continued, "Ethan muttering something about vultures picking at his bones. 'Course, now that I know he's dead, it makes sense."

"It does?"

"Yes'm. I'd guess Ethan had some sense that he was dying and was worried about those he'd be leaving." He cleared his throat. "That brings me to the rest of the talk in the saloon, Miss Cassie."

She waited while he glanced at the children before continuing. "Cyrus Stoner is telling folks that you've taken up with a gun-toting gambler, ma'am." He swiveled his head to peer at Quin.

"You see," Luella cried, "I knew he would bring scandal—"

"And he's saying that you're just doing what comes naturally, since you were..." He shot a glance at Luella and his leathery neck flooded with color. "Begging your pardon, ma'am, I just wanted to warn you about what Cyrus Stoner's been saying."

For a moment Luella looked as though she'd been struck dumb. Cassie watched sadly as her mother stood and walked to the fireplace, keeping her back to the others.

Jedediah continued. "He's also saying that since the gambler came to live here, there are strange things happening out here."

"What strange things?" Cassie tore her troubled gaze from her mother's rigid back.

"Several of Stoner's ranch hands found dead at the edge of town. The bodies of three of his men found frozen in an abandoned barn just over that ridge. And the foreman of Stoner's ranch found floating in the river."

"How many men are dead?"

"Ten, at last count, ma'am."

Cassie glanced over the old man's head to where Quin stood. The Crow had been back to her cabin twice since they brought the cow. Both times they had spoken with Quin before taking their leave as silently as they'd arrived. And both times Quin had been grim faced. But when she had asked him what they wanted, he told her that they were just reporting on the activities of Stoner's men.

Even though a part of her mind told her that Quin had probably been trying to protect her and her family from the brutal facts, another part of her was furious that he had withheld information from her.

"And you came out here to warn me about the gossip."

"No, ma'am. I just came to see for myself that you were getting by." He shot a quick glance at Quin, then back to her. "And now that I've seen, I'll be taking my leave."

"Thank you, Jedediah. For your friendship, and for taking the time to come all this way."

"No trouble, Miss Cassie."

As she took the empty plate and cup from him he said, "If you don't mind, Miss Cassie, I'd like to visit Ethan's grave before I return to town."

"Of course."

She pulled on a buckskin jacket and picked up her rifle before leading him outside. Quin followed. They walked to the edge of the forest in silence. When they reached the snow-covered mound, Cassie knelt while the two men doffed their hats and bowed their heads.

It was a somber group that returned to the cabin a short time later.

As Jedediah pulled himself into the saddle, he leaned down and whispered for Quin's ears alone, "I don't want to alarm Miss Cassie and the others, but I got a look at the bodies of Stoner's men. Most of 'em weren't killed by white men. It looks like the work of Crow to me."

The two men eyed each other for long, silent moments.

A slow smile touched the old man's lips. "I get the idea that you're not surprised."

Quin merely shrugged.

"You look like a man who knows how to handle that gun, McAllister. I think maybe Miss Cassie and her family are in good hands."

"Thanks, Jedediah." As the old man reached for the reins, Quin caught them. "Tell me something. After you brought that assayer's report to Ethan, did he ask you to mail a letter?"

"Letter?" The old man scratched his beard. "Nope. Ethan never gave me any letter."

Looking beyond Quin to where Cassie stood alone, Jedediah called, "Don't you pay any attention to the gossip being spread by Cyrus Stoner, Miss Cassie. No one else will. The good people of Prospect don't bother to judge a person by what others say."

"Thank you, Jedediah," she called. "Goodbye."

Quin took a step back, and the old man touched a hand to his hat. "Goodbye, Miss Cassie. McAllister."

When the horse and rider were gone, she turned a frigid look on Quin. "Ten men, Mr. McAllister. All dead. And all killed by our...good neighbors."

"Would you rather the bodies had been your mother? Your children?"

She flinched.

Regretting his words spoken in anger, he deliberately softened his tone. "I'm convinced that Ethan found proof of his treasure. That's the only reason he'd ask you to stay here. And somehow, Cyrus Stoner found out about it, and wants it for himself."

"Treasure." She turned away, still angry. "You heard Jedediah. When Ethan opened the assayer's report, he looked grim. Does that sound like a man who'd just been informed of a treasure? I won't have men killed for the sake of something that may not even exist."

Quin caught her by the arm. His voice was low with anger. "A man like Stoner will stop at nothing to have what he wants. Without the help of the Crow, we'll be the ones dying. Is that what you want?"

"I don't know." Tears blurred her vision and she drew herself stiffly away. "I don't want any more violence, any more death on my hands. I don't want gossip ruining our good names. I just want to be allowed to live in peace."

"Then sell to Stoner and walk away."

For what seemed an eternity they stared at each other in silence.

Finally she lowered her head. "How can I sell Ethan's dream?"

He lifted her chin and gave her a grim smile. "That settles it then. Starting tomorrow, we devote at least a few hours every day to the mine."

Reluctantly she nodded, then turned and made her way inside.

Heading toward the barn, Cassie paused as Quin brought the ax down, neatly splitting a log. He had shed his parka and rolled his sleeves, revealing muscles that rippled each time he lifted the ax above his head.

Seeing her, he stopped. A breeze ruffled his dark hair and she felt her throat go dry.

In the past days, the attacks from Stoner's men had abruptly halted. Life at their little cabin had fallen into a routine of hard work, followed by an early supper, and then a long night of more work. After morning chores, they all worked in the mine. After supper, when the children were tucked into bed, Quin and Cassie would spend several more hours in the mine. But though they searched the uncharted tunnels below the ground, they found no sign of treasure, and no sign of Ethan's last work site.

The hours were long, but Quin managed to make it all seem like a pleasant diversion. It was a gift he had, Cassie mused. He could make even the toughest tasks seem like fun. Each evening, though he was probably exhausted from the demands made on him, Quin managed to find an hour or two to relax around the fire. He taught the children card tricks, and was able to coax all but Luella to join him in poker.

Underneath his charming smile, however, Cassie sensed a layer of pain that Quin kept carefully hidden from view. It was there, just below the surface. Sometimes, in unguarded moments, she was able to glimpse it as he gently teased her daughters, or turned away to stare silently into the flames of the fire. She found herself wondering, as she often did, what his life had been like before the war.

Quin watched as Cassie disappeared into the barn. He always felt the same familiar jolt at his first glimpse of her in the morning. Despite the faded gown and mud-spattered boots, she was the kind of woman who took a man's breath away. The face of an angel and the body of a temptress. Skin as cool and pale as porcelain; hair that, when brushed loose, reminded him of heat and fire and passion.

The hardest part of being here was working along-side her and never being able to touch her. But he knew if he did, he wouldn't be able to stop, and a fine, decent woman like Cassie would wind up hating him.

With his muscles protesting and his back aching, he stacked the wood neatly beside the cabin, where it joined several more cord of logs he'd chopped and split. By now there was enough wood to see them through the harshest of winters.

Struggling beneath another armload, he cursed and called himself every kind of fool. What in hell was he doing here? He might have the Montgomery family fooled, but he couldn't hide the truth from himself. He was here because of a pair of haunting green eyes that had looked into his and touched his soul. He might tell the others that he worked so hard because he wanted to be prepared, but he knew better. Work was the only release from all the heat and passion that were building inside him.

Chapter Eleven

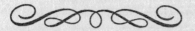

"When I get big," Jen said as she gathered eggs, "I'm never going to be afraid of anything."

"That's just silly," Becky called from the other side of the barn. "Everybody is afraid sometimes."

"Not Mr. McAllister," Jen retorted. "Tell her," she called to Quin. "Tell Becky that you're never afraid."

Cassie, seated beside the cow, looked up in alarm. But before she could interrupt, she heard Quin's voice, low, serious.

"I can't do that," Quin called from the stall. "It would be a lie, Jen. Becky is right. Everybody is afraid at some time in their lives."

"Even you?" The little girl was astonished.

"I've been afraid a lot of times."

"Then how come you stayed here and joined in our fight?" she demanded.

Becky stood, straight and still, watching and listening, her eyes wide.

"Because some things are more important than fear," Quin explained. Seeing the way Becky studied him, he leaned on his pitchfork and said gently, "There's nothing wrong with being afraid. It's as natural as every other emotion. But the measure of a person is how they behave while they're afraid. When something needs to be done, it's up to all of us to do it.''

Cassie closed her eyes and whispered a grateful prayer. Then, lifting the pail of milk, she called, ''Bring the eggs, Jennifer. Your gram is waiting to fix breakfast.''

''Yes'm.''

They departed on a swirl of icy wind.

The barn returned to silence, with only the soft swishing sound of Quin's pitchfork as it moved through the straw.

''Do you think I'm pretty, Mr. McAllister?''

Quin looked up. He'd thought the girl had left with her mother and sister.

''You're very pretty, Becky.''

She walked closer and leaned her arms on the rail. ''As pretty as my mama?''

He spread fresh hay before setting the pitchfork aside and mopping his forehead with his sleeve. ''It's plain to see that you're going to look just like her when you grow up.''

''I am grown-up.'' She ducked under the rail and stepped into the stall beside him. ''Mama and Gram might not think so, but I am in the eyes of the chief and his son.''

Quin picked up a piece of cloth and began rubbing down his horse. His movements stilled when she placed a hand on his arm. Her voice came from directly behind him, where she stood on tiptoe to make herself taller.

''I've never been kissed by a man, Mr. McAllister, and I was wondering—''

''Becky.'' Tamping down on his surprise, he tossed the cloth aside and turned toward her. He caught her by the shoulders and held her a little away, so that she was forced to look into his eyes.

"Don't you want to kiss me, Mr. McAllister?"

His mind raced. He had to find a way to refuse her without causing undue pain or embarrassment. She was troubled enough as it was. "I remember being your age. My body used to run ahead of my mind sometimes. I said and did whatever I thought, without regard to the consequences. And oh, how I wanted. I wanted things I knew I wasn't ready to have, but I wanted them anyway."

She opened her mouth to protest but he continued smoothly, "I know that it's very tough, growing up out here, alone and isolated, to sort through so many confusing feelings. It's true that you're almost a woman, Becky. But you still have so much of life ahead of you. Don't be in a hurry. Take the time to learn, to do, to experience all that life has to offer. And most of all, be stingy with your kisses. Save them for special people. That way, when you finally give your heart, it will be to someone who deserves it."

Her cheeks flamed. "You think I'm just a little girl, don't you?"

"No, Becky. I've seen so many good qualities in you. I think you're a very fine, special person."

"But not as fine and special as Mama."

She lifted her chin in that same defiant way as Cassie, and he bit back a smile. "What do you mean?"

"I mean, Mr. McAllister, that I've seen the way you watch my mother when you think no one is looking. If she was standing here offering her kisses, I don't think you'd refuse."

Instead of the angry denial she expected, he laughed. "You're right, Becky. I sure would enjoy having your mother offer to kiss me." His laughter faded, but his smile remained. "But remember this. Your mother is a very wise woman. Wise enough to know that she shouldn't waste her kisses. And I hope you'll take a lesson from her."

She swallowed, touched by his honesty. "You're not mad at me for asking?"

"Mad? Becky, I'm flattered." He pressed a kiss to the top of her head, then turned her around and said, "Now, you'd better get back to the cabin and give your grandmother a hand with the cooking."

As she let herself out of the barn, Becky shot a last quick glance at the man who had already returned to his chores. In his eyes there had been neither censure nor condemnation. In fact, what she had seen was—the realization stunned her—the look of a loving father.

"Rebecca. Didn't you see these eggs?" Luella pointed to a cluster of eggs in the straw.

"No, Gram. I guess I overlooked them."

"There's no excuse for such carelessness, child. Open your eyes."

"I'm not a child, Gram. I'm almost a woman."

"Then act like one, and take pride in your chores, no matter how menial they may seem." Luella touched a finger to the unlatched barn door. Her eyes flashed. "Did you forget the rule? You're to see to certain precautions at all times. Your carelessness could cause harm to you and, what is worse, to Jen, who depends on you. Now latch this door at once."

"Yes, ma'am." In sullen silence Becky crossed the barn and threw the latch.

"This is another reason why I want you to consider following in my footsteps and studying at Miss Atherton's Conservatory of Music in Savannah. Music is a discipline, Becky. You have the gift, but lack the discipline. At Miss Atherton's, you will become prepared for all of life's hard lessons."

"I told you, Gram. I have no intention of ever returning to the South. And as for my singing..." The girl's voice trembled. "I only sang for Pa. And now that he's gone..." She turned away to hide the tears.

From his position in the stall, Quin watched and listened, wishing he could think of some way to ease the tension.

The war of nerves was beginning to take its toll. Unable to go outdoors alone, the children bickered over the simplest things. They argued over their sums. They argued over who would sit closest to the fire after supper. They even fought for the last biscuit on the plate.

At the most unexpected time, Becky would stare dreamily into the flames, or sulk in the barn. Often after supper she ordered Jen out of the bedroom they shared with their grandmother, declaring that she desired her privacy. To taunt her, the little girl would sneak in and catch her writing poetry on her slate, or staring at her reflection in a chipped mirror. Then the bickering would begin again.

Luella found fault with everything her daughter or grandchildren did. She fretted, too, about the dwindling supplies of flour and sugar. The war and its aftermath had left permanent scars on the old woman's soul. Remembering the terrible hunger of that time, she lived in fear of starvation.

Quin's card games with the children after supper were a constant source of irritation to her, as well. She called cards the devil's tools and threatened to burn them if she found them lying around one more time.

Cassie struggled to soothe, to admonish, to cheer. But the long hours spent in the mine after the others went to sleep, coupled with the added tensions, were beginning to show. She moved through her chores more slowly, often forgetting to make coffee, or burning the biscuits. When that happened, her mother would remind her how much her carelessness cost them.

One evening after supper, Luella began her usual litany of complaints. "We're almost out of flour. And sugar. And I'm almost out of thread. And if we don't soon—"

"Ma." Distressed, Cassie turned too suddenly and felt the plate slip through her soapy hands. Before she could catch it, it shattered on the floor.

"Now look what you've done," Luella cried. "How could you be so clumsy? That was one of the last of my mother's dishes. They're all I have left of her."

With tears stinging her eyes, Cassie bent to pick up the shards of china.

"I'll clean this up." Quin snatched up a broom and gently herded the two women across the room. "Mrs. Chalmers, why don't you tend to your mending? And Cassie, go sit by the fire. It's time you got off your feet."

"I don't need—"

"Never argue with someone bigger than you," he said with a grin.

The two children watched in amazement as he swept up the broken glass, then proceeded to wash the dishes. Turning, he called to them, "Are you going to just sit there? Or are you going to dry?"

At once Becky and Jen picked up towels and began to work alongside him.

"How long has it been since you went to town?" Quin asked as he set a stack of plates in the pan of soapy water.

"A year, I guess." Becky muttered. "The last time I went to Prospect, I was with Pa."

"How about you, Jen?"

"I've never been to town." The little girl set a dry plate on the table and reached for another, being extremely careful. She wouldn't want to have her grandmother direct her anger at her. And she certainly didn't want to see her mama cry again. "Pa said I was too little. I had to stay home with Mama and Gram."

"You mean the whole family never went into town together?"

Becky shook her head. "We couldn't. Pa said somebody had to stay here and tend the animals."

"That does it." Quin dried his hands and unrolled his sleeves, then turned to Cassie and her mother. "Tomorrow we're leaving for Prospect."

For a moment the two women stared at him in stunned silence.

"All of us?" Cassie asked in amazement.

"That's right."

"But what about the animals?" Luella asked.

"We'll ask our neighbors to see to the cow and the chickens."

"Neighbors?" Luella peered at him. "You mean the Crow?"

"That's right. And in payment they can help themselves to the milk and eggs. I'd say that's a fair trade, wouldn't you?"

"What about Cyrus Stoner's men?" Cassie asked.

"They haven't been spotted around here in nearly a week."

"But once they know we're in town, won't they jump at the chance to break into our cabin?" Cassie shivered. "In fact, what's to stop them from burning us out while we're away?"

"The same thing that stopped them before," Quin answered. "It wasn't our guns that drove Stoner's men off. It was our neighbors, the Crow. Besides, this is all part of the game. You have to show Stoner that you're not afraid to leave your cabin. Otherwise, you become a prisoner of your fear."

Cassie frowned. "Do you really think it's safe to go into Prospect? It's almost a whole day on the trail."

"I not only think it's safe," Quin said, "I think it would be good for all of us."

"What about money?" Luella, ever the practical one, began to fret aloud. "Besides the supplies, we'll need lodging and meals in town. We have no money for such frivolous things."

"I'll hunt up a couple of deer right now. And whatever else I can find." Quin crossed the room and picked up his rifle. "We'll barter the meat and pelts for whatever we need. Now, what do you say?"

Cassie glanced at her children. Becky had her hands pressed together in supplication. Jen's eyes pleaded with her, awaiting a response.

She let out a long breath. "I know I'll regret this. But...all right."

With a smile Quin let himself out.

After lifting down the last of the flour and sugar, Cassie began mixing biscuit dough. "I'd better start baking. We'll need enough food to get us all the way to Prospect."

With a yelp, Becky began dancing around the room. Jen broke into a grin so wide it seemed to cover her whole face. Only Luella seemed more restrained than usual as she set aside her mending and joined her daughter at the table. She whispered, "If we're truly going to Prospect, you'll need to have that talk with Becky."

Cassie looked up, and her mother could read the refusal she was about to make.

Clutching her arm, Luella continued, "If, as Jedediah has said, Cyrus Stoner has already spread vicious gossip, you must prepare her."

"Oh, Ma—"

"Now, girl," Luella said urgently. "You must not put this off."

With great reluctance, Cassie dried her hands on her apron and called, "Rebecca, would you give me a hand in the barn, please?"

As she walked, Cassie steeled herself against the inevitable questions. Once inside she leaned against the closed door and studied her daughter in silence.

Becky looked around. "Why are we here, Mama? What do you need my help with?"

"I need to talk to you, away from the others."

"Talk? About what?"

"About... about growing up," Cassie said softly.

"I didn't think you noticed." Becky's frown turned into a smile. "Mama, how old were you when you married Pa?"

"Fourteen. Almost fifteen."

"Why, you—" Becky's eyes widened. "You weren't much older than I am."

"You're only twelve, Rebecca."

"I'll be thirteen in January."

"You're still a little girl."

"Jen's little, Mama. I'm almost grown. Why, I'm taller than you already."

Cassie felt a knife pierce her heart. She wished she could deny the truth, but it was there for her to see. "There are so many things I want for you, Rebecca. A fine home and education. A chance to be young and carefree. A chance to experience life before you settle down and raise a family of your own."

"But what about what I want, Mama?"

Cassie looked startled. "What do you want?"

The girl's voice lowered. "Do you know, Mama, that's the first time you've ever asked?"

Cassie felt tears spring to her eyes, but quickly blinked them away. Moving closer, she said, "I guess I've been so busy seeing to all the things that needed doing after your father died, I forgot about the things you and Jennifer might be wanting or dreaming about." She caught Becky's hand, but the girl tugged it free and turned away. "Why don't you tell me what you want, Rebecca."

"That's just it. I don't know." Her voice quivered with unshed tears. "But I feel things. Things I don't understand. And I want..." She kicked a toe in the straw, searching for the words. "I don't know what I want. I just know I want to be more than your little girl, or Jen's big sister, or Gram's eyes. I want to be treated like somebody who can make her own decisions, even if they're the wrong ones." She glanced up defiantly. "I suppose Mr. McAllister told you."

Cassie stiffened. "Told me what?"

"That I asked him to kiss me."

Though she was surprised, she merely said, "No, Becky. Mr. McAllister never said a word."

Becky's cheeks flamed, aware that she had no choice now but to confess everything.

"I came up to him here in the barn and asked him to kiss me. And he said I should save my kisses for someone special."

Cassie experienced a wave of relief that he had been so gentle with her daughter. It was one more favor she would owe Quin McAllister. "He gave you very good advice," she said tenderly.

"But..." Becky's lips quivered. "How will I ever find someone special out here, Mama?"

In the silence that followed, Cassie watched as her daughter's body shook with the tears she could no longer hold back. For the space of several moments she agonized over what she had to say. Then, stepping closer, she dropped an arm around the girl's trembling shoulders.

"You may not believe this, Rebecca, but I know how you feel. I remember saying something quite similar to my mother." A smile came into her voice as she remembered. "It was such a carefree time. I wish you could have known what it was like then. It was before the war, before the madness...." She took a deep breath. "I was so young. And pretty. Oh," she added quickly, "not as pretty as you are. But pretty, I suppose. And there were young men paying attention. It's very exciting, having young men who notice you." She tightened her grip on her daughter, thinking about the chief's son, and the way he watched Rebecca. "You walk differently, knowing they're watching. And you begin to feel things...." She sighed. "I was looking forward to dances, and parties. But my mother was worried, as all mothers worry, that such things would turn my head. You see, Rebecca, my mother knew all too well what can happen to a pretty, carefree girl. Though you wouldn't know it now, your grandmother was a rare beauty when she was young. And there was a young man who hurt her. He..." Cassie swallowed. "There are always callow young men who want a pretty girl, just so they can boast to their friends. But they don't really care about her. And when they have satisfied their own needs, they leave her... soiled."

Shocked, the girl's head came up. "Gram was hurt by a man?"

Cassie nodded. "He claimed to love her, then, when he discovered that she was carrying his child, he abandoned her."

"Oh!" For the first time in her young life, Becky could see her grandmother not as an old woman, but as a young, beautiful girl. "What did she do?"

"It was a terrible, desperate time for your grandmother. Her family turned against her, claiming that she had disgraced them. People who had once been her friends turned against her, as well. But one man didn't care what others thought. He saw only goodness in her, and offered her his love and protection. Though you don't remember your grandfather, he was a wonderful man who married her and loved her and her baby with all his heart."

"What happened to the baby?"

Cassie blinked, aware that her daughter, so caught up in the story, had no idea. "I was that baby, Rebecca."

"You!"

"Yes. And I grew up with a special burden. I always felt that I had to prove to my mother that I would not repeat her mistake. So when she saw that boys had begun to notice me, and that I was responding to them, she insisted that it was time I married. She said that she had found the perfect man for me. And though I argued and wept and pleaded, in the end I did as I was told. I married your father, even though I hardly knew him.''

''Oh, Mama.'' Becky threw her arms around her mother's neck and began to cry.

For a moment Cassie was almost overwhelmed by all the old feelings that swamped her. Her pain was as fresh as it had been all those years ago, when she had felt hopelessly trapped.

Then she gathered her strength. ''Hush. It's all right. Your father was such a good man. He truly loved me. And he loved you and Jennifer, as well.''

Cassie wiped her daughter's tears, then drew her close and murmured, ''I give you my word, Rebecca. You will never be asked to pay for the sins of others. Whatever choices you make in your life, I will stand behind you.''

''Oh, Mama,'' the girl sobbed. ''I love you.''

''I love you, too, Rebecca. I will always love you.'' They stood, clinging to each other for long, silent minutes. Then, swallowing back her tears, Cassie said, ''Your grandmother asked me to tell you, so that you would be prepared before our visit to Prospect. Cyrus Stoner may have spread ugly gossip.''

''Knowing doesn't change the way I feel about Gram,'' Becky said. She sniffed back her tears and, pausing at the door to the barn, asked, ''Mama? Did you love Pa?''

''I...'' Cassie paused. It was a question she had never allowed herself to probe too deeply. But now she no longer feared the answer. Taking a deep breath, she looked into her daughter's eyes. ''Yes, Rebecca. Your

father was a good man. I will carry his memory always
in my heart.''

They left, arm in arm.

When the door closed behind them, Quin stepped
from the stall where he'd been saddling Cutter. He
hadn't meant to eavesdrop, but there had been no way
to make his presence known.

Leaning against the stall, he took a cigar from his
pocket and held a match to the tip. Secrets, he thought
as smoke curled upward. Everybody had them. And if
you lived long enough, you stopped being shocked by
them. But now that he'd overheard, he faced an even
worse dilemma than before. He would have to be more
diligent than ever to see that he kept a tight rein on his
feelings.

By the time Quin returned from the forest, it was well
past midnight. He had fashioned a travois behind Cutter to haul the game—three deer, a bear and half a
dozen rabbits.

The little cabin was filled with the fragrances of biscuits and beef and venison and the sharp, pungent odor
of lye soap. A rope had been strung across the length of
the cabin. On it hung dresses and several feminine frilly
petticoats, as well as a little girl's shirt and patched
britches.

Luella and the children, despite their eager anticipa-
tion, had retreated to their beds. Cassie, wearing a prim
nightgown covered by a modest shawl, was asleep in the
rocking chair.

Quin dropped to his knees beside her and drank in the
vision of her as she slept. Her hands rested on top of the
shirt she'd been mending for Jen. Such small hands. So
work roughened. Quin placed one of her hands on his

and gently lifted it to his lips. She smiled in her sleep but didn't awaken.

A lock of hair had fallen over one eye. He lifted a finger to it, brushing it aside, and allowed himself the luxury of studying the smooth brow, the curve of cheek, the full sculpted lips that begged to be kissed.

She stirred, then opened her eyes. Seeing him so close, she was jolted fully awake. "I'm sorry," she murmured. "I meant to stay awake until you returned. I've left the bucket of water over the fire to wash your clothes."

As she started to stand, he placed his hands on her shoulders and eased her back into the chair. "You've done enough for one day, Cassie."

"But your clothes—"

"I'll wash them."

"No. You've already done more than you should. Please," she whispered furiously. "Let me wash your clothes before you go into town. You arrived here looking so splendid. And now, you look—"

"Like a tired, dirty rancher." He smiled. "Don't worry yourself over it. I'm capable of washing my own clothes. The only thing you're going to do is sleep." To prevent any further protest, he bent and lifted her in his arms. For a moment, as he cradled her against his chest, he felt a rush of heat that left him stunned.

Cassie, too, felt the jolt, and was troubled by it. But though she wanted to resist, there seemed nothing to do but wrap her arms around his neck. That simple movement was followed by the press of her cheek against his.

She breathed in the musky, male scent of him, filling her lungs with him.

"I'll never be able to sleep," she whispered. "I'm too excited . . . about tomorrow, I mean."

"Mmm-hmm." He could have stood there like that for hours, holding her just so. "Trust me. You'll sleep." His breath was warm against her temple as he carried her to her bedroom. After drawing back the covers, he deposited her in her bed.

For a moment, as he tucked the blanket around her, he felt a sudden, violent arousal that had his pulse racing. The thought of lying with her, of spending the night loving her, was almost more than he could resist.

He rubbed the back of his knuckles across her cheek in a gesture that was achingly tender. "Good night, Cassie."

It took all of his willpower to turn and walk from the room. She was asleep before he lowered the blanket that served as a door.

Chapter Twelve

A leaden sky threatened snow. A north wind blew across the plains, stinging the eyes, reddening cheeks to the color of berries. But the little party, bundled into furs in the wagon, was as festive as if they were on their way to a summer picnic.

The two plow horses easily pulled the wagon across the frozen ground. Quin was astride Cutter, who pranced eagerly alongside the wagon.

"I see no Indians, Mr. McAllister," Luella called.

"No, ma'am. But they're there." Quin knew, by the prickly feeling along his scalp, that they were watching nearby. And though they would leave everything exactly as they found it, he knew that the Crow would enter the cabin and satisfy their curiosity about its occupants. He smiled. For that reason he had left a cigar on the table, as a gift for the chief.

"All this land you see now belongs to Cyrus Stoner," Cassie said. "It stretches from here all the way to Prospect."

Quin scanned mile after mile of rolling plains. "If a man's worth is judged by how much land he owns, I'd say Stoner is a very wealthy man. Why would he need yours?"

Cassie looked away. The same thought had occurred to her.

"How long before we're there?" Jen called.

"We have hours to go. And more miles than you can count." Quin urged Cutter up a hill and surveyed the vast empty land that lay before them. Glancing back at the wagon, he took pity on the little girl, wedged on a hard seat between her sister and grandmother. He wheeled his mount and retraced his steps. "How'd you like to ride with me, Jen? We'll scout the trail ahead."

The little girl's eyes lit. Turning to her mother, she whispered, "Please, Mama."

Cassie stared at Quin, astride his magnificent stallion, bundled into his cowhide duster, the wide-brimmed hat casting his eyes in shadow. This morning, before dawn, when she had ironed his shirt, she had held the fine fabric to her face, breathing in the scent of him that still lingered in the folds. There was a time when she had taken such finery for granted. Now her faded gingham gown seemed all the more shabby by contrast to his expensive apparel.

"I think the child should stay with us," Luella said sternly.

"She'll be fine, Ma. You may go with Mr. McAllister, Jennifer."

At her mother's words Jen gave an excited yelp before being lifted in Quin's strong arms.

"Think you can hang on?" Quin asked.

"Yes, sir."

In one smooth motion Quin settled Jen behind him. The girl wrapped her thin arms around Quin's waist, and Cutter took off at a slow, easy pace.

"It might be rough going at times." Quin guided his mount up a steep, slippery incline. "You let me know when you get tired, Jen."

"I'm never going to get tired of this." Jen's voice quivered with excitement.

"Look." Quin pointed and the child was suddenly rendered speechless at the sight of hundreds of buffalo spread out on the plain below. Their great shaggy bodies moved slowly as they pawed the blanket of snow in search of precious bunch grass.

When she finally found her voice, Jen asked, "Are you going to shoot some?"

Quin shook his head. "We have more than enough meat in our wagon. We'll leave the buffalo for our friends, the Crow. Their survival depends upon the buffalo."

"Why?"

"They use the buffalo for food and clothing. They even build their tepees with their skins." Quin chuckled. "And though I enjoy buffalo meat occasionally, the truth is, I much prefer beef or venison."

"Me, too," Jen said emphatically. Right now, she loved everything Quin McAllister loved, even if she didn't know why. But somehow, riding behind this man, astride his big black stallion, Jen felt safe and warm and secure, the way she had before her father had died. And her heart was beating as though it would burst from excitement.

Unlike her older sister, Jen could no longer remember the place of their birth. The stately mansions, the opulent life-style, the slow, gentle rhythm of the South, were completely wiped from her memory. She stared down at the vast panorama spread out below and drank it in, feeling a welling of love. From the stark mountain peaks around them, swarming with sheep and goats, grizzlies and cougars, to the waterfalls and clear lakes, this strange, foreign land had become home.

Overhead a hawk made slow, lazy circles and Jen pointed a finger as it suddenly plummeted to the ground, only to lift into the air again, holding a squealing rabbit in its beak.

"Breakfast," Quin said with a laugh. "That reminds me. Are you hungry yet?"

"No, sir."

"Good. Hang on, then. I'd like to take a look at what's ahead."

With a flick of the reins, Cutter broke into a run, and the little girl clung to the man, blissfully unaware of the wind in her face.

Several hours later, when Quin noticed the press of Jen's cheek against his back, and felt the girl's grasp go slack, he gathered her into his arms and made his way to the wagon. There, Jen was tucked into a nest of furs in the back of the wagon, where she slept.

"Prospect." Quin pointed and the little party studied the town in the distance.

After spending so much time in their cramped cabin in the wilderness, they were impressed by the distant cluster of buildings. But as they drew nearer, they realized that the town was small, even by their standards. As the wagon rolled along the main street, which was really only a wide dirt road, each of them focused on a different building.

For Luella, the only building that mattered was the church, with its crude wooden cross. It had been so long since she had heard the rich, resonant tones of a preacher exhorting her to more lofty ideals, or the voices of a congregation raised in song, touching a chord deep in her soul. More than anything else, she had missed the comfort of her church.

Becky's gaze was caught and held by Sutter's Mercantile. Through the window she could see bolts of brightly colored fabric, and pretty bonnets adorned with lace and feathers. She was old enough to remember Atlanta before the war, when the city had been every bit as fine as New York or Boston, or so her father had told her. Though she had never been to those other places, she had thought Atlanta the prettiest city in the whole world. In her drab, faded dress, which had been made over from one of her grandmother's, she thought there could be nothing more wonderful than a trip to the mercantile, where she would wish and dream and pretend.

Jen stared hungrily at the tiny schoolhouse, wondering what it would be like to hear the voices of other children talking, laughing, teasing. Playing. Learning. There was so much she didn't know. And she wanted to know everything. Maybe that was why she loved listening to Quin McAllister. He had been everywhere, had done everything. And someday, Jen vowed, she would be like this man, roaming the land in search of adventure.

For Cassie, it was the row of neat houses, with smoke curling from chimneys, and curtains at the windows. She was unaware of the look of hunger that crossed her face as she watched women and children bustling about inside, preparing supper. How she missed the comfort of a real home and hearth. She had once presided over dozens of servants while she entertained hundreds of Atlanta's finest citizens. Her dinner parties had been the talk of the town. Her gowns had come from Paris and

London, as had her furnishings. And now...she glanced down at her hands, rough and callused from ranch chores. Now she was lucky to survive one day at a time.

As he led them through town, Quin's attention was drawn to the gaudy lights of the saloon. His eyes narrowed at the sound of a woman's laughter and tinny piano music drifting on the evening air. A scuffle erupted, and a towering hulk of a man could be seen hurling a second man through the swinging doors, where he landed in the dirty snow in the road. At once Quin's pulse quickened, his lips curved into a smile.

He turned. Seeing Cassie watching him, he cleared his throat. "We'll find a boardinghouse first. Then I'll see to the horses."

As he continued along the dusty road, his smile fled. He'd once boasted that there was nothing that excited him like a game of chance. And now? Now, he thought grimly, there was something else...someone else, he corrected himself, that excited him far more.

"Evening." The blacksmith stepped out of his shed, eyeing the wagon and its occupants. "You folks planning on staying the night?"

"We'd like to. Is there a boardinghouse in town?"

"Just down this road. The widow Claxton keeps a clean place." His teeth flashed in a quick smile. "Good cook, too. That's where all the men in this town go to eat if they aren't lucky enough to have a wife to cook for them."

"Thank you." Quin turned to Cassie. "I'll settle everyone in first, then bring the horses back here."

After discussing price with the blacksmith, they settled on a deer in payment. Quin mounted and led the way to a large rambling house at the edge of town. Besides the main house, of two stories, there were several large outbuildings in back.

A knock at the door brought a quick response. The door was opened by a plump woman whose dark hair was pinned into a neat knot. A plain white apron was tied around her ample middle. She dried her hands on the apron before asking, "Are you folks looking for just food, or food and lodging?"

"Both, ma'am." Quin indicated the women and children in the wagon. "Is there room for all of us?"

"Indeed there is." She glanced at his rifle and side arm. "I have two rules. Neither whiskey nor guns permitted in my house. Can you abide by that?"

"Yes, ma'am."

"Have you made arrangements for the horses and wagon?"

"I've already stopped by the stable and paid the smith."

"Fine. My son Willy will see to them."

She stood aside and a boy of about fourteen or fifteen stepped outside, pulling on a parka. He was tall and rangy, with a dusting of fine blond hair that spilled over a wide forehead.

After catching Quin's reins as he dismounted, the boy took the lead harness and held the horses still while Quin helped everyone from the wagon. His blue eyes looked startled when he caught sight of Becky, seated between her mother and grandmother. When she looked up, he flashed her a bright smile.

Becky blushed and turned away.

"Come in," Mrs. Claxton called.

"Before we go inside, ma'am, I'd like to settle our payment." Quin indicated the two deer. "I hope this

will cover our rooms and meals. I'd like to use the rest
to buy supplies."

The woman looked them over carefully, admiring the
size and quality. "These will more than cover everything, including tubs of warm water. I usually charge a
dollar extra for such luxuries." She strode to the porch
and held the door. "Please, come inside."

Removing his holster, Quin handed it to her as he
stepped past her.

The formal parlor boasted a horsehair sofa and several inviting, overstuffed chairs. A fire crackled in the
fireplace.

"Please sit and warm yourselves. Supper won't be
ready for another hour, but I'll bring you tea and some
biscuits before I show you to your rooms. The tubs and
warm water will be brought up shortly." The woman
extended her hand to Quin. "My name is Florence
Claxton."

"Quin McAllister."

"Welcome, Mr. McAllister. And Mrs. McAllister,"
she added, extending her hand to Cassie.

Cassie felt her cheeks grow hot. "My name is Cassie
Montgomery. And these are my children, Rebecca and
Jennifer. And my mother, Luella Chalmers."

"Forgive me. I just thought..." The woman arched
a brow. "Mr. McAllister is your...?"

"Ranch foreman," Quin put in quickly.

"I see."

Just then a muscular youth of sixteen or seventeen
entered the parlor with an armload of logs for the fire.

"You met my son Willy. And this is my son Zack,"
Florence said. "Zack, say hello to Mr. McAllister."

The youth deposited the wood beside the fireplace,
then wiped his palms on his pants and extended his

hand to Quin. "Mr. McAllister." Like his younger brother, Zack had fine blond hair. But there the similarity ended. His arms were already corded with muscle. He stood nearly as tall as Quin.

"And this is Mrs. Montgomery and her mother, Mrs. Chalmers, and her children, Jennifer and Rebecca."

The young man acknowledged everyone with a smile, but his smile grew when he caught sight of Becky.

"I'll need logs for the upstairs rooms, Zack. And tubs of hot water," Florence said briskly. "These folks are staying the night."

"Yes, ma'am." The youth nodded and left the room. A few minutes later they heard his heavy footsteps as he carried wood to the upper floors.

"I'll get that tea now," Florence said, "and then I'll show you to your rooms."

She returned a short time later with a silver tray loaded with cups of steaming tea and biscuits spread with butter and jam. For Jen there was a mug of warm milk. The little girl was so enchanted by the sweet jam that she managed to down at least four biscuits before her grandmother scolded her.

"Enough, Jen," she said sharply. "Leave something on the plate for the others."

"Yes'm." Jen kept her eyes downcast until a little boy of six or seven years, with fine, corn silk hair and an infectious grin, danced into the room.

"My name is Oren," he called. "What's yours?"

"Jen."

For a moment he seemed taken aback, and it was clear that he'd thought the little figure in the cap and britches was a boy. Then, with the resilience of the very young, his broad smile returned. "Want to see our puppies?" he asked.

Jen's eyes were suddenly alight with pleasure. She jumped up, then cast an anxious glance toward her mother, who nodded her assent. With a delighted laugh, she dashed off behind her newfound friend.

Florence Claxton appeared in the doorway. "If you're ready, I'll take you to your rooms." As they climbed the stairs she said, "I've given you four ladies the big bedroom." She opened a door to reveal a large, airy bedroom with two big beds, each covered with a colorful handmade quilt. In addition there was a chest in one corner, holding a porcelain basin and pitcher, and in the other corner a tall looking glass. The wood floor was softened with colorful rag rugs. A cheery fire burned in the stone fireplace. On a rug in front of the fire was a tub filled with steaming water.

"I'll leave you to freshen up in here, while I show Mr. McAllister to his room."

"Thank you, Mrs. Claxton."

"It's Florence," she said.

"Thank you, Florence."

The woman closed the door and led Quin along the hall toward a second, smaller bedroom. Inside was a sturdy bed made of rough timbers, in a room made cozy by the addition of a huge stone fireplace. As in the other room, a tub of warm water stood on a rug in front of the fire.

"Supper in an hour, Mr. McAllister," Florence said as she started down the stairs.

"Thank you, ma'am."

He closed the door. Before she had even made it to the bottom step, he'd stripped off his clothes and was immersed in warm water. He leaned back, eyes closed, while the rich smoke from a cigar curled above his head.

At a knock on his door he called, "Come on in. It isn't locked."

"Mr. McAllister. I wondered if..." Cassie's skirts swirled around her ankles as she bustled in and closed the door behind her. Turning, she let her word trail off. Her face flushed several shades of scarlet. She lifted her hand to her throat. "You should have told me you were . . . not decent."

"There's nothing indecent about this, ma'am," he said with a humorous drawl. "It's just the way God intended."

"Perhaps, but I do not intend..." Before she could turn away his hand clamped around her wrist, holding her still.

"I was just wishing for someone to scrub my back. Want to volunteer?" He drew her down until she was forced to her knees beside the tub. With a lazy, sardonic smile that had her breath hitching, her heart racing, he handed her a soapy cloth.

She was constantly being surprised by the strength in him. Though he always gave the impression of easygoing humor, she knew it masked an iron will. Right now it was evident in the press of his fingers around her wrist. It would be useless to struggle. Her strength was no match for his.

"You are too bold, Mr. McAllister."

"Did you ever think you may be too timid?"

"Timid?" She drew back, but he held her firmly. Her head came up, her chin jutting in that way he'd come to recognize. "If it is timid to refuse to play the part of a wicked, painted saloon girl, then I am timid. And if it is timid to blush at the sight of a naked man, then I am timid. But I will not play your game, Mr. McAllister."

She took aim with the soapy rag. Seeing what she intended, he caught her hand in a viselike grip until the rag dropped into the water.

"That wasn't nice, Cassie." Laughing, he dragged her close until she was pressed against the edge of the tub. "I may have to teach you a lesson."

For one startled moment she stared at him, her eyes growing round with fear. Then she saw his laughter fade. His eyes darkened; his gaze fixed on her mouth. Before she could pull back, his arms were around her. His lips covered hers in a hot, hungry kiss that hinted of the passion smoldering just below the surface, waiting to erupt.

She was so aware of him. She could feel him in every part of her body. She kept her hands balled into fists, which she held firmly between them. But at the press of his naked torso, her hands slowly opened until her palms were splayed across his hair-roughened chest.

"Oh, God, Cassie." His words were ground out against her mouth as he changed the angle of the kiss and took it deeper.

She gave no thought to resisting. All she could do was cling to him and offer her lips. Water sloshed over the rim of the tub, soaking the front of her gown. But still she clung to him, returning his kisses with a fervor that matched his.

He lifted his head. His eyes were the color of slate and she could see herself reflected there. As he drew her close, she felt the tiny threads of excitement and fear. How could she have allowed this to go so far? When she had entered his room, it had never occurred to her that he would be naked. Naked. There was something deliciously wicked about such a thing. She was shocked at her own boldness. And yet, as he raised his mouth to hers, she couldn't find the will to pull back. All she could do was twine her arms around his wet, warm neck and allow herself the pleasure.

His lips and hands were able to weave magic. At the first taste of him, there was no doubt that she wanted more.

He studied the way she looked, her cheeks flushed, eyes glazed. The wet fabric clung provocatively to the soft curves of her breasts, making them as visible as if she wore nothing.

He felt a rush of heat as his hands moved along her back, drawing her even closer.

"I don't believe I can stop, Cassie. I have to keep on touching you, kissing you."

Before she could protest, his lips covered hers in the softest, gentlest kiss she'd ever known. Despite the passion that raged between them, he held her gently, like a fragile flower. The only sound in the room was the quiet lapping of the water as it sloshed perilously near the top of the tub, and the soft, barely audible sound of her sighs.

Cassie had never believed a kiss could be this tender. Quin touched his lips to the corner of her mouth, to her nose, then pressed a kiss to her cheek. With his tongue he traced the outline of her lips until he heard her sigh of impatience. Still he didn't take the kiss deeper, but moved his lips instead to her ear, where he tugged on her lobe before circling her ear with his tongue. His breath sent little tremors along her spine, and she clutched blindly at his waist when he darted his tongue inside her ear. When she would have pulled his mouth to hers, he pressed moist little kisses along her throat until she moaned and arched her neck, giving him easier access.

With his tongue he licked at the little drops of water that dripped at her throat.

Steeped in such pleasurable feelings, she clung to him and moved in his arms. Never had she known such feelings. Still, she didn't know what to do about them. She longed to touch the mat of hair on his chest, but she was afraid. She was aching to kiss his cheeks, his throat, to explore his ear as he had explored hers. But fear held her back.

When his lips bent to the swell of her breast, she let out a little gasp. Through the wet cloth his lips found her already hard nipple. At the first touch of his lips she felt as if a fist had tightened deep inside. Pleasure pulsed through her body; her blood roared in her ears.

All her years as a wife had not prepared her for the shock that rippled through her at his touch. Ethan, aware of her youth and inexperience, had been a far different lover than this man. Out of respect for her need for modesty, their only lovemaking had been at night, under cover of darkness. Never before had she experienced such mindless pleasure, such hard, driving need. And all of it by the light of the fire and the soft glow of lanterns.

She wanted him to go on touching her like this forever. But she knew she had to stop him. How long, she wondered, could they continue this love play before she lost all sense of reason? There were so many things she didn't understand. Oh, if only there were someone to talk to. But there was no one. Her mother, she knew, would be scandalized by such behavior.

Calling on all her willpower, she pushed herself free of his arms. Lowering her face, she refused to meet his gaze. Her cheeks burned with shame.

"Cassie." Tipping her face upward, Quin stared into her eyes and saw a glimmer of unshed tears. "Look at me."

Her lids fluttered, and for a moment she met his look before lowering her gaze.

"You're a beautiful, desirable woman." He caught her wrists, holding her when she tried to pull away. "It's the most natural thing in the world to share what we shared."

To cover her embarrassment she resorted to the only weapon she had. Anger. "Let me go, Quin."

As he bent to kiss her again, her hand hit the water, sending a spray across his face. "I said let me go."

His hands fell away, leaving her to fall backward in a puddle that had formed on the floor.

Stunned, she sat a moment, then, eyes narrowed, mouth a thin, tight line, she scrambled to her feet. She seemed puzzled by the grin that suddenly split Quin's lips. Then, looking down, she realized that her gown was soaked, both front and back.

"You did that on purpose."

"I believe I did, ma'am." His smile was swift and teasing. "I kissed you on purpose, too. And if you're not careful, I'll do it again."

"Oh." She whirled and headed for the door, striving for as much dignity as possible. Her soaked petticoats and gown clung to her rounded bottom with every step.

Behind her, Quin felt a rush of heat and wondered if she had any idea just how seductive that haughty walk of hers was. When the door slammed behind her, he plucked the soaked cigar from the water and tossed it into the fire. With a muttered oath he stepped dripping from the tub and, ignoring his nakedness, strode across the room and picked up a thick square of linen. As he began to dry himself he paused, hands in midair.

What the hell had she done to him?

God in heaven. Did he love her? Was that it?

In the beginning, it may have been simple lust, he admitted logically. But now his feelings went much deeper. But love?

Through the window came the tinny sounds of the piano from the saloon. He pulled on his pants and boots, then leaned against the sill and stared at the men below walking through the swinging doors. Ordinarily his first thought after a satisfying bath would have been to mingle with the men and women who frequented the saloon. Now he hesitated. Even the thought of a game of poker had lost its appeal.

Damn this miserable snow-covered wilderness. And damn the woman who'd enticed him into staying.

With a savage oath he turned away and finished dressing.

Chapter Thirteen

Cassie was grateful for the time alone in her room. It was a rare luxury, and one she intended to savor. Thank heavens her mother and daughters had already gone downstairs. Their voices could be heard in the dining room, where they chattered and laughed as they helped set the table for supper. She could have never explained her wet clothes. Worse, they would have known, by the high color on her cheeks, who had been responsible for her disheveled state.

She lingered in the tub, then slowly dried herself. What did Quin see when he looked at her? Dropping the towel, she studied her reflection in the looking glass. It had been so many years since she'd taken the time to really look at herself. What she saw startled her.

She had lost her youthful roundness. Her figure was now that of a woman. Far too slender for her taste. High, firm breasts. Tiny waist. Long, slim legs, and almost no hips. She thought her features plain, with cheeks too high, lips too large. She never knew if her eyes were green or yellow. Cat's eyes, her mother called them. As changeable as her moods. And her hair. She had always yearned for dark, silky curls, or a lion's mane of flax. Instead, thick hair the color of autumn leaves tumbled to her waist. She glanced down at her hands, callused and work worn. Cringing, she held them behind her back for a moment, wishing Quin could have seen her as she'd been before the war. Young, pretty, carefree. No, she thought suddenly. That wasn't quite true. Even as a child she had sensed her mother's need for perfection. Life had never been completely carefree. But compared with her life today, she had lived like a pampered princess.

With a sigh she studied her hands. There was no sense trying to hide what she'd become. She was almost twenty-eight years old. No longer a girl. Her own daughter was almost a woman. And yet, there were times, like now, when she felt all the confusion of a child, while possessing all the needs and desires of a woman. She had no right to the feelings that swirled about inside her, tempting her to go against everything she had ever believed in. Yet the man in the next room could, with a simple touch, cause her to throw caution to the wind and believe, for a little while, that she was young and beautiful. His boldness seemed to reach a need deep inside her. A need to take risks. A need to taste and feel and—experience. A need that had her behaving in a most indecent manner. Just thinking about the kiss they shared had her cheeks flaming.

Such nonsense. Next she would be sulking and dreaming like Rebecca. She stepped into her petticoats, pulled on her faded gown, ran a brush through her hair, and tied it back with a simple ribbon. Then she resolutely turned away from the looking glass, chiding herself for her vanity.

But as she descended the stairs, the sound of Quin's deep voice had her heartbeat quickening, and she wished, fleetingly, that she could be young and pretty again, if only for one brief moment.

"There you are," Florence Claxton called from the parlor.

Cassie paused in the doorway and felt her cheeks redden when Quin glanced up. Though she was aware that there were others in the room, her gaze was drawn to him.

"I...was enjoying the luxury of a warm, leisurely bath," she confessed.

"That's just what Mr. McAllister was telling us."

Cassie's mouth dropped open. Quin's knowing smile had her quickly looking away, but not before he caught the blush on her cheeks.

Unaware, Florence Claxton went on with her conversation with barely a pause. "Mr. McAllister said he couldn't recall when he'd enjoyed a bath more. Isn't that right, Mr. McAllister?"

"Indeed it is, Mrs. Claxton."

"Florence," the woman corrected with a smile.

"Florence," Quin repeated. "Call me Quin."

Cassie's lips thinned. It was plain to see that Quin McAllister had already managed to charm the widow Claxton.

Turning to Cassie, Florence said, "I believe you know Jedediah Taylor."

"Yes." Cassie smiled at the old man standing with his backside warming before the roaring fire. "Jedediah has been a friend since we first came to Montana."

"And this is Sheriff Clayton Wilson." Florence indicated a bewhiskered man whose stomach protruded over his belt. A leather holster was empty. Out of deference to his hostess, he had been forced to deposit his pistol on a shelf by the front door.

"Mrs. Montgomery." He inclined his head and studied Cassie as she took a seat on the sofa beside her daughter.

"I'm surprised that a town as small as this would need a sheriff," Quin remarked.

"We may be small," Florence said, "but some, like Cyrus Stoner, have a lot of valuable land to protect."

"So you were hired by Cyrus Stoner."

The sheriff swiveled his head to peer at Quin. "I was hired by the town of Prospect to keep the peace and protect its interests."

Cassie had the impression that the sheriff was angered by Quin's remark.

When the front door opened on a gust of icy wind, everyone turned to watch the arrival of their latest guest. A tall figure in a long cowhide jacket leaned his weight against the door, then turned to their hostess with a smile.

"Forgive me, Florence. I didn't mean to hold up supper."

"Not at all, Reverend Townsend. We were just about to go into the dining room." Handing his coat to her son, Florence said, "The reverend, being a widower, is staying at my place until his parsonage is built. Reverend, come and meet these nice folks who just arrived this evening."

Leading him around the room, she made the introductions.

"This is Mrs. Montgomery, and her daughter, Rebecca. And her mother, Luella Chalmers. And this is their ranch foreman, Quin McAllister."

The reverend was an impressive figure. Tall, ruggedly handsome, with dark hair just beginning to gray at the temples, he looked more like a prosperous rancher than a man of the church.

"Nice to meet all you good folks."

"Where were you today, Reverend?" Florence asked.

"Burying Lester Cleat's father."

"So the Lord finally took him."

"Don't know about the Lord, but somebody shot the old man in the back, and helped themselves to a herd of unbranded cattle," Reverend Townsend said as he followed the widow into the dining room.

"Who do you think did it, Sheriff?" Florence asked.

The lawman shrugged. "I'm still investigating. Indians, most likely."

The others trailed behind. While they took their seats, Jen and Oren, their hands and faces glowing, their hair slicked back, came racing into the room, then skidded to a halt.

"Well, don't you two look clean," Florence said with a smile.

"Oren showed me his puppies." Jen's voice was high with excitement. "And he let me hold one. Mama, it was this big," she said, moving her little hands a few inches apart. "And it licked my face and fell asleep in my arms."

"That's nice," Cassie said.

"I think he likes me," Jen whispered. "Oren says Mr. Sutter over at the mercantile has offered to buy him for a dollar. Do you think I could—"

"That's enough, Jennifer," Luella said sharply. "Say hello to Sheriff Wilson and Reverend Townsend."

"Hello." Jen shot them quick smiles, then returned her attention to her mother. "I even thought of a name for the puppy."

"All right, folks," Florence called. "Reverend Townsend will lead a prayer, and then you can all help yourselves."

Everyone bowed their heads while the minister offered a prayer of thanks for the food. Then, with the aid of her two older sons, Willy and Zack, Florence Claxton began serving the food. There were mashed potatoes and carrots and platters of roast beef and gravy. And a pan of biscuits still warm from the oven.

"If the puppy was mine, I'd name him Whiskey," Jen continued, as though there had been no interruption, "because he's the color of Mr. McAllister's whiskey."

Luella was clearly shocked. "We will not permit such a name to be spoken in our house, child."

"All right. Then I guess I could call him—" the little girl studied the biscuit in her hand "—Biscuit. He's the color of Mrs. Claxton's biscuits."

"There is no point in this discussion," Luella said, glancing toward her daughter for support. "The puppy belongs to Oren. It's his to name."

When Jen opened her mouth to protest, Cassie touched a hand to her arm. There was a pained expression on her face as she whispered, "Your grandmother is right, Jennifer."

The little girl fell silent.

Sheriff Wilson studied Cassie across the table. "Florence tells me you and your family live out on the plains. What brings you to Prospect?"

"We needed supplies. Flour, sugar."

"And thread," Luella interjected. "Don't forget my thread."

"Long way to come for a few simple things."

For some unexplained reason, Cassie resented the sheriff's intense scrutiny. He was studying her the way a lawman might when taking the measure of an adversary.

"They may be simple, but they are necessary to our survival." She abruptly changed the subject. "Did you know my husband, Reverend Townsend?"

"No, ma'am, I didn't."

"And you, Sheriff?"

"No, ma'am. Never had the pleasure. 'Course, I've only been here a few months. Florence tells me he's dead. How did it happen?"

"A lingering illness. After the war he was never robust."

"A pity you didn't send for the reverend to give him a decent burial."

Again Cassie felt the piercing stare. Had the sheriff heard that she had kept Ethan's death a secret for all this time? Ignoring Sheriff Wilson, she turned to Reverend Townsend. "I couldn't ask you to spend an entire day on the trail."

"But I'd have been happy to do it, my dear. I've traveled farther than that to carry the word of God to people who need marrying or burying."

"Speaking of burying..." Sheriff Wilson turned to Quin. "We've been doing a lot of that lately. A number of Cyrus Stoner's men have been turning up dead."

Quin helped himself to a second serving of meat and potatoes. "Some people just seem to have a string of bad luck." He turned the full force of his smile on his hostess. "Florence, the blacksmith wasn't exaggerating when he said you were a fine cook."

Her cheeks bloomed. "Thank you. But I can't take all the credit. Luella gave me a hand in the kitchen. I've already decided I like her recipe for beef better than mine. Try the biscuits. Luella baked them.''

The sheriff, refusing to be put off by easy banter, persisted. "There are a lot of rumors in town, McAllister. Some say you've cast your lot with the Crow.''

"Now who would say a thing like that?" Quin lifted a cup of coffee to his lips and studied the sheriff over the rim.

Sheriff Wilson shrugged. "Cyrus Stoner is a powerful man in these parts. He doesn't take kindly to having his men attacked and his cattle rustled.''

"Rustled?" Quin set his cup down but kept his eyes narrowed on the sheriff. "Is that what this is about? Cattle rustling?''

"The Crow, especially during the long winter, need meat to survive. And they're not above helping themselves to the property of others.''

"They have all the game they need. Just today we passed a herd of hundreds of buffalo.''

"According to Stoner, it's easier for the Crow to shoot the white man's cattle than it is to hunt buffalo on the plains.''

Quin's tone remained conversational, but there was a thread of steel in it. "According to Stoner. I suppose it was Cyrus Stoner who suggested that the Crow were responsible for the death of the man the reverend buried today, too.''

"I believe it was. I'll remind you, McAllister, in these parts, cattle rustling is a hanging offense.''

"I surely will keep that in mind." Quin drained his cup. "Fine coffee, Florence.''

"Wait 'til you taste my ma's apple cobbler," Willy boasted.

"With cinnamon and sweet cream," Oren added.

"My mouth is watering already." Effectively dismissing the sheriff, Quin accepted a second cup of coffee and winked at the little boy across the table.

Beside him, Sheriff Wilson could hardly contain his temper. "You don't strike me as a fool, McAllister. But only a fool would side with thieving Indians against white men. Especially when one of the whites is as powerful as Cyrus Stoner."

Quin said blandly, "I've been called worse things than a fool, Sheriff."

Becky and Zack helped Florence serve the cobbler, to the raves of everyone at the table.

"My wife used to bake cobbler," Reverend Townsend said as he took his first bite. "I still miss it."

"How long has your wife been gone?" Luella asked.

"Five years. And your husband?"

Luella thought about the man who had stood beside her for twenty years. With his gentle humor he could always tease her out of her little fits of temper. "He's been gone for nine years now."

"That's a long time to be alone."

"Yes. Well, I have my daughter and my grandchildren. Do you have any family, Reverend?"

"Please call me Matthew. And the answer is no," he said a bit wistfully. "My wife and I never had any children, though we'd always hoped the Lord would bless us. You're a very lucky woman to have your family." He glanced around the table. "And you're all very lucky to have such a fine grandmother."

At his words Luella felt a warm glow. She dipped a spoon into the cobbler and took a bite. "Oh, this is wonderful." She sighed as she leaned back in her chair. "I haven't eaten anything like this since before the war."

"Well, this is a festive occasion," Florence said as she walked around the table, refilling coffee cups. "Children, will you clear the table, please?"

Jen and Becky pushed away from the table and began to help clear away the dishes, along with Zack, Willy and Oren.

"Special occasion?" Luella prodded.

Florence bobbed her head. "I've been busy baking for over a week now, what with Christmas just a few days away."

"Christmas!" Jen and Becky stopped in their tracks.

"Why, yes. Don't tell me you two forgot." Florence smiled at Luella. "I knew all along why you folks came to town today. To load your wagon with all the special things you'll need to celebrate."

"Christmas. Of course." Luella busied herself with her napkin.

"Let's take our coffee in the parlor," Florence said, leading the way.

Quin glanced across the table at Cassie, who had remained silent. He was surprised by the stunned look on her face.

Sensing his probing stare, she pulled herself together and got to her feet. Squaring her shoulders, she followed the others into the parlor.

Shirtless, Quin stood by the darkened window of his room, listening to the sounds of music and laughter that drifted from the saloon. It seemed strange that he wasn't tempted. After all, he couldn't sleep. He wanted a cigar. What's more, he wanted a glass of whiskey. And when it came to poker, he was the best there was. So why wasn't he at the saloon?

The thought of winning didn't heat his blood. It wasn't cards or whiskey he craved.

He wanted Cassie.

The thought came in a rush. At once he dismissed it. Cassie Montgomery wasn't the kind of woman a man merely played with. She was the sort of woman who made a man think about home and family. Roots. Permanence. All the things he had always disdained. A man could never have a woman like Cassie and then walk away. Her memory would linger, like the taste of fine wine, like the essence of French perfume, haunting him to his last breath.

He clenched his hand into a fist and turned away from the window. After quickly pulling on his shirt and boots, he made his way downstairs, intent upon smoking a cigar on the front porch. As he passed the darkened parlor, a sound caused him to halt. Peering inside, he saw that the fire had died to embers. In a chair pulled close to the fireplace was a hunched figure.

As he drew closer he realized it was Cassie, her face buried in her hands. She was sobbing as though her heart would break.

"Who did this to you? Who made you cry?" His voice was gruff as he dropped to his knees in front of her and dragged her hands away from her face. "Tell me who hurt you."

"Quin..." Tears streamed down her cheeks and she struggled to find her voice.

"Was it the sheriff? If that bastard—"

"No. Oh, Quin..." The tears started again and she was powerless to stop them.

Desperate to ease her pain, he stood and drew her into his arms. At once he felt the jolt. It was the most purely sexual feeling he'd ever known. Heat consumed him.

He was aware of her as he'd never before been aware of a woman. The soft contours of her body pressed against him. His hands were actually shaking. She was so small, so helpless. He would fight anyone, kill anyone, who made her cry.

At his sudden, shocking arousal, he cursed and called himself every kind of fool. What Cassie needed at the moment was tenderness, not passion. And he would, by heaven, give her whatever she needed, if it was in his power. At the moment she needed his quiet strength, his comfort.

She was racked with sobs. He felt a moment of panic. She had always been so brave, so stoic in the face of every danger. Whatever had caused her pain, it was more terrible than anything she had yet been forced to endure. And all he could do was hold her and murmur words of endearment until her tears had run their course.

"Now tell me, Cassie." He handed her his fine monogrammed handkerchief, and waited while she wiped her tears. "You have to tell me what's happened."

"It's…" She sighed and swallowed and dabbed at the tears that stained her cheeks, before attempting to continue. "It's Christmas."

He waited, expecting something more. But when she said nothing else, he studied her with a puzzled look. "That's it? Christmas?"

She nodded, and had to struggle with fresh tears. "Don't you see? Florence said that the day after tomorrow is Christmas Eve, and we didn't even know. It has become just another day of hard work and misery for my mother and my children. Oh, Quin, what has this place done to us? What have we become?"

He realized that, until this moment, he'd been holding his breath, afraid to hear what disaster had befallen her. But now that he knew, he felt as though some terrible weight had just been lifted from his shoulders.

He placed a hand under her chin, tipping her face up for his inspection. His tone was gruff with a welling of unexpected tenderness. "Stop being so hard on yourself, Cassie. You've survived a war that devastated this land. You've lost your husband, your home, your friends. You're carving out a life for yourself and your family in a hostile wilderness. And on top of all that, you've held on to the ability to laugh, to love, to hope for something better." He touched a hand to her cheek. "Is it so terrible that you forgot about Christmas?"

"Yes." Her eyes filled and she blinked rapidly to keep from crying again. "It tears my heart out to think that my children will not celebrate Christmas as I did when I was a child."

He didn't smile, though laughter lurked in his eyes and warmed his tone. "I can see that we'll have to do something about this."

"But don't you see? There's nothing we can do." Her eyes were troubled and for a moment he feared she might begin to cry again. Then she pulled herself together, lifting her chin in that way he'd come to recognize. "I'm sorry. I didn't mean to burden you with my problems, Quin. It won't happen again. I'm fine now. I guess I just needed a shoulder to cry on."

He framed her face with his big hands. "You can use my shoulder anytime."

Now that the storm had passed, she became aware of a strange, new emotion. Not desolation. Not despair. Not even the comfort Quin offered. Cassie was suddenly aware of the hands that touched her so gently, of the warm breath that feathered her hair, of the inviting lips that hovered just above hers.

Heat coursed through her veins, leaving her weak-limbed. Her legs were rubber. Her fingers seemed to have a will of their own as they wrapped around his arms, clinging for a moment before inching upward until they were twined through the hair at his collar.

Her tone softened, invited. "I should...go up to bed now."

"Mmm-hmm." He made no move to release her. Instead, his arms came around her, drawing her closer.

"Ma might notice I'm gone." Her gaze fastened on his lips. Such firm, tempting lips. Still, he made no move to kiss her. "Or Rebecca. Or Jennifer."

"They might."

She wanted desperately for him to kiss her. But still he waited, watching her in that strange, silent way he had. "I..." She lifted herself on tiptoe until her lips were even with his. "I don't want to go up yet, Quin."

"And why is that?" His eyes narrowed slightly. He wouldn't make the first move this time. The decision had to be hers.

"I...want to kiss you first." She pressed her lips to his.

For the space of a heartbeat, he didn't respond, and she drew away to slant a look at him. Then, bringing her lips back to his, she kissed him again, this time more fully.

She heard his quick intake of breath before his arms tightened around her, dragging her against him until their bodies fused. His mouth moved over hers with a hunger that matched her own.

"Dear God, Cassie, I want you." The words escaped his lips before he had time to think. Once said, there was no way to snatch them back.

Her heart soared at his admission. He wanted her. And she knew in her heart that she wanted him, as well. Wanted him as she'd never wanted anyone or anything before. With a sigh she gave herself up to the pleasure of his kiss.

He felt the gradual change in her as she relaxed in his arms and offered her lips. It was not an act of submission, but rather a sharing of pleasure. Lost in the kiss, she lowered her defenses. It was his undoing. Heat danced through him, quickening his pulse. At once his arms tightened, drawing her so close he could feel her erratic heartbeat inside his own chest.

He knew if he didn't soon find the strength to step away, he would take her here, now, like a savage. And still he lingered over her lips, savoring the sweet, fresh taste of her, unlike anything he'd ever known before. He wanted her. Wanted her so desperately, he had to call on every bit of willpower to resist the urge to take them both over the line. His hands were almost bruising as he caught her roughly by the shoulders and drew her away.

Cassie's lids slowly opened. She felt breathless. And slightly exhilarated. As though she had just tempted fate, and stepped back from the very edge of a steep precipice. Would she have fallen? Or would she have soared?

"I'd... better go up to bed now."

Quin merely nodded. The truth was, he was afraid to trust his voice.

"Aren't you coming up?"

He cleared his throat. "Not yet."

"Good night, then."

"Good night, Cassie."

On legs that still trembled, she made her way to the door. She turned. "Quin?"

"Yes?"

"Thank you. For listening. For...everything." She turned away quickly, before she said something she'd regret in the morning.

He listened to the sound of her quick, light footsteps on the stairs, and the sound of her bedroom door as it was opened and closed.

For long minutes he stood very still, considering. Then he pulled on his duster and wide-brimmed hat. His hands, he noted, were unsteady. Not exactly the cool, steady hands of a gambler. But maybe a walk in the frigid night air would have the desired effect.

With a steely look of determination in his eyes he made his way outside. And headed straight to the saloon.

Chapter Fourteen

Florence Claxton's boardinghouse was perfumed with Sunday morning breakfast. Thick slabs of bacon sizzled in a pan, along with potatoes and eggs. There were freshly baked biscuits ready to be smothered in gravy. Stacks of wheat cakes dripped butter and blueberry preserves. A blackened coffeepot sputtered over the fire, emitting its heavenly fragrance.

Jen and her new friend, Oren, could hardly contain themselves as they watched the women putting the finishing touches on the table. When everyone began assembling for the meal, their mouths watered at the stack of wheat cakes.

The sheriff, who lived in a small room in back of the jail, and regularly took his meals at the boardinghouse, hurried in accompanied by a gust of icy wind. Reverend Townsend followed him a minute later.

Florence looked up from the stove. "Now that everyone is here, I guess we'll begin. Matthew, will you lead the blessing?"

His rich, warm voice flowed around the room as he led them in prayer. Afterward, as they started to take their seats, Florence hesitated. "I don't see Mr. Mc-

Allister. Jen, would you go upstairs and call him to breakfast, please?"

"Yes'm."

Afraid that all the wheat cakes would be devoured before she returned, the little girl took the stairs two at a time and knocked on Quin's door. Hearing nothing, she timidly opened it and looked inside. Finding it empty, she raced back downstairs.

"He isn't there," Jen announced as she sat down and reached for the stack of wheat cakes. Her plate was filled almost before the words were out of her mouth.

"Not there?" Florence glanced from Cassie to Luella, then back again. "Did he say where he was going?"

Cassie shook her head. "I didn't see him this morning. I just assumed he was in his room."

"Did anyone see Mr. McAllister last night?"

Cassie's cheeks flooded with color. "I saw him. Before I went up to bed," she added quickly. "But he didn't say anything about going out."

She saw her mother staring at her, and lowered her gaze to her plate, knowing she would have to deal with questions and recriminations later.

"Nowhere to go in Prospect except Lottie's place," the sheriff mumbled around a mouthful of biscuit.

"What's Lottie's place?" Jen asked.

"Nothing you should know about, Jennifer," Cassie said quickly. But she knew. Everyone else at the table knew. Quin had given in to the urge to drink and gamble and . . . whatever else men did in such places.

"We should have expected as much." Luella sniffed and lifted her cup to her lips. "Can't change a skunk's stripes."

"How long has McAllister been your foreman?" Sheriff Wilson asked suspiciously.

"A few weeks." Luella's tone revealed her disdain.

"How much do you know about him?"

The older woman's voice lowered. "Only that he's a gambler."

"He was a very good friend to my husband," Cassie said in Quin's defense. Though she was stung by the knowledge that he had spent the night at a saloon, she would not allow others to demean his name.

"I don't mean to frighten you good ladies," the sheriff went on. "But a man like McAllister is certainly aware that women and children, so far from their nearest neighbors, would be no match for him. No telling what a man like that might do."

Becky and Jen, glanced wide-eyed from their mother to their grandmother, before turning to stare at the sheriff.

Sheriff Wilson, pleased that he had everyone's attention, continued in his most authoritative tone of voice. "Seems to me a lot of strange things have been happening since this gambler drifted into Montana."

"What are you suggesting, Sheriff?" Cassie's food lay forgotten.

"Only that I'd be real careful if I was you, ma'am."

"I trust Mr. McAllister," she said softly. "Unless he proves otherwise, I believe him to be our friend."

"Yes'm." The sheriff forked another helping of meat, potatoes and eggs onto his plate. His tone rang with sarcasm. "I guess there's a good reason why your . . . friend spent the whole night at Lottie's place."

Subdued, Cassie sipped her coffee and tried to banish the images that were torturing her. Images of Quin smoking a cigar, a whiskey in one hand, cards in the other, surrounded by beautiful women who knew how to please a man. Women in revealing gowns, who smelled of French perfume. Women with painted faces and soft hands.

She clenched her own callused hands together in her lap.

Hoping to smooth over the tension, Florence motioned for her sons to begin clearing the table. "There's just enough time to wash the dishes and get dressed for Sunday services." She glanced around the table. "You folks will be joining us, won't you?"

Luella answered for all of them. "We wouldn't miss it."

"What about Mr. McAllister?" Jen asked worriedly. "Do you think he'll be there, Mama?"

"I don't know, Jennifer. But I hope so."

"So do I," the little girl said softly.

Luella frowned. "Don't go getting your hopes up, child. A man like Quin McAllister has probably never seen the inside of a church."

"Ma. That isn't fair," Cassie began, but her mother cut her off.

"And you know better than to encourage your daughter to wish for the impossible," Luella said with a sigh of impatience. "Honestly, Cassie, when are you going to stop defending that gambler? Is that the sort of man you want your children to admire?"

As the others left the table and made their way upstairs, Cassie trailed slowly behind, deeply troubled.

Cassie and her family followed Florence Claxton and her boys up the aisle, aware of the curious stares from the congregation.

Zack and Willy managed to sandwich Becky between them as they took their places. Each brother offered to share his hymnal with her, and it was plain that Becky was enjoying their attentions. She was wearing a pale pink gown, which had been made over from her mother's best Sunday dress, and around her shoulders, her grandmother's favorite shawl. Her long hair had been brushed until it gleamed. There was a sparkle in her eyes, and color on her cheeks that turned the head of every man, young and old, in the church. It was easy to see she would grow to be a beauty.

Cassie, determined to separate her younger daughter from Oren, so that these two new friends wouldn't be tempted to whisper or giggle or otherwise distract, caught Jen by the arm and held her back until the others were seated. Then she allowed the little girl to precede her into the pew, while she took a seat next to the aisle.

"Mr. McAllister's going to come, Mama," Jen whispered. "You'll see."

Cassie dropped a hand to her shoulder, as if to spare her. Her mother was right. The longer she encouraged such thinking, the more painful would be the little girl's disappointment when Quin let her down. "You mustn't expect so much of Mr. McAllister, Jennifer. He's just..." She struggled to find the words. But what could she say? That he was a friend of Ethan's, who had been tricked into coming to this harsh land against his judgment? That he was a gambler, who would rather spend his nights in a saloon? "He's just a man who doesn't always believe as we do."

"He'll be here," Jen said, turning away.

The simple wooden benches were crowded with townspeople and ranchers from nearby, who took a break from their chores to worship together.

Reverend Matthew Townsend was resplendent in a dark suit. Standing on a raised platform at the front of the church, he made a striking presence as he offered a word of welcome.

Spying an organ, Luella leaned toward Florence. "Where is your organist?"

"We haven't found anyone who can play," the plump woman admitted. "The congregation bought the organ almost a year ago, but so far, the Lord hasn't seen fit to send us anyone who can play it."

"I could try," Luella said softly.

"You?" The other woman's eyes widened. Scrambling to her feet she called, "Reverend Townsend, our prayers have been answered. Mrs. Chalmers can play the organ."

All eyes turned to Florence and the woman seated beside her.

"Can you truly play?" the preacher asked.

"I can, though I haven't had the opportunity to play in years." Luella got to her feet. "I studied piano and organ many years ago at Miss Atherton's Conservatory in Savannah, Georgia."

"Praise be." Reverend Townsend motioned toward the organ. "Please, Mrs. Chalmers, if you would honor us with a song."

Luella walked to the front of the church and settled herself at the organ, allowing her stiff fingers to roam the keys. Looking up, she said loudly, "I'd be proud if my granddaughter, Rebecca, would come up here and lead us in song."

Becky's cheeks turned bright scarlet as everyone in the church strained to see her. But seeing the pride on her grandmother's face, she knew she couldn't refuse. She moved slowly out of the pew and made her way to her grandmother's side.

Luella began to play the first notes of a familiar hymn. At first Becky had to fight back a wave of fright at the sea of faces turned toward her. But as the organ swelled, she thought of her father, who had always been so proud of her talent.

"This is for you, Pa," she whispered before she sang the first tentative notes. Then her voice rose. Her nerves were forgotten and she lost herself in the music.

Hearing the rich, clear voice, Luella felt a shiver of pure joy. Oh, how her prayers had been answered. She had missed her church and its soul-stirring music. She had longed for the comfort of tradition. Caught up in the moment, her fingers flew over the keys while her granddaughter's voice soared like an angel. After the first verse, the congregation joined in the chorus, their voices swelling to the rafters in the tiny church.

From his position in the pulpit Reverend Townsend watched and listened while Luella played. All her features were transformed. On her face was a look of ecstasy.

When the last notes died, he allowed the silence to settle over them before he said, "God has truly blessed us this day. What we have been given is a very special gift. It is gratifying to see the gift of musical talent used to praise our Creator. We can only pray that these fine women will grace us with their presence again in the future, for they have added much to our service."

Lifting his voice, he led the congregation in prayer. His voice rang with a plea for peace among men, for forgiveness among neighbors, for love and understanding among family members.

Beside her, Cassie felt Jen shifting and turning to glance frequently toward the door. Each time, she shot the little girl a disapproving look until Jen managed to return her attention to the minister.

At last, with the prayer ended, everyone settled down and stared expectantly toward the crude wooden pulpit.

"My dear people..." As Reverend Matthew Townsend began to speak, the door opened. The reverend paused. Every head swiveled to see who would dare to arrive so late, causing the preacher to interrupt his sermon.

Quin, hat in hand, strode up the aisle until he came to the row where Cassie and her family sat. To make room for him, everyone was forced to scoot down. Jen leaned around her mother, beaming with pleasure.

"My dear people," Reverend Townsend began again. "I was reminded of something this morning. And it is the basis for my sermon." He paused. A smile softened his eyes and warmed his voice. "How fortunate we are to have found each other in this splendid, untamed land. How great are our blessings. As we look around this church today, think of all the fine people we now call friend, who were not known to us a year ago, or even a few months ago. And think how these same strangers, who are now friends, have enriched our lives."

Cassie shuffled uneasily beside Quin. Friend indeed. His hair and clothing bore the unmistakable odor of tobacco and whiskey. His eyes, when he glanced at her, were bloodshot. She felt a wave of fury that he should have caused her family such humiliation.

Beside her, her youngest daughter beamed with joy. Somehow, Quin's arrival made their little family seem ... less alone, less incomplete. Now if only her mother wasn't so angry.

Feeling Cassie's angry stare directed at him, Quin glanced over. And winked. At once her cheeks flamed and she looked down at her hands, squeezed tightly together in her lap. When would she ever learn that he was nothing more than a charming rogue? He could not even give this place of worship its due. Instead, he was as relaxed as if he were still in that ... in that den of wickedness.

Across the room she caught sight of the thin, tight line of her mother's mouth. To a woman like Luella, the proper image was so important. She had learned a painful lesson in her youth. Rules were not meant to be broken. Woe to those who did not walk the line. The censure of others could be a painful thing to endure. And now, just as Luella was being singled out for honor among these strangers, she was being forced to endure another public humiliation.

Cassie's displeasure grew as the preacher's voice washed over her, reminding them of their duty to God, to country, to each other. Now that Quin had displayed this weakness, she must face some truths. It was time she realized that Quin McAllister was not some gallant knight riding to her defense. He was a mere mortal. A man who, by circumstance, was forced to endure a few weeks in a snowbound wilderness. To him it must seem a prison from which he was eager to escape. And soon enough, she realized, he would. He would ride off as abruptly as he had arrived, leaving them to face the future alone.

The congregation was on its feet, singing. Startled out of her reverie, Cassie stood and began fumbling with the pages of her hymnal. Quin stood quietly beside her, then reached up to share the book.

His voice was low and deep and melodic, with traces of his Southern heritage. Her own rich voice blended perfectly with his, and she found herself enjoying the familiar hymn until she glanced up and caught him looking at her. She stopped singing and was forced to swallow several times before she could continue.

When the song ended, the people bowed their heads while Reverend Townsend led them in another prayer. Then they were seated and the preacher began his second, related sermon. Again he spoke of the need for love, brotherhood and a community that stood by one another through good times and bad.

Quin's shoulder brushed Cassie's. It was the merest touch, yet Cassie had to struggle against the rush of heat. At once she felt her annoyance growing. What sort of fool was she, that she could respond shamelessly to a man who had just spent the entire night in the saloon? Not only that, but everyone in this church had seen him swaggering up the aisle, reeking of smoke and whiskey and cheap perfume.

She glanced at her young daughter, who was staring adoringly at Quin. At last Jen snagged Quin's attention. With a sly wink Quin gave the girl a quick smile. It was immediately returned.

Cassie sighed. It was plain that Jennifer looked up to this man. The longer she permitted it, the more harmful it could become. Perhaps Quin couldn't help being what he was, but she certainly didn't want her daughter to grow up believing that it was perfectly normal to play cards for a living, or spend the night in a saloon.

Besides, she warned herself, what would happen to the little girl when the man she adored left her? She had witnessed the pain of Jen's loss at the death of her father. How much worse would it be when Quin McAllister, the only other man in her young life, calmly rode away forever?

She experienced a wave of guilt when she realized that the sermon had ended. Instead of listening, she had allowed her mind to wander. Something she had permitted far too often lately.

"Please, my dear people," the reverend called out, "help me thank our dear friends, Luella Chalmers, and her lovely granddaughter, Rebecca, for the beautiful music which added so much to our service this day."

There was applause, and the room was filled with the sound of shuffling feet as the congregation began to file from the church.

"Mama, aren't we going to go?" Jen tugged on her mother's sleeve.

"Yes. I . . . yes."

Taking Jen's hand, Cassie got to her feet and walked down the aisle, with Quin beside her. Once outside she paused to thank the reverend for his fine sermon, but Jen's words stopped her.

"Gram said you wouldn't come to church, Mr. McAllister. But I knew you would."

"Did you now? And how did you know that, when I didn't even know it myself?"

The little girl brushed a wisp of bright red curls from her eyes. "I asked my pa."

"Your pa?"

Both Cassie and Luella stopped in their tracks.

Jen's head bobbed up and down. "Mama said my pa is in heaven now, like the angels. So I figured, if I can

ask the angels for favors, why not ask my pa? I ask him
for all kinds of things.''

"And you asked him to see that I made it to church.''

Pleased that Quin understood, Jen's smile widened.

Luella pointed a finger at her daughter. "Do you see
what sort of lessons you've given that child? She can't
even tell the difference between her father and her
heavenly Father. And as for you.'' Her anger had been
simmering throughout the entire service. Now she
swooped down on Quin, poised to attack. "How could
you embarrass us like that?'' she demanded in a loud
whisper. "Didn't it occur to you that everyone in that
church would know where you spent the night? Look at
you! Unshaven, unwashed.'' She wrinkled her nose with
disgust. "You reek of whiskey and cigar smoke.''

"Yes, ma'am.'' Quin shot her a lazy grin. "I guess I
do.''

She was in a fine fury now. The full force of her temper exploded. "Oh! When I think of you parading up
the aisle, holding up the reverend's sermon, drawing
attention to all of us, I could just die from the humiliation of it all. Didn't you stop and think what the people of Prospect would think of us?''

Noting Jen's stricken look, Reverend Townsend
stepped between Quin and Luella. With a gentle smile
in the little girl's direction he said, "I couldn't help
overhearing what you said to Mr. McAllister. I'm
pleased that your mother has taught you how to pray,
Jen.''

Luella was clearly shocked. "You don't think it
wicked that she prayed to her dead father?''

"Not at all. I believe in the power of prayer,'' Reverend Townsend said gently. "And I believe that our
Father hears our prayers and answers, often in strange,

unexpected ways. As for Mr. McAllister." A wide smile split his lips. "I used to indulge in a bit of high living myself, before I found my calling." He shook his head. "There is still nothing like a fine cigar, a sip of spirits, and a pair of aces. Unless, of course—" he turned his full gaze on Quin "—it's the love of a good woman."

Quin merely smiled.

"Reverend Townsend!" Luella appeared scandalized.

"I think we sometimes forget," he said, taking her hand, "that we are a congregation of sinners, not saints. Until, like Ethan, we join the angels, we must be forced to acknowledge our shortcomings."

He turned to Quin and offered his hand in friendship. "Personally, I much prefer the company of men who admit they are somewhat less than perfect. I hope you'll come back to our church, Quin, whenever you're in Prospect."

"Thanks, Matthew," Quin said, accepting his handshake. Taking a cigar from his pocket, he handed it to the preacher. "Maybe you'll enjoy this after Christmas services."

"Thank you. I will." Reverend Townsend took Cassie's hand and looked into her eyes, seeing the lingering clouds of worry and anger. It would be some time, he figured, before Quin would manage to redeem himself. "I hope you and your lovely family will return to our church often, Mrs. Montgomery."

"Even me?" Jen asked.

"Especially you, Jen. I hope that all your prayers are answered this Christmas."

"Come on, Oren," the little girl called, grabbing her friend's hand. The day had suddenly taken on a glow. "Let's go look in the windows of the mercantile."

Cassie watched the two children scamper away. Then she turned to where her daughter stood with Zack and Willy. The two youths were showing off, pelting each other with snowballs. They looked so incredibly young and carefree. But when a snowball glanced off Becky's head, Zack immediately became her fierce protector. In order to shield her from further attacks, he stepped between her and his younger brother. When he'd driven Willy away with a barrage of snowballs, Zack turned and lifted a hand to her cheek to brush away the snow.

"You will stay for supper, won't you?" Florence's voice had Cassie whirling.

Reluctantly she shook her head. "We can't spare any more time away from our home."

Becky, walking between Zack and Willy, overheard and called out, "Please, Mama. Can't we stay another day?"

"I'm truly sorry," Cassie said softly. "I wish we could." She saw the regret in her daughter's eyes before she turned away.

"Come along," Luella called briskly. Despite the reverend's words, she wasn't about to let Quin forget his indiscretion. "It's time we loaded the wagon so we can make it home by nightfall. If," she added in her most strident tone, "Mr. McAllister isn't too weary after his night of debauchery."

Quin rolled his eyes. "I'm sure I can manage. I'll bring the wagon around to Mrs. Claxton's in a little while, as soon as I've picked up our supplies at the mercantile."

As he sauntered away, he could still feel the heat from their angry stares. The ride home, he knew, promised to be long and cold.

Chapter Fifteen

"I wish you weren't leaving." With a sigh, Florence placed several plucked chickens in a large roasting pan, in preparation for a big Sunday supper. She turned to Luella. "All my life I've been surrounded by men. Not only my husband, God rest his soul, but three sons, and all these men who room here and take their meals with us."

She glanced at Reverend Townsend, who always took Sunday supper with her family. For some reason, he'd come back to the kitchen, something he'd never done before, and was seated at the table, sipping coffee. "Nothing against you, of course, Reverend. We love having you."

"Thank you, Florence. I'm grateful to have a place where I feel welcome."

"I hope you know you'll always have a place with us here, even after your parsonage is completed." Florence trimmed a piecrust and began rolling a second. "Luella, you're the first woman I've had staying here who enjoyed helping me in the kitchen. I can't tell you what a joy it's been having you."

"I enjoyed it, too." Luella finished stirring her special biscuit dough and began dropping spoonfuls onto a flat tin. When she was finished, she carried the baking tin to the oven. Turning, she spied Reverend Townsend licking the bowl, and stopped in midstride.

"Why, Matthew, my husband always did that same thing."

"I can see why. I do believe you make the best biscuits in the world, Luella. My wife used to make biscuits like this, and I always thought nobody would ever top hers. But there's just something about these..." He went back to licking the spoon, allowing his words to trail off.

Luella felt overwarm and blamed it on the heat from the oven.

"I can see that you're enjoying yourself here," Reverend Townsend said.

"If truth be told, I think this is the happiest I've been in a long time. There is something so satisfying about cutting, peeling, washing, stirring." Luella took a deep breath, inhaling the wonderful aromas. "The rich variety of foods in this house has restored my soul almost as much as the Sunday services." When she realized what she'd revealed, she shot the minister an apologetic look. "Forgive me, Matthew. I know nothing should be as inspiring as our faith."

He lifted a hand. "Not at all. I can see that you derive great satisfaction from seeing others eat your cooking, in the same way that I derive much pleasure from seeing others find solace in my ministry. It is as important to feed the body as the soul."

It was true, she realized. She loved watching others savor her cooking. Especially a man like Matthew Townsend, who ate the way he seemed to do everything—with great joy.

Upstairs she could hear her daughter and grand-daughter laughing and talking easily together while they made up the beds and tidied up the room. She glanced around the big, cheery kitchen. "It's so cozy here. You have no idea how I'll miss this. It's been so good for all of us."

"Do you think you could ever make a home here in Prospect?" Reverend Townsend asked.

Luella shook her head sadly. "How I would love to. But I couldn't leave my daughter. She needs my help. Besides, since the war, nothing feels like home. Although I must admit this is the closest—"

They all looked up at the sound of the wagon wheels. Luella struggled to hide the feelings of regret that filled her. It was time to return to the bleak little cabin and the endless work.

Removing her apron, she walked to the stairway and called, "Cassie. Becky. Mr. McAllister is here."

When they descended the stairs, Luella said to her granddaughter, "As usual, you'll have to hunt for your little sister."

"She's probably out in the shed with Oren." Florence called to her oldest son. "Zack, go with Becky to fetch the young ones."

"Yes'm." He and Becky started outside together.

As soon as they were out of sight of their families, Zack boldly caught Becky's hand. "Careful," he muttered, "it's slippery out here."

Becky looked up and, seeing the shy smile on his face, walked alongside him in silence. Even though it felt good having her hand held in his, she wondered if she ought to allow it. But after a moment's hesitation, she decided that he was, after all, only seeing to her safety.

They took as much time as they could walking to the outbuilding. From inside came the sounds of childish laughter. Instead of going in, the two slipped around to the back, where they stood a moment, silent and breathless.

"I wish you weren't leaving." Zack kicked a toe in the snow.

"I'll come back someday."

"When?"

Becky shrugged. "The next time we need supplies. Springtime, I guess."

"Springtime." He stared at their linked hands. "I wish..." He stopped, embarrassed.

"Wish what?" Becky studied the way his fine blond hair spilled across his forehead when he ducked his head.

"I wish you were older." He lifted his head until their eyes met.

"I will be." She gave him a tremulous smile. "Will you wait for me, Zack?"

At her words, all his features seemed to be infused with light from his radiant smile. It was the knowing smile of the young, the innocent, who have just discovered the secrets of the universe.

"I'm not going anywhere," he said simply. "I'll be here."

She tugged on his hand. "Come on. We'd better get Jen before Gram starts hollering."

She started to turn away but he dug in his heels. "Don't go yet," he whispered. "I'd like to...kiss you."

"I'd like that, too." As he impulsively stepped closer, she remembered what Quin had said and added, "But not just yet. I'm...not ready yet."

Spying Willy walking toward them, they stepped apart.

"Here you are. Ma's looking for you," he said.

"We just came out here to get Oren and Jen."

"Uh-huh." Fourteen-year-old Willy glanced from Zack to Becky. Neither would meet his eyes. Both looked flushed and guilty.

His Adam's apple bobbed up and down as he cupped his hands to his mouth and shouted, "Come on Jen, Oren. Time to go."

The door to the shed was flung open and two laughing children spilled out. A minute later, with Willy, Jen and Oren trailing them, Zack and Becky walked slowly toward the house, taking great care to see that they didn't touch or even look at one another.

"You come back soon, you hear?" Florence Claxton stood on the steps, wiping her hands on a towel.

Zack held the horses still while everyone climbed aboard. When Becky pulled herself up to the seat, he caught a glimpse of ankle before she smoothed down her skirts. He stood very straight and very tall, wishing with all his might that some miracle would prevent them from leaving. Not that he wished them ill. But springtime seemed like a million years away.

Reverend Townsend watched Luella as she took a last, lingering gaze around the parlor. "Our town needs fine people like you and your family, Luella," he said, coming up behind her. He surprised her by placing his hand on her shoulder.

She whirled, her eyes round and wary.

To ease her fears he removed his hand and gave her a reassuring smile. "You take care of yourself, Luella. And someday soon, I hope, I'll hear your sweet music again in church." His voice lowered. "When you first started to play, I thought I was hearing heavenly music."

Flushed with pleasure she said, "I will miss your Sunday services, Matthew."

"And I will miss your special biscuits." He paused, considering, then added, "A man who lives alone would think he'd found heaven if he could have a woman like you waiting for him each night, filling his home with good food and music."

She was too shocked to say a word.

He cleared his throat. "I know that you know very little about me. But I have been alone for a number of years, and this is the first time that I have given a thought to the empty space in my life. I think, since you are also alone—"

Luella stepped back a pace, halting his words. "You do not know me, Matthew. I'm sure you have heard. There are shameful things in my past that I regret."

He touched a finger to her lips. "Shh. I care nothing about the past. I set no store by gossip. If we were to trade stories, I think my own would make yours pale by comparison. No one can live as long as the two of us without having regrets. But remember this, Luella. We would not be who we are now if we had not made those mistakes in our past."

"But—"

"I care only for the woman you are now, Luella."

They both looked up at Florence's voice, summoning them.

"And I know this," he said softly. "You are a woman I would like to know better. I hope you allow me that opportunity."

He offered his arm and she accepted. Outside, he helped her into the wagon, then stepped back, keeping his gaze fixed on her.

Oren good-naturedly tagged Jen as she climbed into the wagon. At once, Jen climbed back down to tag Oren. Within minutes the two little ones were chasing each other around and around the wagon.

"Jennifer," Cassie called more sharply than she'd intended. Her emotions colored her words. And right now her emotions were playing a tug-of-war. She was dejected about leaving this warm, cozy house with its lively, interesting people. Worse, she was furious with Quin for publicly embarrassing all of them. Everyone, including these good people, knew that he'd spent the entire night at a saloon. She simply couldn't get that thought out of her mind. "Jennifer, get in here now, please."

At once she regretted her harshness. It wasn't Jen's fault that this was so painful. It was hard enough leaving all this comfort to return her family to their rough cabin. Harder still was the thought that the sweetest of holidays would be just another day of hard, back-breaking work.

She couldn't help but notice how reluctant everyone was to leave their newfound friends. Luella had displayed more tenderness toward both Florence and Reverend Townsend than she had displayed toward her own family in recent years. Becky was basking in the attentions of the Claxton boys. And poor little Jen had never before had a friend to play with. It was wrenching to have to drag them away.

"Jennifer," she called again in a softer tone.

"Yes'm." With a hurried touch to Oren's back, Jen scrambled up into the wagon, evading the boy's attempt to tag her.

"I won," Jen taunted.

With shrieks of giggles, Oren tried to climb up. At a word from Florence, Willy caught him and hauled him backward.

"That's enough," Florence said to the kicking, struggling little boy. "Don't make a nuisance of yourself, Oren."

Quin tipped his hat to her, then handed the reins to Cassie, who gave him a dark look.

"It took you long enough to pick up our supplies."

"Yes, ma'am. I certainly didn't want to miss anything on that list you gave me."

The horses leaned into the harness and the wagon jolted ahead.

"Goodbye. Godspeed," Matthew Townsend shouted.

Luella stared straight ahead and blinked rapidly, blaming the moisture in her eyes on the stinging wind. It did make a body's eyes smart.

Becky, seated between her mother and grandmother, chanced a glance at Zack. When she realized that he was staring at her, she blushed and looked away.

Horses and wagon picked up speed, and Becky gathered her courage and turned to wave until the boardinghouse and its occupants were out of sight. Then she drew the blanket around herself and hunched into its warmth, shutting out the voices of the others, losing herself in a jumble of thoughts.

Cassie, too, was lost in thought. Most of it centered on the man who rode the trail ahead of their wagon. The image of Quin spending the night in wicked pursuits had cast a pall on the entire trip. Added to that was the knowledge that tomorrow was Christmas Eve, and she and her family would spend the day, as they did every day, struggling to survive.

"Oren said Mr. Sutter gave him a job sweeping the mercantile. He's saved up almost twenty-five cents and he's going to buy his mama some rose water for Christmas." Jen glanced at her mother's pinched features. She hadn't smiled since they'd left Prospect. Neither had her grandmother or Becky. In fact, Becky had crawled into the back of the wagon, loaded with sacks of flour and grain and sugar, and hadn't spoken a word to anyone in hours.

"Would you like rose water for Christmas, Mama?"

"No, Jennifer. We don't have twenty-five cents."

"I know. But if I lived in town, and worked at the mercantile, and had some money, would you like rose water?"

"Yes," she said wearily. "Yes, I would."

"How about you, Gram? Would you like rose water too?"

"Hush, child. Stop talking about things you can't have."

"But someday, when I'm bigger, and I have lots of money, maybe even a whole dollar, would you like rose water, Gram?"

The older woman gritted her teeth. "Yes. Rose water smells very nice."

"How about you, Becky?" the little girl persisted. "Would you—?"

"Be quiet, Jen," she shouted. "I'm sick and tired of hearing about what you're going to buy for Christmas

someday. Don't you understand? There isn't going to be
any Christmas this year."

Jen's eyes went wide. "You take that back, Becky.
There will too be Christmas. Tell her Mama. Tell her
she's wrong."

Cassie flicked the reins and the horses started up a
steep incline, their breath pluming in the frosty air.

"Mama?" Jen waited with all the impatience of a
five-year-old, but Cassie remained silent.

"Becky's right." Cassie flinched as her mother spoke
in quick, staccato phrases that lashed like a whip.
Sometimes the only way to deal with pain was to face it
head-on. "Times are hard, Jen. Even though your
mother disagrees with me, I think you're old enough to
understand that this year—"

"Jen." Quin slowed his mount as he drew alongside
the wagon. "I was going to wait until Christmas, but I
don't think I can keep it a secret much longer. Would
you mind holding something for a little while?"

"What?" The little girl barely looked up, so great was
her despair.

Reaching inside his coat, Quin withdrew a wrig-
gling, squealing bundle of yellow fur.

"Biscuit!" Jen let out a squeal of delight. "Mama.
Gram. Becky. Look. It's Biscuit." She pressed the
puppy to her cheek. In return the pup licked her nose
and whimpered happily.

"You'll have to keep him warm," Quin said.

"I will. Biscuit can share my blanket," Jen promised.

"And see that he gets some of this every couple of
hours." Quin reached into his pocket and withdrew a
small bundle of linen. Inside were bits of chopped meat
that Florence had given him for the journey home.

"Yes, sir."

All Cassie's anger melted. She shot Quin a grateful look.

With a delighted shout Jen climbed into the back of the wagon beside her sister, where the two burst into laughter at the antics of the clumsy little puppy. Whatever tension they had felt earlier was quickly forgotten in the excitement of the moment.

With a tip of his hat Quin urged his horse into a run and was soon far ahead of the wagon. Cassie watched with a mixture of joy and sadness. Joy that her youngest daughter had been spared the truth for a little while longer. Sadness that, despite the excitement of the moment, her mother was right. There would be little to celebrate this Christmas. But at least for now, their troubles were forgotten. And a little child's heart had been spared.

It had been snowing for hours. The night was bitter cold, and the temperature was still dropping.

With his hat pulled low, Quin rode in silence alongside the wagon. Becky and Jen slept snugly under a layer of furs in the back of the wagon, with Biscuit between them. Cassie hunched in her blanket. Her fingers holding the reins were stiff. Beside her, Luella's head bobbed.

"Ma," Cassie whispered.

At once the older woman's head came up.

"Climb into the back with the children and go to sleep."

Luella shook her head. "And leave you up here alone?"

"I don't mind. And I'd feel better knowing you were comfortable."

"I'm fine right here." The older woman straightened her spine and faced into the wind.

Cassie sighed. Stubborn. Her mother had always been stubborn. And she supposed she'd inherited that same trait from her. Why else would she drag her family out here in the middle of a wilderness?

"I'm sorry, Ma."

Luella turned to look at her. "Sorry for what?"

"For the mess I've made of things. I shouldn't have agreed to come all this way with Ethan just to follow some silly dream. I should have insisted that we stay in Atlanta and start over. At least there we wouldn't have to fight a dangerous man like Cyrus Stoner. And at least there we wouldn't see all this snow. We'd be warm and safe and..." Her voice wavered.

"And what?" Luella prompted.

"The thought keeps haunting me. Maybe if we had stayed there Ethan wouldn't have died."

"Now you listen to me, girl." Luella's voice rang with righteous indignation. "It is true that if we had remained in Atlanta, we would be safe from Cyrus Stoner. But we would still have to deal with villains. The city must be swarming with them by now. Scavengers ready to pick the bones of a dead city and its unfortunate citizens. As for this snow." She stared out at the sea of white that glistened like an ocean in the darkness. "I do admit I find it a cross to bear. But think of how precious the springtime shall be when it comes." She cleared her throat. "Now about Ethan. Don't ever think that it was this place that caused his death. It was the war."

"But Ma—"

"I know," she said, nodding her head for emphasis. "He survived the war. Nevertheless, it was the war that killed him, as surely as if he'd taken a musket ball in the chest. And you can take comfort in the fact that he died surrounded by the ones he loved, here in this untouched wilderness, far away from the scars of battle."

"Oh, Ma." Cassie's cry caught in her throat.

"I know." Luella draped an arm around her daughter and drew her close to press a kiss to her cold cheek. Her voice thickened. "Now, let's stop talking about what might have been and talk about what we can salvage for celebration."

"What celebration? You said yourself there will be no Christmas."

"So I did. And thanks to Mr. McAllister's generous gift of that animal," she said, nodding toward the sleeping puppy, "we'll have one more mouth to feed. But we need not despair. It might not be grand, but at least we will not go hungry."

Cassie blinked back a tear as her mother went on in that same matter-of-fact tone. "Florence gave me a little basket of apples and a cinnamon stick. I shall bake an apple pie and add cinnamon to my biscuit dough. Won't that make the cabin smell nice?"

"Yes, Ma."

"We'll cook venison and roast beef and..."

In the darkness Quin slowed his mount, allowing the wagon to pull ahead. He studied the two women, heads bent against the cold. Despite all their tough talk, they loved each other without question. And despite their bleak existence, they were determined to find a glimmer of hope, to bring a small measure of joy, to those they loved.

He shook his head in admiration. They were two remarkable women. And damned if he wasn't hopelessly in love with one of them.

Chapter Sixteen

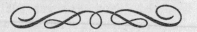

The cabin was little more than a dim outline in the darkness. As they drew closer they could see that it was still standing exactly as they'd left it. For some odd reason, Quin felt reassured by the sight of it. Could it be that this crude shelter was actually becoming home to him? A dangerous thought, he reminded himself. It was just because he had spent the past few weeks here, had taken risks to defend it. He was still more at home in a saloon, holding a winning hand, he assured himself, than he'd ever be mucking a stall or handling a pick and shovel.

The wagon rolled to a stop at the door. Quin dismounted and took the reins from Cassie, then helped her down. Beside her, Luella stirred, then accepted Quin's hand as she made her way from the wagon. She moved slowly, her muscles stiff.

"Don't bother waking the children," Quin muttered. "I'll carry them inside and get a fire started."

Luella let herself in and struck a match to the lantern. A small thin flame chased away the darkness.

While Cassie held the door, Quin carried Jen to her bed. Even in sleep the little girl never loosened her hold on the puppy, cradled against her chest. When they were tucked into Jen's bed, Quin returned to the wagon for Becky, who yawned and snuggled against his chest. While Cassie covered her, Quin hauled an armload of logs and kindling to the fireplace. Soon a cheery fire crackled.

"I'll help you unload the wagon," Cassie said as she started out the door.

"No." Quin caught her roughly by the arm.

At her arched look he softened his tone. "You've done enough. It was a long, hard ride. I'll take care of the supplies."

It took him more than an hour in the bitter cold to unload the wagon, as he dragged barrels inside, then tossed the heavy sacks over his shoulder one at a time. After that he led the horses to the barn, and fed and watered the weary animals. A check of the cow in its stall showed that the Crow had taken their obligation as good neighbors seriously. The animal had been carefully tended. Quin hoped the Crow children had enjoyed the milk.

It was well past midnight before he made his way to the cabin. Inside, coffee bubbled over the fire and a meal of dried beef and biscuits had been left on the table for him. Cassie and her mother were nowhere in sight, but he knew, from the lowered blankets at their doorways, that they had retired for the night.

He poured himself a cup of coffee and held it between his hands, warming them, then drained the cup before prying off his boots. Stretching out his feet toward the fire, he ate, then drank a second cup more slowly, and afterward enjoyed a cigar.

It was then, when he was warm, refreshed, relaxed, that he sensed her presence.

Turning slowly, Quin watched Cassie walk across the room until she was standing in front of him. She wore a pale woolen night shift, and over that, a shawl for modesty. Her hair spilled, long and loose, across her shoulders, down her back.

"I want to thank you," she said softly, "for taking us to Prospect, and for seeing us safely home."

"You're welcome."

"I especially want to thank you for what you did for Jennifer. She will never forget you. Nor will I." She took a deep breath. "And now it's time for you to think about leaving."

"Leaving? Now? Before Christmas?"

She flinched, but refused to back down. "I think the day after Christmas is soon enough."

"I see." He dragged smoke into his lungs and exhaled slowly. "Is there some reason why?"

"I think you know, Mr. McAllister."

"No, but I'm sure you'll enlighten me."

"It isn't just the fact that you spent the night at the saloon, though that would be reason enough," she said sternly. "It's the reason why you did such a thing."

"The reason." He studied the way she held herself, rigid, unyielding, as though her spine would snap if she dared to relax even a fraction.

"I cannot blame you for gambling." She fought to keep her tone even. "Right from the start, you made it plain that you're a gambler who doesn't stay in one place very long. So we should not have been surprised by your behavior in Prospect. It is as my mother said. You cannot change. But by your actions you let us know that you have been confined here for too long. It is plain that you are eager for your freedom. We have no right to hold you here any longer."

"I didn't know I was being held." She was so solemn, so serious. He got to his feet and set the cup on the mantel with a clatter.

To her credit she held her ground, although she lifted her hand to her throat as if reluctant to stand so close to him. "You feel an obligation to Ethan's memory. I can appreciate that."

"An obligation." He lifted a hand to her hair and watched the fiery strands sift through his fingers.

She was caught off guard by the heat that flared, but forced herself to go on with the speech she'd rehearsed. "It is not fair of us to expect you to give up your own way of life for us. We must accept the fact that it's time for you to move on."

He knew his touch had surprised her. He could almost see in her eyes all the emotions that were churning inside her. "That's very noble of you. What about Cyrus Stoner?"

"Cyrus is our problem, not yours. You have to get on with your life, Mr. McAllister. And..." She turned away. The hem of her shift swirled about her ankles as she sailed toward her bedroom, effectively breaking contact and ending further discussion. "We must get on with ours. Good night."

He stood for long minutes, smoke curling over his head. A smile touched his lips. What would have been her reaction if he'd done what he wanted just then? What he'd wanted, he thought, his smile growing, was to pull her into his arms and kiss her until all that pent-up anger dissolved and she was purring like a kitten.

A kitten? Hardly. He chuckled. A wildcat. The most amazing little wildcat he'd ever met. All that fire, all that passion, hidden under a very proper demeanor and a carefully controlled temper. He'd give her her due. No matter what, she was always a lady.

He took a final drag on his cigar, then tossed the rest of it into the fire.

It was suddenly cold in here. Maybe frigid air had seeped through the chinks between the logs. He'd have to seal them with moss and hot pitch in the morning.

He grinned. Maybe the frigid air in here was due to Cassie. She'd certainly tried her best to make him believe she wanted him to go.

Go? How could he leave, when there was still so much to do?

He smiled again, just thinking about her. Funny. He'd convinced himself that the only kind of woman who attracted him was an earthy, bawdy saloon girl, who knew how to laugh and tease and please. Now, none of the women he'd ever known could hold a candle to this very proper woman who wanted no part of him.

Tossing the last of his coffee into the fire, he made his way to the nest of blankets and furs in the corner of the room. After the day he'd put in, he was asleep instantly.

Cassie awoke from a fitful dream. For the next hour she tossed and turned, unable to get her mother's warning out of her mind.

"Girl, that man is a gambler. A wanderer. If you couldn't face up to that fact before, at least now you can no longer deny it. The man proved it in Prospect, in front of everybody in town. Show his kind a saloon and everything else will be forgotten. Men like that never settle down. They just take their pleasures where they can find them, and then move on. And if you don't dig up the courage to send him packing soon, you'll be hurt by him. And not only you, but those two children. You can see how much influence he already has over a fatherless girl like Jen.''

That had been like an arrow to her heart, wounding her deeply.

Everything her mother had said was true. Nothing had been the same since Quin McAllister had entered their lives. They'd begun to depend on him. Trust him. And that was dangerous. Hadn't she learned anything from her mother's mistake?

Restless, she slipped out of bed, drawing a blanket around her shoulders, and walked from her room.

The fire had burned low. Red-hot coals painted an eerie glow across the ceiling. Outside, the wind had picked up, sending gusts of snow whipping against the cabin walls.

Spotting the coffeepot on the warming shelf, Cassie poured herself a cup and settled into the rocker. Her gaze was fixed on the glowing coals, as though, somehow, they held the secrets to all life's worries.

''Nothing can be that bad.''

At Quin's deep voice, her head came up sharply. ''I thought you were asleep.''

''I was. But I have this peculiar habit of reaching for my gun when I hear someone walking around the cabin at night.''

''I'm sorry.'' She returned her gaze to the fire. ''Go back to sleep.''

''That's not going to be easy to do now.'' He tossed back the covers and got to his feet, wearing only tight black pants. After pulling on his boots, he crossed to the fireplace and added another log. Sparks leapt and danced until the bark caught fire. He turned to face her.

"Now, tell me what has you walking the floor before dawn."

"I have some decisions to make."

"Want to talk about them?"

She couldn't meet his eyes. "I'm thinking about accepting Cyrus Stoner's offer."

"What? After his men tried to burn you out?"

"I know." Her words were anguished. "But think what we could do with five hundred dollars."

He felt a wave of guilt. He'd often risked more than that on the turn of a single card.

Mistaking his silence for recrimination she said in a rush, "I know it doesn't sound like much to you, Quin, but it would be enough to move my family to town. They would be around people. My mother would have her church and music, and the children would have friends."

"And you, Cassie? What would you have?"

In agitation she set aside her cup. Getting to her feet, she gathered her blanket around her and began to pace. "I don't know. Sometimes I think I'll stay and keep on searching for Ethan's treasure. But other times I realize what a fool I've been for sacrificing everything for a dream. I don't mind for myself. But it isn't fair to ask my family to suffer like this."

"I don't hear them complaining."

"That's just it." She drew her arms around herself, hunching deeper into her blanket, wishing she could chase away the chill that seemed to have settled deep inside her. "They never say a word. But it tears at my heart to see what they've become." Her voice lowered. "You saw how happy Ma was when she was playing the organ in church. And the pleasure she took in Florence's kitchen. And then there are Jennifer and Rebecca. They opened up like flowers around the Claxton boys. They need to be around people. They need the comfort of church and school. And I'm standing in their way."

"You're too hard on yourself, Cassie."

"No." Her head came up. "I've been selfish. But no more. It's time to make some decisions."

"You'll regret this."

"Maybe." She started to brush past him. "But it has to be done."

His fingers closed around her wrist, stopping her in midstride. "Cassie."

That was all he said, but the sound of her name spoken so urgently had her heart pounding. Beneath his fingertips he felt her pulse leap.

"It's time I got dressed." She kept her face averted, afraid of what he might see in her eyes. "It will be dawn soon, and I'd like to get started early on my chores."

"Why do you keep turning away from me?"

She stiffened, then slowly faced him. Fear mixed with anger, deepening her tone. "Don't confuse me with your saloon women. I should think you've had enough...pleasure to satisfy you until you reach the next town."

"Is that what this is about?" Humor sparked in his voice and he caught her by the shoulders, staring deeply into her eyes.

She flushed and tried to pull away but he held her fast. The corners of his lips curved in a hint of a smile. "If I didn't know better, Mrs. Montgomery, I'd say you were jealous."

"Jealous!" She hoped she looked properly horrified. "Of you and some painted woman in Lottie's Place?"

"Lottie's Place." His smile grew. "My, my, Mrs. Montgomery. I'm impressed. You even learned the name of the saloon. It would appear that you indulged in a bit of gossip with the good people of Prospect."

"And how could we not gossip? Everyone in town was witness to your stroll up the aisle of church, reeking of tobacco and whiskey, and looking as pleased with yourself as the cat who just skimmed the milk bucket. And everyone in that church knew what you'd been up to."

"Did they now? Tell me. What had I been up to?"

"Drinking. Gambling. Forni—" She stopped, her cheeks going bright red.

"The word is fornicating," he said with a laugh. "And I wish now I'd indulged myself, since I'm already guilty in the eyes of you and the town busybodies."

"I am not interested in your guilt or innocence."

Her mouth pursed in a little pout, and he felt as if he'd just taken a blow to the midsection. He knew there and then that he could no longer resist the urge to kiss her.

Though his smile remained, his tone was rough. "What are you interested in?" He lowered his mouth to hers. "This?"

The heat was so swift, so sudden, she had no time to react. The kiss was hot and hungry, his lips firm and possessive. Even though her first instinct was to break free, the unaccustomed rush of desire overruled and won.

Heat. Strength. Carefully controlled passion. She'd discovered all these things each time he'd kissed her. Her body seemed to become fluid as he dragged her against him.

Without any logic, without any reason, without any thought to the consequences, she leaned into him, wrapping her arms around his neck.

It seemed so easy, so right. Though his kiss was anything but gentle, though the hands that held her were almost bruising in their intensity, she knew no fear. She knew so little about him, and yet she felt as if she'd known him forever. Needs grew. Needs so long denied. To be held. To be loved. To be cherished.

Quin questioned his sanity. He must be losing his touch. Earlier tonight this woman had ordered him to leave. Now, with the taste of her on his lips, the scent of her filling his mind, he was thinking about home and family and forever after.

He could feel both their heartbeats racing until their breathing became shallow. He heard a hoarse voice whispering her name, and realized it was his. He tore his mouth from hers to hurry desperately over her face, her throat. The need grew inside him until it was a rage. He wanted her, here and now. And he wanted all of her. Mind, body, soul.

This was madness, he knew. At any moment her mother would be waking up. Her children would be strolling out to begin the day. It didn't matter. Nothing mattered except to hold her, to kiss her, to feel the fire. He indulged himself for a moment longer, drawing out the kiss, feeling her body pressed firmly against his.

"Do you still want me to leave?"

Her eyes snapped open. For a moment she felt strangely disoriented. Then, wrapping herself once more in dignity, she took a step back.

"I think it would be best."

"For me?" He reached out and tipped up her chin, staring into her eyes. "Or for you?"

She backed away, breaking contact. "For both our sakes I want you to leave. But not until after tomorrow. It would be too upsetting for the children."

"Fine. The day after tomorrow." His voice was a low, fierce whisper. "That suits me just fine."

She turned and walked stiffly toward her bedroom.

Behind her, Quin watched with a feeling of frustration. She was the most damnably independent woman he'd ever met. It would be impossible to stay now that she'd ordered him to leave. And yet, how could he leave her in this desperate situation? How could he leave, when everything he'd ever wanted was here?

The little figure stood in the doorway of the bedroom and watched her mother walk away. Then her glance turned to Quin, who pulled on a parka before stomping out of the cabin.

With the puppy pressed firmly to her chest, the little girl hurried across the room and crawled into Quin's bed, snuggling into the heat that still lingered in the folds of the blankets. She breathed in the scents of leather and tobacco, all the scents she had once associated with her father, and squeezed her eyes tightly shut. It would be wrong to go against her mother's wishes and yet . . .

"Please," she silently pleaded, "don't let Mama send Mr. McAllister away."

Chapter Seventeen

The snow began just after dawn on Christmas Eve.

Cassie and the children pushed their way into the barn for their morning chores and found Quin mucking the stalls.

"Thought I'd get an early start," he muttered. "Looks like we're in for a norther."

Cassie reached for a bucket, avoiding his eyes. As she milked the cow she listened absently to the children's questions and Quin's replies.

"What's a norther?" Jen asked as she set Biscuit down in the hay and watched the puppy scamper after a chicken.

"A big snowstorm blowing down from Canada."

"How big?"

Quin spread fresh hay and filled a trough with water. "Sometimes it dumps so much snow, you can barely see the roofs of the barns when it's over."

Jen was clearly intrigued now. "You mean it could bury our cabin?"

"It could."

Instead of being concerned, the little girl seemed overjoyed. "I guess, if we get that much snow, it might take days before we can dig out."

"It might." Quin finished his chores and set the pitchfork in a corner of the barn. "I think I'll seal all the cracks between the logs before the snow gets any higher. No sense losing more heat than we have to."

"I'll help," Jen said, scooping up the puppy before he could tumble into the trough.

"Me, too." Becky snatched up her parka.

Quin seemed about to refuse their offer. It was a bitter day to be out of doors. But when he caught sight of the eager looks on both their smiling faces, he didn't have the heart. "Thanks. I could use some help."

"My pa hated the cold," Becky said as she worked alongside Quin. "He said it always reminded him of the prison camp."

"Yes, I guess it would." Quin turned up his collar against the driving wind and snow and bent to his work, lost in thought. What business was it of his if Cassie sold this place to Cyrus Stoner? Didn't she have the right to do whatever she thought necessary to protect her family? He had no right to try to influence her decision.

"How come you never talk about it?" Becky asked.

Quin was jolted out of his reverie. "About what?"

"The prison camp where you and Pa were sent during the war."

"It's not something I like to talk about."

"Were the Yankees mean to you?"

"Some were. War changes some men. They become less like men and more like animals."

"Weren't you afraid?" Becky demanded.

"Sometimes. Everybody is afraid sometimes. But remember this, Becky. Being afraid doesn't mean we can't act. No matter how much we might fear someone or something, we still have to do what we know is right."

"Is that why you saved my pa's life?" Jen asked.

Quin went very still. "What makes you think I saved his life?"

"I heard Mama talking to Gram. She said she owed you for saving Pa's life. What did you do?"

Owed. The word grated. "Nothing special." Quin sealed the final row of logs.

"I bet you killed a man," Jen said suddenly. "And that's why you won't tell us."

"Did you kill a man, Mr. McAllister?" Becky asked.

Both children were watching him carefully.

"Yes, I killed a man."

"Was he a bad man? Did he hurt my pa?"

Quin knelt down, so that his eyes were level with the little girl's. "He hurt your pa, and a lot of other innocent men."

"Then I'm glad you killed him."

Quin caught Jen by the shoulders, forcing the little girl to meet his eyes. "Remember this, Jen. Taking a life isn't something you can do lightly. Don't ever be glad for someone's death."

"Even if they're bad, like Cyrus Stoner?"

"Even then."

"Are you sorry you killed the bad man?"

"I don't regret what I did," Quin said, choosing his words carefully. "But I'm not proud of it, either. I just did what I had to do to survive."

"So what does that make you, Mr. McAllister?" Jen's eyes revealed her confusion. "Gram says you're a no-account gambler. And Mama says you're a hero for saving Pa's life."

"I'm just a man, Jen. Not the worst, not the best. Just a man."

Before either of the children could ask any more questions, Quin got to his feet and turned away. But as he turned he found himself face-to-face with Cassie. From the look on her face he surmised that she had overheard more than she'd intended to.

For the space of several seconds they stared at each other in silence.

"You'll be wanting something hot," she said at last. "There's a pot of soup on the fire."

"Sounds good." Brushing past her, Quin led the way to the cabin door.

Cassie and the children followed slowly, their thoughts as tumultuous as the storm that raged.

"Something smells wonderful. Is that apple pie?" Quin breathed in the aroma of apples and cinnamon.

"It is." Luella ladled soup into bowls and cut a thick slice of bread. "I baked two of them with the apples Florence gave me."

The little pup scampered up from a rug in front of the fire where he'd been sleeping and launched himself into Jen's arms.

Quin and the children hung their parkas and washed, then took their places at the table. Soon the cold outside was forgotten in the cheery warmth of the little cabin.

"Cassie and I are going to spend the rest of the day cooking and baking," Luella announced. "And if you children have finished your chores, we could use your help."

"Doing what?" Becky asked.

"Shelling nuts. Cutting up bits of dried fruit."

Becky's interest was piqued, but Jen looked decidedly unhappy at the prospect of spending the rest of the day in the kitchen.

"If this storm keeps up, I'll be going down in the mine," Quin said. "I could use some help."

At once Jen's head came up. An eager smile lit her eyes. "Can I help?" she asked.

"I'd like that. Unless..." Quin glanced at Cassie. "Do you really need her to help with the cooking?"

Cassie shook her head. "I think we can do without Jen. Ma and Rebecca and I can manage just fine."

The little girl gave Quin an adoring look. Somehow, the mere presence of this strong, silent man made her forget all her loneliness and isolation.

By midafternoon the sky was as dark as night and the snow had drifted to the windowsills.

"No sense trying to go outside," Quin muttered as he turned from the window. "I guess I'll go work in the mine."

Quin pulled on his parka and Jen did the same. Scooping up the puppy curled in front of the fire, the little girl climbed down the ladder behind Quin, who carried a torch. They moved easily along the familiar tunnels and passageways until they came to the site of Quin's latest work.

"There's just one rule," Quin said firmly. "I want you and Biscuit to stay close by. Don't go wandering off. If you ever got lost in this maze, there's no telling how long it would take to find you. Do you understand, Jen?"

The little girl nodded solemnly.

Setting the lantern on a stone ledge, Quin lifted a pick and began to cut away at the rock. Close by, Jen amused herself by holding up her fingers to the light and making pictures on the shadowy walls, just the way Quin had taught her.

Biscuit scampered about underfoot, stopping every few inches to sniff the walls of the tunnel. When the pup ambled off to explore, Jen followed, always keeping Quin's warning in mind. As long as she could see the light from the lantern, she knew she was safe.

"Where are you, Jen?" came Quin's voice.

"Over here, following Biscuit."

"Bring him back this way. I want you to stay close enough to see."

"All right." The girl turned to pick up the puppy. But all her good intentions fled when Biscuit scampered away. One minute she could see the pup plainly, sniffing at a blackened hole in the wall. The next, the little animal disappeared.

"Biscuit!" With a cry of alarm, the little girl raced off into the darkness.

Behind him, Quin heard the cry and dropped his pick. Peering around the small circle of light cast by the lantern, he felt a flicker of annoyance. "Jen," he called loudly. "Where are you?"

He snatched up the lantern and began to run.

Though the darkness was frightening to a small child, Jen was even more afraid of losing her beloved puppy. Racing along the tunnel, she began calling frantically, "Here Biscuit. Here boy."

Suddenly she stopped running and listened. Close by she could hear the dog's muffled barking. It sounded as though it came from under the ground. Dropping to her knees, she listened. The sound was closer.

In front of her was a narrow, chiseled hole in the rock wall. She peered around, expecting the interior to be shrouded in darkness. Instead, her eyes widened at the vision before her.

"Mr. McAllister!" she shouted.

Quin paused and held the lantern aloft, staring into the pale circle of light. "Jen? Jen, where are you?"

"In here." As if from a great distance, the child's voice seemed to bounce off the walls.

Quin raced on, calling out more urgently, "Jen, answer me. Where are you?"

"In here."

The voice was closer but still very faint.

When he spotted the small opening, Quin dropped to his knees. "Jen, are you in here?"

"Yes, sir. Wait 'til you see."

"Are you all right?"

"I'm fine. But hurry."

Lying flat on his stomach, Quin thrust the lantern ahead, then crawled through the opening. When he was inside, he scrambled to his feet. Jen, holding the puppy in her arms, didn't look at all contrite. Quin grabbed her by the shoulders, intent upon scolding her for her foolishness. Before he could say a word, he stared around with a look of wonder.

They were standing in a huge cavern. Light filtered down from above, bathing the entire scene in an ethereal glow. Evidence of earlier mining was everywhere. A pick and shovel rested against the far wall. Leather pouches were scattered about, overflowing with rocks.

"It's like a city beneath the ground," Quin said in hushed tones. "How did you find this place?"

"Biscuit found it," Jen said simply. "What do you think it is?"

"I'm not sure." Lifting the lantern high Quin said tersely, "Follow me. And stay close." He muttered,

"There has to be an opening up there, covered by snow. Probably a mine shaft dug many years ago, and then forgotten."

He led the way across the wide expanse, noting the gashes in the earth where great quantities of rock had been removed and broken into stones small enough to carry.

Quin knelt and examined one of the stones, holding it close to the lantern while he turned it over and over in his hands.

When he got to his feet he slipped one of the leather pouches over his shoulder. As he continued to circle the cavern, his look grew more thoughtful.

"Come on, Jen," he said at length. "I think we've been down here long enough."

They crawled through the narrow entrance to the cave, then, after marking the spot, made their way along the maze of tunnels until they came to the ladder.

Quin held the lantern while Jen carried the puppy up the ladder. When the little girl reached the top, Quin followed.

"I was just going to climb down and call you two," Cassie said. "Wash up. It's time for supper." Catching sight of the leather pouch she arched a brow. "Rocks, Mr. McAllister?"

"Not just rocks. I suspect they may be what Ethan sent to the assayer's office."

Across the room Luella and Becky, busy setting the table, glanced up. For a moment no one moved. No one spoke.

At last Cassie found her voice. "What makes you think that?"

"Jen found a cave. It's bigger than the cabin and barn put together. And inside are tools. My guess is they're Ethan's tools, lying just as he left them."

"Jen, you found your father's site?" Cassie hugged her daughter fiercely.

Embarrassed, the little girl said, "It wasn't me, Mama. It was Biscuit. I just followed him."

"Then Biscuit deserves a reward."

"See, Gram," Jen said in all innocence. "And you thought Biscuit was just one more mouth to feed."

Luella joined in as the others burst into laughter.

Cassie eyed the contents of the pouch. "Is that what Ethan was mining? Those rocks don't look like gold to me."

"Not gold," Quin said. "We won't know for certain until the assayer has a chance to test one. But if my hunch is right, Ethan found his treasure before he died."

"Oh, praise the Lord." Luella caught her daughter and hugged her, then hugged both her grandchildren.

Cassie looked a bit dazed. When she glanced at Quin, standing apart from the others, he winked at her and her heart tumbled over.

"Well now," Luella said, taking charge. "Let's get washed up and get ready to enjoy Christmas Eve supper, such as it is."

"You mean Christmas is coming this year after all?" Jen asked.

"It will be Christmas tomorrow whether we celebrate it or not," Luella said matter-of-factly. "But Mr. McAllister's hopeful news will certainly add to the festivities, even though there won't be church services or presents."

"Presents." Looking startled, Quin headed toward the door. "I'll just be a few minutes."

Puzzled, the others watched as he stepped out into the storm, catching hold of the rope that ran from the cabin to the barn. A short time later he returned, his hair and clothes white with snow. Under his arm were several parcels.

"I picked these up in Prospect. I was going to wait until morning, but I think the celebration should begin now. Merry Christmas," he said as he handed a package to each of them.

"Now what in the world...?" While Cassie and Luella merely stared at their packages, Jen and Becky tore into the wrappings.

Jen opened her parcel and stared at it for long, silent moments.

"What is it?" Luella asked.

"It's a gold locket," the little girl said.

"Open it," Quin said softly.

When her little fingers had managed to open the locket, she gave a gasp of surprise. On one side was a miniature portrait of her mother, her sister, and herself painted when she was an infant. On the other side was a portrait of two handsome Confederate soldiers.

"That's my pa," she cried, hurling herself into his arms. "And you, Mr. McAllister."

"That's right." He scooped her onto his lap and fastened the gold chain around her neck. "Ethan gave it to me when we were released from the prison camp. He asked that I keep it, so I'd never forget him or his family. I thought it was time I returned it to its proper home."

"Thank you," Jen said, wrapping her arms around his neck.

For a minute he seemed to freeze. Then, enfolding her in his arms, he hugged her fiercely before releasing her.

Across the room, Cassie watched in silence and struggled to swallow the lump in her throat.

"Aren't you going to show us your gift, Becky?" Jen demanded.

"Oh, Mr. McAllister." Becky held up a silver-handled comb and brush and silver-framed oval mirror. "I've never seen anything so fine."

"I'm glad you like them, Becky. I thought, since you're becoming a beautiful young lady, you might have a use for them."

"Thank you. I love them." She held the mirror aloft and studied her reflection as she danced around the room.

Jen pointed to the gift that lay in her grandmother's lap. "Are you going to open your gift, Gram?"

"Indeed I am." Luella unwrapped the small parcel. For a minute she was unable to speak. Then she held her gift aloft. "Spectacles." Slipping them on, she peered through them, unable to believe how clearly she could see. "Lands," she said with a sigh as she examined the intricate stitches on one of the faded dresses in her sewing basket, "I can even thread my own needle." After carefully removing them, she surprised Quin by kissing him. "Thank you, Mr. McAllister. I can't think of anything I would have liked more than these."

"I'm glad, ma'am."

They all turned to Cassie.

"Well, Mama," Becky demanded. "Open your gift."

"Yes. Of course." Cassie felt the heat rising to her cheeks as she tore the wrappings from her package.

When the paper fell away she let out a gasp. "Oh, my." In her hands was a beautiful pale pink gown.

"Put it on, Mama," Becky urged.

"I couldn't. It's far too pretty to wear. I can't possibly accept something like this, Mr. McAllister."

"But it's Christmas Eve," Becky argued. "Besides, how will we know how it looks unless you try it on?"

Cassie looked to her mother, expecting her to show her disapproval. Instead, the older woman nodded encouragement. "I agree," she said. "There will never be a better time to wear such a lovely gown. It's Christmas Eve, girl."

Cassie walked into her bedroom and lowered the blanket at the doorway. A short time later she emerged, flushed and slightly embarrassed at the thought of modeling her new gown in front of the man who had bought it.

It had a high, modest neckline and long sleeves cuffed with white lace. A pale pink sash encircled her tiny waist. The full skirt was gathered here and there by deep rose bows, revealing a deep rose underskirt.

She had gathered her long hair up on top of her head with combs. Soft wisps of hair escaped to curl around her forehead and cheeks in a most beguiling fashion.

"Oh, Mama," Becky sighed. "You look—"

"Beautiful," Luella breathed. "More beautiful than a song."

Cassie blushed. "I feel . . . beautiful," she admitted.

"What do you think, Mr. McAllister?" Becky turned to Quin and saw the stunned look on his face.

It was the first time in his life that Quin had ever felt speechless. But the woman before him took his breath away. "You look . . . like Christmas."

Cassie lowered her gaze, afraid to meet his eyes. Nervously touching a hand to her hair, she said, "Thank you. But I don't know how you could afford such beautiful gifts. All you had were a few pelts...."

The poker game. It hit her with all the force of a storm. He had spent the night gambling because he had found her crying. He hadn't gone to the saloon to satisfy his own needs. He had risked her anger, and that of the town gossips, so that she and her family could have Christmas presents.

She turned away to hide the tears that threatened. How could she have been so blind?

"Are you crying, Mama?" Jen asked.

"No. I'm just...overcome." She swallowed the lump that had lodged in her throat. "Mr. McAllister, would you care to lead us in prayer before we eat?"

They stood around the table, hands grasped, heads bowed.

As Quin spoke the words of blessing, Cassie glanced at him from beneath lowered lashes. She felt such a welling of love for this man, and thought again of the things she had overheard him telling her children. He claimed to be neither hero nor villain. He was just a man. But what a man. He had come unbidden into their lives, had saved them from peril and, with his irreverent charm, had brought them warmth and tenderness and laughter.

And she loved him. Sweet heaven, she could no longer deny the truth. She loved him.

Chapter Eighteen

"**O**ne more hand of cards, Gram. Please."

Luella surprised everyone by agreeing. With her spectacles perched on her nose, she seemed to be having a grand time learning to play poker.

"This is the last game," Quin insisted.

"You're just tired of being beaten, Mr. McAllister." Luella picked up her cards and began sorting them.

"You're right. I am. It's a good thing we're not playing for money."

"You mean you aren't happy about doing two days of kitchen chores?" she asked with a perfectly straight face.

"Not to mention the cow I'll be milking." He shot Cassie a look and she demurely glanced at the cards in her hand. But he could see the laughter glinting in her eyes.

"I do recall hearing you say that you always win, Mr. McAllister."

"I used to. Until I ran into the Montgomery Gang."

That brought a round of laughter from the children.

"All right. Who can open?" Quin looked around the table. "Cassie? Luella?"

"I'll open," Becky said with the air of one who'd been playing poker all her life. She dropped a piece of straw in the center of the table and announced, "Ante up, everyone."

"I don't believe it." Quin added a piece of straw to the pile in the middle of the table, and everyone else followed suit. They were playing a game Quin had named Cutthroat. Whoever won each jackpot could assign chores to the losers. "How many cards?"

"I'll take three," Becky said, discarding the same number.

Quin dealt, then turned to Luella. "How many?"

She shook her head. "I'll keep these."

He managed a straight face as he dealt to the others, then picked up his hand. Placing the ace next to the pair he already had, he said aloud, "I smell victory. Becky, what do you have?"

"A pair of queens."

"I don't have anything," Jen said.

"Neither do I." Cassie dropped her cards.

"Sorry, Becky. It looks like I win. Three aces." Quin set them down, then began to reach for the pile of straw.

As he dragged it toward him, Luella said, "Tell me again what it takes to beat three of a kind."

"Oh, Gram," Becky giggled. "You have a full house?"

"Indeed I do." Luella dropped her cards, saying, "It's still hard for me to understand how two little old threes and three fives can beat all those pretty aces."

Cassie and the children roared with laughter as Quin surrendered the straw to Luella, who doled out a list of chores like a hardened wagon master.

"That's it," Quin said, gathering up the cards. "I think we've had all the fun we can stand for one night."

"Who would like warm milk and cookies?" Luella asked as she pushed away from the table.

With the children eagerly following her, she placed a pan of milk on the fire and began filling a plate with cookies.

"You cheated, didn't you?" Cassie whispered.

Quin looked offended. "How can you say such a thing? Did you see me cheat?"

"Of course not. You're too good to get caught. But it was you who decided that the loser would have to assume all the burdensome chores on Christmas morning. I know you cheated so we'd all win."

He gave her a roguish smile that had her heart leaping to her throat. "A gentleman never cheats."

"And you're always the perfect gentleman, aren't you?"

He winked and slid the deck of cards into his pocket. "Yes, ma'am."

"Sit over here, Mama, Mr. McAllister." Becky and Jen moved apart to make room on the bench. When they sat down, Jen climbed onto Quin's lap, while Becky sat beside her mother.

Luella settled herself into the rocking chair, a fur robe over her lap, a cup of warm milk in her hands. Despite the howling of the wind outside, they were snug and warm. Biscuit was curled into a ball of fur on a rug in front of the fireplace. It was a scene of perfect contentment.

"Mama," Jen coaxed, "tell us what Christmas was like before the war."

The war, Quin thought. Everything in their lives was defined by the war. Life before the war. Life since.

Cassie stared into the flames, remembering. Her voice took on a dreamy quality. "Friends would come from miles around to our Christmas Eve supper. Robert always came. General Lee," she added, seeing the children's questioning looks. "Oh, the food. We always killed several geese, which I stuffed with sage dressing. Ethan and some of the men would hunt pheasant and partridge and doves. The governor always personally delivered a whole roasted pig, which became a tradition. There was punch and wine and even French champagne. And the sweet table was a wondrous thing to behold, with pies and rum cakes and fancy cookies."

"I can almost remember," Becky said with a sigh.

"Was I there?" Jen asked.

"Oh my, yes," Cassie said. "Your father was so proud of his baby daughter. He carried you in for all to admire, and watched as you and the other children scampered off to enjoy the taffy pull and play a game of tag. And at midnight, Saint Nicholas came, dressed in his bishop's robes, to distribute candy and presents to all the good boys and girls."

"That's the best part," Becky said with a sigh.

"I don't know." Jen yawned and leaned her head back against Quin's shoulder. Her hands rested atop Quin's big hands. "I don't think it sounds as nice as this. I think this was the best Christmas ever."

For a moment everyone fell silent as they looked at her. Cassie felt tears spring to her eyes. "You're right, Jennifer. This has been a fine Christmas. We are truly blessed. We have this snug cabin and more than enough to eat. And best of all, we have each other."

"Don't forget Mr. McAllister," Jen said.

"Yes," Cassie said softly. "We are grateful for Mr. McAllister."

"Do you remember the songs we used to sing at your Christmas party?" Luella asked suddenly.

Cassie nodded.

"Sing with me, Becky," Luella urged.

In her clear voice Becky began to sing, of a wondrous night, of humble shepherds keeping watch over their flocks, of a host of heavenly messengers heralding the birth of an infant who would change the world.

As Luella joined her, she stared into the flames, the cup in her hands empty, the plate of cookies forgotten. Soon Cassie and Quin joined in, their voices lifting, filling the little cabin with rich, beautiful music.

When the song ended, Cassie glanced at the little girl nestled against Quin's chest. Though she was making a valiant effort to stay awake, Jen's eyes blinked, then closed.

"I think it's time to say good-night." Cassie got to her feet.

Before she could reach for Jen, Quin stood and effortlessly lifted the little girl in his arms. With Cassie leading the way, he carried Jen to her bed. Cassie drew the covers over her, and Biscuit jumped onto the foot of the bed, where he promptly curled up, fast asleep. Cassie pressed a kiss to her daughter's cheek, and Quin did the same before he tiptoed out.

"Good night, Mr. McAllister," Luella called as she draped an arm around her granddaughter's shoulder. "Thank you again for my spectacles. I can't believe how much I've been missing."

"You're welcome. Good night, ma'am."

"Thank you, Mr. McAllister." Becky surprised him by brushing a kiss across his cheek. "Merry Christmas."

Luella and Becky made their way to the bedroom. Quin heard the whispered words of endearment before Cassie emerged a short time later.

He tossed another log onto the fire, then stood a moment, deep in thought as the flame licked along the bark. When he turned, Cassie was standing across the room, looking flushed and a little breathless.

"Where do you go," she asked softly, "when you get all quiet like that and stare into the fire?"

When he didn't answer, she said, "You never talk about your family, and what your life was like before the war."

He shook his head and began to turn away. Instantly she crossed the room and touched a hand to his arm. "Forgive me, Mr. McAllister. I had no right..."

She felt him stiffen at her touch. The look on his face was so bleak, it seemed to pierce her heart.

"I'll say good-night now, ma'am." He drew away, breaking contact. "I'm going down in the mine to work for a while."

"But it's so late." She gripped her hands together, feeling helpless. Her impulsive question had caused him to turn away from her, but she had no idea how to make amends. "Why, it's almost midnight. After the day you've put in, you can't possibly feel like going back to the mine."

"I'm not tired yet. Besides, it will give me a chance to work off all that good food." He pulled on his parka and called, without looking at her, "Good night, ma'am. A happy Christmas."

"Yes. A happy..."

She watched as he picked up a lantern and lifted the trapdoor. Within minutes he had disappeared.

* * *

Quin set the lantern on a shelf of rock and removed his parka. Rolling his sleeves, he took up the pick and began to chisel away at the entrance to the cave. Each time the point bit into the wall of rock, straining his muscles, he welcomed the release of hard physical work. It would help to take his mind off the images that tormented him. Images made all the more painful tonight, while a little girl slept in his arms and a beautiful woman sat beside him.

He pushed himself beyond the pain, working until his muscles ached from the effort. In no time the entrance had been enlarged from a tiny crawl space to an opening that could accommodate a man and wheelbarrow.

Satisfied, he set aside the pick and turned to retrieve the lantern.

That was when he saw her. She had draped a blanket around her shoulders. She stood now, clutching it tightly about her, watching him with the wariness of a frightened doe.

His voice was gruff. "I thought you'd be asleep by now."

"I can't sleep." She moistened her lips with her tongue and took a tentative step closer. "I never properly thanked you for this—" she touched a hand to her gown, then lifted her eyes to him "—and all the other things you've given us."

"I've been properly thanked." His manner was brusque. He spun on his heel. "Now go up to bed. This is no place for you, dressed like that."

She would not be ignored again. She'd had time to gather her courage. Lifting her chin, she walked closer and placed a hand on his arm. "What is it? What have I done to upset you?"

She felt him flinch, but he kept his back to her as he said, "You haven't done anything."

"I'm not leaving until you tell me honestly what's wrong."

He turned. Very deliberately he kept his tone rough. "What's wrong? You look entirely too fetching in that gown, Mrs. Montgomery. That's what's wrong. And unless you get out of here now, I'll have you out of that gown and into my arms so fast your head will be spinning." His eyes blazed. "Is that honest enough for you?"

He saw the stunned look in her eyes before he gripped her roughly by the shoulders and turned her around. There was no gentleness in his touch as he gave her a shove. "Now leave me and go back to your safe haven before I do something . . . unforgivable."

Without another word he grabbed up the pick and stormed into the cavern. If he worked through the night he could have enough rocks to fill the wagon. With that goal in mind he bent to his task with a vengeance.

"I understand now." The sound of her breathless voice, so near, sent shock waves through him. "You want me. But you think somehow you'll hurt me."

The gentle touch of her fingers on his arm caused him to drop the pick. He swore as he swung toward her. "Woman, leave me. Now, before it's too late."

The blanket slipped from her shoulders and fluttered to the floor of the cave.

Her voice was hushed. "Don't you see? It's already too late."

He clenched his hands into fists and, through sheer force of will, kept them at his sides. "Damn it, Cassie, you're confusing gratitude with love."

"I'm not confused. And what I feel is not gratitude."

Still he resisted. "It sure as hell isn't love. A woman like you . . . it isn't possible for you to have feelings for a man like me."

"I'll be the judge of my feelings."

His nerves were stretched to the limit, but he gave no indication, except for the clenching of his jaw. "I'll hurt you."

"Oh, no." In an achingly sweet gesture she wrapped her arms around his waist and pressed her cheek to his. "You could never hurt me." But even as she spoke those words, she knew that he could. He was the only man who could, if she dared to open her heart to him. She pushed aside that thought. For this one special night she didn't want to think. She wanted only to feel. "I want you to hold me."

He swore again, softly. "If I do, I won't be able to let you go. And in the morning, nothing will be the same."

"I know. But this is what I want. What we both want." She stood on tiptoe to reach his lips.

The moment her lips brushed his, he knew he had lost. The arms that crushed her were almost bruising as he dragged her against him and savaged her mouth.

For a moment she was startled by the roughness of his kiss. Then she leaned into him, giving herself up to the moment. His lips moved over hers, taking until she was drained, then filling her with the dark, mysterious flavor of him, until all she could taste was him.

"Quin." She breathed his name.

At once his touch gentled. His name on her lips was the sweetest sound.

"Say it again," he murmured against her lips. "Say my name."

"Quin. Quin."

His kiss cut off her voice. His mouth moved over hers, slowly, deliberately, drawing out the kiss until she sighed and her lips parted. His tongue tangled with hers, drawing out all the sweetness until they were both lost in the pleasure.

He lifted his head and for a moment she felt bereft. Then his lips whispered over her face, pressing light kisses to her eyelids, her cheeks, the corner of her jaw.

"Oh, Cassie. Do you have any idea how sweet you are?" He was determined to show her, by word, by touch, how precious she was to him. And so he forced himself to go slowly, to keep his kisses, his touches, as gentle as he could manage. But inside a storm was brewing. A storm of passion that he knew, once unleashed, would devour them both.

With his tongue he traced the curve of her ear, nibbling, tugging, then darting inside until she gasped and pushed away. He dragged her close, burning a trail of kisses down her neck. When he buried his lips in the sensitive hollow of her throat, she gave a little moan of pleasure and clung to him, afraid that at any moment her legs would no longer hold her.

As if reading her mind, he lowered her to the blanket and kissed her until she was breathless.

"There's still time to change your mind, Cassie." Even as he said it, he knew it was a lie. He would beg, he would crawl, to keep her here with him.

"I've already given you my answer, Quin."

She twined her arms around his neck, but still he held back.

"I can't make you any promises."

She felt the knife-edge of pain and shrugged it aside, offering her lips. "I won't ask for any."

He took her offering with a hunger that shocked them both. His kisses were by turns punishing, then gentle, as he waged a war within himself. He wanted her. More than anything in the world. But he knew that what she offered was too precious, too priceless, to squander. He wouldn't merely take; he would give. All the pleasure, all the gratification, all the rapture, he could manage.

Outside the wind raged, but inside, the cavern was silent, with only the sounds of their whispered sighs. The light from the lantern made shifting patterns on the walls of the cave, bathing them in a pool of amber light.

Quin struggled to bank the needs that raged within him, seeking release. For her sake he would go slowly, allowing her to set the pace, allowing them both to savor each moment.

His kisses became gentle, almost reverent. With teeth and tongue and fingertips he explored her face, her neck, her throat. And with each touch he felt her body grow more tense, her breathing more shallow.

Time stood still. There was no tomorrow. No yesterday. There was only now, this place, this woman in his arms.

"Cassie. Cassie." Her name was a prayer on his lips.

She lay in his arms, steeped in pleasure. She wouldn't allow herself to think about tomorrow. For now there was just Quin, his touch, his taste, the pleasure he brought her. And if she repeated the mistake of her mother, there would be no regrets. For this one special night, she was loved.

As his kisses intensified, her breathing grew more rapid. The thought of what she was about to do had fear leaping into her eyes. Seeing it, he soothed, caressed, calming her fears, easing her tension, until she relaxed in his arms.

He felt the gradual change in her. Trust. She trusted him. The knowledge excited him. With mutual trust they could take the next step. Together.

He reached for the buttons of her gown and, with infinite patience, undressed her. As he slid the gown from her shoulders he brushed his lips across her naked flesh. She trembled and sighed, exciting him more, and he reached for the ribbons of her chemise. When that last barrier fell away, he was at last able to see the body she had kept hidden from his view.

She was so beautiful, so perfect, she took his breath away.

With her eyes steady on his, she reached for the buttons of his shirt. She slipped it from his shoulders, then bent to brush her lips across his hair-roughened chest. She felt him tremble as a moan escaped his lips. When her fingers fumbled with the fasteners at his waist, he helped her until his clothes lay discarded with hers.

They knelt facing each other. He reached up and removed the combs from her hair, watching as fiery curls tumbled loose, spilling down her shoulders. Without a word he plunged his hands into the tangles and pulled her head back, then covered her mouth with his.

The kiss was hot, hungry. It spoke of loneliness, of needs so long suppressed, of a deep, abiding need to touch and be touched.

She wrapped her arms around his waist and clung to his strength. At that simple contact, she felt his muscles contract violently. Then his hands began moving over her, enticing, arousing, until her body hummed with need.

Ever since he'd first seen her he had fantasized about making slow, torturous love to her in a big feather bed in a gilded saloon. But now, with a fire blazing inside

him and a hunger that bordered on madness, he had no
need of fantasies. This was real. This was now. She
possessed him, body and soul.

Now she understood why he had struggled so long to
remain aloof. Always before he had revealed only the
charming gambler. Now it was as though a stranger had
emerged from some deep, cavernous prison to devour
her. This dark, dangerous side of him excited her.
Knowing that it was her touch, her taste, that aroused
him, made her bold. She pressed light kisses across his
shoulder, down his chest, exploring his body as he had
explored hers. His low groan of pleasure made her even
bolder.

Half-starved, they feasted. Half-mad, they took and
gave and took until they slipped beyond reason.

His body was alive with needs. Though he had intended to go slowly, he could no longer rein in the desire that smoldered. With her own passion unleashed,
he was free to lead her higher, to take her to new places.
Together they would taste and touch and feel. If he
could give her nothing else, he could bring her this one
night of exquisite pleasure.

With great care he lay her down on the blanket and
brought his lips to her breast, moving his tongue across
her nipple until it hardened. Then he moved to the other
breast, nibbling, suckling, until she moaned and
writhed beneath him. Her breath came faster now, as
she clutched at the blanket and moved in his arms.

The cave was cold, but the heat rose between them,
clogging their throats as he drove her higher, then higher
still, keeping release just out of reach.

She trembled as he moved over her, warm flesh to
warm flesh. He felt her stiffen and gasp as, with lips and
fingertips, he brought her to the first peak.

There was no time to think. Now there was only Quin. His taste, his touch, his voice, low, urgent, as he took her to places she had never been before. He gave her no time to recover as he moved over her, dragging his lips back to hers.

Her eyes were steady on his, glazed with passion. She hadn't thought it possible to want more, but she did. As he entered her, she enfolded him in her arms, moving with him, matching his strength.

He filled himself with the fresh clean taste of her. He knew that in the years to come, wherever his journeys took him, he would think of her, of this, and be warmed by the memory.

And then all thought fled. They moved together, strong, sure, chasing a distant light. Her name was torn from his lips as he began to soar. At last their bodies shuddered, quaked, as they reached the sun, embraced it, and shattered into a million glittering fragments.

Chapter Nineteen

They lay, still joined, feeling their heartbeats slowly return to normal. The enormity of what they had shared brought a mist to Cassie's eyes.

Quin pressed his lips to the corner of her eyelid. Feeling the moisture, he immediately levered himself above her. "I've hurt you. I know I was rough—"

"No." She caught him before he could roll away. Pulling his head down, she brushed her lips over his. "These are happy tears."

"You're sure?" His heart began to beat again. "You aren't having regrets?"

"I'm sure, Quin. No regrets." No matter where life took them, she knew, they would always have this memory, this special bond. Even though they had made no promises, there would never be room for anyone else in her heart. Her man, she thought fiercely. Hers. And the love she felt for him would warm her through all the cold, lonely winters of her life.

He pressed his lips to the sheen on her forehead, then rolled to one side and drew her into the circle of his arms. Mistaking her silence, he whispered, "I'm sorry. I didn't plan for this to happen."

"I know. I did." When he leaned up on one elbow to stare down at her she began to laugh. "Well, what choice did I have? All of a sudden you had become the very stern, righteous, noble gentleman."

He joined in the laughter. "If I'd known about your change of heart, ma'am, I could have saved myself a lot of long walks in the snow." His tone became serious. "You are so very special, Cassie. Do you know how long I've wanted you?"

Intrigued, she sat up. Her hair spilled in disarray around her shoulders. "How long?"

He caught a handful of her hair. "Since the minute I laid eyes on you, looking so fierce, aiming that rifle at me."

"Why, Mr. McAllister," she said in her best drawl, "if I'd known that, I could have had my way with you days ago. All I would have had to do was get out my little old pistol and aim it at your...heart."

He was so delighted by her wicked sense of humor, he threw back his head and roared. "Mrs. Montgomery, you do continue to surprise me."

"I'm glad you don't object. Because I have a few more surprises in mind." Reveling in her newly discovered power, she leaned forward and began to press kisses along his shoulder, his collarbone, his chest.

The laughter died in his throat. He gave a low moan of pleasure. "Do you know what you're doing to me?"

"Good. I can't think of anyone more deserving."

He brushed his lips lightly over hers. At once he felt the rush of desire. He was amazed that he could want her again so soon. But the truth was, he would never have enough of her. A lifetime of loving would not be enough.

She felt a surge of power. Knowing it was her touch, her kiss, he craved, she straddled him and began to move over him.

"Woman, have you no shame?"

"None." Realizing that he was fully aroused, she flashed a dangerous smile. Her hair swirled around him as she ran hot, nibbling kisses across his collarbone and down his stomach. When she moved lower she heard his quick intake of breath.

"I can see that there's only one cure for this," he muttered as he suddenly rolled her over and covered her mouth with his.

Her smile fled. She gasped as he entered her. And then they were lost in a world of quiet sighs and passionate kisses. A world of endless pleasure. A world of love.

Quin studied the woman in his arms. Her eyes were closed, her breathing slow and steady. There had been so little time for sleep. As the hours sped past, they had loved with a desperation born of the knowledge that all this would soon end, for he had already told her of his plan to leave at first light for the assayer's office in Virginia City, the territorial capital.

Their lovemaking had been at times a frenzy of emotions that sent them into a swirling storm. At other times they had been as gentle and as tender as old, comfortable lovers.

It was cold and damp in the mine, and Quin knew they would both be more comfortable in the cabin, in Cassie's bed, or in his bedroll of furs. Yet neither of them had made any move to leave. This cave had become their sanctuary. Despite the cold, they were warmed by each other's bodies, and by their love.

Love. Quin wondered when the passion, the desire, had become love. It felt so right, so natural, to love this woman.

Cassie stirred, and he saw the look in her eyes as she glanced at the hazy light in the mine. "What are you thinking about?"

"Freckles," he muttered, running kisses across her shoulder. "There's something intriguing about all these freckles. I'm going to have to kiss every one."

She sighed her pleasure at the touch of his lips. "Is it dawn?"

"Almost."

She surprised him by wrapping her arms around his neck. "I like waking up in your arms. In fact, I can't think of a nicer place to be."

"I was just thinking the same thing." He kissed the tip of her nose. "Which must mean that we've both lost our senses. Do you realize there's a warm fire just above us, while we have nothing more than this blanket and the heat from our own bodies?"

"Mmm-hmm." She touched her lips to his and stretched contentedly. "But you must admit, we've managed to generate a great deal of body heat."

Laughing, she brought her hands down, running them along his body, anticipating his response. Her teasing suddenly stopped when her fingertips encountered a raised scar that ran along one side from shoulder to thigh. Until now, she hadn't had the confidence to ask about it.

"What is this, Quin?"

"Nothing. Just an old wound."

"Oh, Quin." She could feel him closing up, turning away from her again, as he had the previous night, before their lovemaking. And again she felt helpless. As her fingers moved along the ridge of flesh, her eyes grew troubled. "I hate the war and what it did to you."

"How can you say that, love? You don't even know what it did."

Love. She was warmed by his use of that endearment. It gave her the courage to whisper, "I know that whatever it was, your pain is so deep you can't even bring yourself to speak of it."

Without a word he drew her against his chest and wrapped the blanket around the two of them, enveloping her in warmth. For long minutes they remained that way, neither of them willing to break the silence.

Just when she thought that he would keep his secrets, he gave a deep sigh and began to speak. The pain was evident in his voice.

"You have a right to know, Cassie." He twirled a strand of her hair around his finger, avoiding her eyes. "Ethan and I had much in common. Maybe that was why we were drawn into such a close friendship. I was the only son of a wealthy plantation owner. I adored my two younger sisters, and they adored me. When I think back, I realize how young, how foolish I was. I thought everyone was open and generous and fun loving like my family."

Cassie heard a slight change in his tone.

"When a beautiful, aloof young woman pursued me, I was more than a little flattered. We were soon married, and shortly thereafter, expecting our first child."

Though Cassie was stunned at this revelation, she forced herself to say nothing, for fear that he would draw back into silence.

"It should have been a wonderful time in our lives," Quin muttered, "but the truth soon became apparent. She didn't love me. In fact, she was incapable of loving anyone. She had married a man of means because her father was deeply in debt. After I cleared his debts, she became even more aloof, often falling into black moods that would last for days or weeks. By the time our beautiful little daughter was born, ours was a marriage in name only. She had no interest at all in our baby."

Thinking of her own children, and her boundless love for them, Cassie felt a wave of compassion. Without realizing it, she rested her cheek against his chest and tried to find comfort in the strong, steady beat of his heart.

"And then came the war," Quin said softly, "which I saw as a means to escape my personal unhappiness. I must admit that I thought of the war as little more than a brief adventure. I gave no thought to the reason why we were fighting. I was not only willing, but eager, to join the fray. Leaving my wife and daughter with my family, I accepted an assignment no one else wanted, as a courier between General Lee and General Longstreet. I found myself constantly in enemy territory."

She shivered. "It must have been frightening."

"Not at first," he admitted. "I still thought of it as no more than a fine challenge. It satisfied my need to take risks. But as the war dragged on, and I saw the carnage, the thrill of adventure was replaced by a kind of numbing horror. I saw so many good men killed, so many others left to suffer. I saw limbs severed, young healthy bodies shattered beyond recognition. And then, suddenly, I was captured and found myself spending the rest of the war in a prison camp."

"Where you met Ethan," she said in hushed tones.

"Where I met Ethan."

He fell silent for several seconds, and she could see that he was back, reliving the horror. Then, with a deep

sigh, he continued, "I discovered that my skill with
cards could be useful in securing food, blankets, and
whatever else we desperately needed to stay alive in that
filthy place. And except for a few ... ugly incidents ...
the treatment was tolerable. I remember after the war,
heading home, still believing I could put the war behind me." His voice lowered. "By the time I reached
Atlanta, everyone and everything I loved was gone. All
of them dead. Some of my neighbors thought my family had been murdered by roving bands of former soldiers. But others suggested that they'd been killed at the
hands of a woman driven further into madness by the
war."

Cassie felt a wave of revulsion. "Are you saying your
wife killed your family?"

His voice trembled with emotion. "I will never know.
But if it is so, then their deaths are really on my hands.
My parents, my sisters, even my beautiful daughter,
died because of my arrogance."

"Your arrogance? You blame yourself?" Sitting up,
she stared at him, tears welling in her eyes. "But why?
What could you have done?"

"Oh, Cassie, don't you see?" He turned his head to
hide the anguish in his eyes. "I didn't go off to war for
any noble reasons. I went to escape an unhappy marriage. And because of it, all those who depended on me
had to suffer. If I had been there with them—"

"You could not have stayed there, Quin. Even if you
had not gone voluntarily in the beginning of the war,
you would surely have been forced to join the battle as
the war raged on." She touched a hand to his cheek and
felt him flinch. "You are not to blame for their deaths,
Quin, any more than I am to blame for Ethan's. It is as
my mother said. It was the war." She felt her lips trem-

ble but forced herself to go on. "Ethan felt much the same way as you when he returned. He could not forgive himself for the things we'd been forced to suffer while he was gone. Can you imagine? He was more tortured by what we had endured than by what he'd been forced to live through. I thought..." She shivered, remembering the torment in her husband's eyes. "I thought it was just the sickness. But I realize now it was a sickness of the soul. He could not let go of this need to protect us, even when his health was ebbing. He truly believed that he could continue to watch over us, even after his life was over. This torment, this dedication is, I believe, what really killed him." She was quiet for a long time. Lifting a finger to Quin's forehead, she traced the lines of worry as she said, "I have seen that same look in your eyes, Quin. If you would free yourself from these demons, you must first forgive yourself."

"How can I forget that I failed all those who trusted me?"

"The failure was not yours. Whatever else you believe, you must know this. However your loved ones died, it was ordained by one greater than you. You must accept that they have found their eternal peace."

"Oh, God, Cassie." His voice trembled with emotion. He pulled her close, his mouth seeking hers. The kiss spoke of pain, of anguish, of soul-wrenching torture. But as the kiss deepened, it became something else. Passion, need, dark desire.

They came together in an explosion of raw emotion. And as the light of dawn filtered into the cavern like a benediction from heaven, they moved in each other's arms, absorbing each other's pain, healing each other's wounds. And when at last they lay, spent, arms and legs tangled, they felt a rare kind of peace.

"Tell me honestly," Cassie murmured against Quin's throat. "Did Ethan speak of me?"

He ran a finger along her arm, studying the fine porcelain skin. "He spoke of nothing else. You were his reason for living." And mine, he realized with a shock. Though Quin had never before admitted it, it had been Ethan's description of his wife and children that had kept them both sane in that place of insanity. And though he hadn't realized it until now, he had fallen in love with Cassie all those years ago. Her goodness. Her sweetness. Before he had ever seen her face or heard her voice or felt her touch, he had fallen in love with another man's wife.

For a moment he was rocked by the knowledge, and experienced a sense of shame that he should be given such a gift. Then the shame was replaced with a sense of humble acceptance. He would always be grateful to the fate that had brought him here. For it was with Cassie that he had at last found peace.

He studied the thin rays of light that streamed from the ceiling of the cave. His arms tightened around Cassie, and he pressed a long, lingering kiss to her lips before muttering, "It's time."

Cassie sat up and shoved the hair from her eyes while he dressed. "I can't bear to think of you spending Christmas Day on the trail."

"Don't think about that." He watched as she slipped into her dress and buttoned the row of tiny buttons. The temptation to linger, to taste her lips one more time, was great, but he knew that the day could no longer be put off. "Just remember, by the time I reach Virginia City,

Christmas will be over. And as soon as the assayer's office opens, I'll have the answer and be on my way home.''

Home. She wondered if he realized what he had revealed.

Cassie handed Quin a linen towel wrapped around an assortment of biscuits and dried meats. He stuffed the food into his saddlebag, then turned for a final good-bye. After he embraced Jen and Becky, and tipped his hat to Luella, he merely touched a finger to Cassie's cheek.

It was then that Luella sensed something different. Standing a little to one side, she glanced from Quin to her daughter. She felt a sudden shock as realization dawned. There was no denying the truth. It was there in their eyes. In the way their bodies strained toward each other, though they steadfastly maintained a proper distance.

They had become intimate.

The old woman felt a tightening in her throat. She could understand how it had happened. Two lonely people. A desperate yearning to be held, to be comforted. Had she not experienced similar feelings? But, oh, how she had prayed that it would not be the fate of her beloved daughter. Luella knew only too well what could happen to a woman foolish enough to let her emotions overrule common sense.

''Look for me tomorrow night,'' Quin said as he pulled himself into the saddle.

''You can't possibly make it to Virginia City and back in that length of time,'' Cassie protested. ''Unless you don't bother to sleep.''

"Don't worry about me. I'll be here. Just take care of yourselves until I get back."

He nudged his horse into a run. They all watched until he was out of sight. As the others returned to the cabin, Cassie stood alone in the biting cold, her spine straight and stiff beneath her shawl. But from her vantage point inside the cabin, Luella watched as the thin shoulders suddenly sagged, then shook, as her daughter gave in to the need to weep.

The trail was steep and slick. Cutter picked his way through several feet of snow.

Quin, hunched into his long duster, spoke words of encouragement while the horse strained to the top of the rise. Despite fatigue and the biting cold, a smile touched Quin's lips at the sight of the darkened outlines of the familiar barn and cabin in the distance. He touched a hand to the assayer's report tucked in his pocket. Christmas festivities were about to be extended another day. Or a lifetime, if truth be told.

As they began the long descent, Quin felt a prickly feeling along his scalp. What was wrong with the scene before him? He peered through the darkness, straining to put his finger on the problem.

It wasn't unusual to see the cabin in darkness. After all, it was well past the time when Luella and the children would have retired for the night. Still, he'd expected a lantern burning and Cassie waiting up for him.

The feelings of unease increased as he drew closer. It wasn't just the lack of light. Something else was wrong. And then it dawned on him. There was no smoke coming from the chimney.

His mount, sensing his urgency, broke into a run. When they came around the barn, Quin spotted a patch

of darkness against the white snow. A human form.
Unmoving. His heart forgot to beat. He leapt from the
saddle and sprinted toward the darkened form.

"Cassie. My God..." The words died in his throat as
he knelt in the blood-spattered snow and lifted the life-
less form in his arms. He realized at once that it wasn't
Cassie. The body was that of a handsome young Crow.
The son of the chief. Rage bubbled, hot and furious, at
the knowledge that this fine young brave had given his
life in defense of others. Quin's memory flashed back
to the war and he experienced once again his fury at the
inhumanity of needless bloodshed.

A little beyond was another dark form, and another.
Quin bent to each. They all bore the unmistakable signs
of gunshot. And each time, his rage grew. The bodies
of the Crow warriors formed a trail of blood all the way
to the cabin.

The cabin door stood ajar.

Dreading what he would find, he drew his pistol and
strode inside. The interior of the cabin bore testimony
to a terrible struggle. The table lay on its side, dishes
smashed, chairs scattered about. In the bedrooms, beds
had been overturned, blankets tossed in a heap.

At his footsteps, a tiny bundle of fur lifted its head
and, whimpering, crawled out from beneath a blanket
where it had been huddled.

"Biscuit." Quin gathered the trembling puppy into
his arms, his feeling of dread growing. Jen would have
never willingly allowed herself to be separated from her
pup. When the whimpering stopped, he stowed the little animal inside his parka where it nestled against his
chest.

Lifting the trapdoor, he listened to the silence, then
descended the ladder. A lantern hung on a peg, a thin

Chapter Twenty

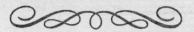

Quin's rage grew with every mile. He had no way of knowing whether Cassie and her family were still alive. And he had no plan. He knew only that if they had been harmed, Cyrus Stoner would pay dearly.

He was a man who'd known little fear in his life, but he was afraid now. Afraid for Cassie, for Luella, for those two sweet children. As a gambler he'd always lived impulsively, accepting winning and losing with equal grace. But now, recalling Ethan's deep and abiding faith, he found himself praying that he was in time to make a difference.

Even before he reached Stoner's land, Quin spotted the guards, silhouetted against the snow. Keeping to the high ground, which was heavily forested, it was an easy task to avoid being seen.

He skirted the barn and bunkhouse, moving in the shadows. When he reached the main house, he dismounted and led Cutter to a stand of trees, where the horse would be hidden from view. After wrapping the puppy in his parka, he slipped his rifle from the boot of the saddle, then made his way on foot to the back of the house.

As he peered into windows, he was puzzled by the lack of activity within. The kitchen was dark. In Stoner's parlor he spotted Cassie and Luella, bound and gagged, seated stiffly in wooden chairs on either side of a fireplace. For the first time in hours Quin felt alive again. Seeing them gave him his first ray of hope. His gaze shifted. Across the room, Stoner sat behind his desk, looking perfectly at ease as he tended to his paperwork.

Quin circled the big house, and found, to his dismay, that the other rooms were empty. Where were the children? He tipped his head to study a spill of light from the second-story windows.

He slung his rifle over his shoulder and climbed to the balcony. With the stealth of a cat, he moved from window to window until he located Jen and Becky, flung across a big bed, their hands and feet bound.

When Quin slid open the window, the curtain billowed inward, causing the children to cry out. Cursing the wind, Quin touched a finger to his lips and their cries ended abruptly. He worked quickly to free them. Once free they wrapped their arms around his neck and he hugged them fiercely.

"Mr. Stoner has Mama and Gram," Becky cried.

"I know. I'll see to them in a minute," he whispered. "First, I have to make certain that the two of you are safe."

"Why can't we stay with you?" Jen asked.

"Because Cyrus Stoner won't give up without a fight. And I won't have either of you in the line of fire. Now," he said as he led them toward the balcony, "Cutter and Biscuit are down there, hidden among those trees."

The children looked where he pointed, and could see several dark shadows moving and shifting in the wind.

Though they were clearly afraid, they uttered not a sound of protest.

"I want you to climb down and stay with Cutter, no matter what you hear." He handed Becky his rifle. "I know how you feel about guns, Becky. But if any of Stoner's men should find you, you know what you have to do."

The girl gathered her little sister close and nodded. Quin waited until the two children climbed out the window. Then he pulled open the bedroom door and headed toward the stairway.

Cassie was still reeling from the events of the past few hours. At first, when Stoner and his men had approached the cabin, she'd expected to deal with them as she had in the past. Always before, she'd been able to hold them at bay with stern words issued at the point of her rifle. This time, however, he had come with an army of men who surrounded the cabin. Though she and her family had scrapped with a frenzy born of desperation, Stoner's men had simply overpowered them.

The Crow, who had been keeping watch over their new friends, had fought valiantly to defend them, but in the end, had been brutally shot down. Cassie knew she would never be able to wipe the memory of that bloody massacre from her mind.

The ride to Stoner's ranch was little more than a blur. She could hear her mother's voice, angry, outraged, as she was lifted into a saddle. And the children crying as they were roughly herded into a wagon. Stoner had wisely separated them, so that they couldn't comfort each other or plot an escape. Cassie had been forced to endure Cyrus Stoner's arms holding her as they sped across the frozen plain. What was even worse was his boast that, at long last, he would have everything he wanted.

Now Cyrus folded his hands on the desk and looked at her with an air of supreme confidence. "Miz Montgomery, isn't this cozy?"

Seeing the anger in her eyes, he laughed. "What a fine joke this is. When I think of how long you lied to me, keeping your husband's death a secret, I do believe this is my moment of sweetest vengeance."

Cassie closed her eyes against the knot of fear that threatened to choke her. When she thought of the exquisite joy she had felt—was it just a night ago?—she had thought she had it all. Quin's love. Security for her family. How was it possible that she was now cast into the very depths of despair? She struggled with the terror that lurked in the dark recesses of her mind. All the torturous work, all the sacrifices, had been in vain. Ethan's dream had fallen into the hands of a monster.

Quin heard the sound of Stoner's laughter and his finger tightened on the trigger. The thought of that brute touching Cassie, tormenting her, nearly blinded him with rage.

He had intended to move cautiously, to take the time to assure himself that there would be no guards. But the sound of Stoner's voice changed all his plans. Without regard to his own safety, Quin put his shoulder against the door and forced his way into the room.

Cyrus half rose, then, seeing Quin's gun aimed at him, slowly sank back down to his chair. It occurred to Quin in that fleeting second that something was very wrong. Stoner's smile hadn't been wiped away by the sight of him. In fact, his smile had actually widened. Quin glanced across the room to make certain that

Cassie and Luella were unharmed. Though they couldn't make a sound, their eyes looked wild and troubled, and they were trying desperately to cry out. Or to sound an alarm. As he turned back to Stoner, he realized his mistake.

A voice from the doorway commanded sharply, "Drop the gun, McAllister."

Quin whirled and found himself facing half a dozen of Stoner's men standing in the doorway. All were holding guns pointed directly at him.

"Welcome to our little trap, McAllister," Cyrus said. "As you can see, we've been expecting you."

Quin felt the butt of a rifle crash against his skull. He staggered, dropping to one knee, but refused to lower his weapon. He heard a strange whimper, and recognized Cassie's muffled cry. It seemed important that he get to her, to shield her from this violence. But before he could take a step, a second blow to his head brought a shower of stars. And then, as pain engulfed him, he sank into merciful blackness.

"Do whatever you have to." Stoner's words sounded as though they were coming from a great distance. "I want him awake, to witness this."

Whiskey fumes stung Quin's nostrils as the rim of a glass was forced between his lips. He gagged on the first few drops, then managed to swallow the rest. He struggled through layers of pain, shaking his head to clear the confusion. That only made the pain worse.

"He's coming around" came a voice directly beside him.

Quin's eyes opened, then squinted against the brightly colored lights that moved and danced. He blinked several times and the swirling lights steadied and stilled.

He was tied to a chair, his hands so tightly bound the leather strips dug into his flesh, drawing blood. Still he raged against his bonds, bringing a smile to Stoner's lips, and a murmured, "That's better."

Someone forced his head up so that he could see Cassie, standing beside Stoner's desk.

"Now, Miz Montgomery, I'll free you and your family," Cyrus said, "as soon as you agree to sign over your property to me."

"Will you free Quin, as well?" she asked. Though her hands were still bound, there was nothing meek in her demeanor. Her head was high. Her eyes flashed with defiance.

"What's McAllister to you except a hired gun?" Cyrus remarked. "Once you sign this paper, you won't have need of him."

"I won't sign it unless you agree to allow Quin to go free, as well."

Cyrus gave an imitation of a smile. "You drive a hard bargain, Miz Montgomery. But if you insist..."

"If you sign that, Cassie—" Quin struggled to get the words out through a swollen, bloody lip. His mouth felt stuffed with cotton "—you'll sign your own death warrant. Stoner can't afford to let any of us live."

"Now why would I want your deaths on my hands?" Cyrus asked in careful, patient tones. "I just want your land." He shoved the paper into Cassie's hands. "Read it and sign."

Quin's mind raced. "Go ahead," he said suddenly. "It doesn't matter anyway."

Both Cassie and Cyrus lifted their heads to stare at him.

"Sign it away," Quin muttered. "It's just a piece of worthless land. Not worthy of the time and effort you've put into it."

"Worthless! What do you mean?" Cyrus snarled. "Is this another one of your jokes?"

"You can see for yourself." Quin knew that he had Stoner's complete attention now. "I have the assayer's report right here in my pocket."

Cyrus stormed across the room and fumbled in Quin's pocket until he found the paper. As his fingers closed over it, Quin brought his knee up with such force, Cyrus gave a grunt of pain and collapsed on the floor. At once Stoner's men aimed their guns at Quin's head.

"No," Cyrus said between painful gasps of breath. "Don't kill him yet. I want to save that pleasure for myself."

Stoner stumbled to his chair and sat down heavily. Then he unfolded the document and read. When he'd finished, his eyes glittered with greed. "You lying bastard," he said to Quin. "I knew you were lying."

"And how would you know that?" Quin asked.

"Everybody used to laugh about the crazy old man searching for his treasure. But though my men and I searched the entire area, we could never find the entrance to the mine, so we figured it was just a myth. But when the Montgomery family came all the way from Atlanta, and settled in the same spot, I figured I'd wait and watch and see if there might be something worthwhile after all." A slow, evil smile curled his lips. "And there is. Silver," he announced, holding up the document. "The highest grade silver the assayer has ever tested."

Cassie's eyes filled with tears. "Truly, Quin? Ethan's fortune wasn't just a foolish dream?"

"It's real," Quin said bleakly. He thought of the eagerness with which he'd left Virginia City to head back to the cabin. The thought of the joy he would bring Cassie and her family had filled him with such happiness. Now he would give anything if the assayer's report had found nothing but useless rocks. The fortune they'd worked so hard to find would guarantee that they would die. "And the minute it becomes Stoner's, it seals our fates."

Cyrus opened a desk drawer and removed a pistol. "You're meddling in something that isn't any of your business, McAllister. I guess what I heard about you is true." With his eyes steady on Quin's, he fondled the gun. "The information I received is that you thought you were pretty tough during the war. The hero who carried secret information across enemy lines."

"How would you know that?"

Cyrus laughed. "Oh, I made it my business to learn all I could about you, McAllister. With enough money, a man can learn plenty. Your nickname was Gambler, and the rumor was that there wasn't any risk you wouldn't take. The greater the odds, the more you enjoyed your work. General Robert E. Lee called you his avenging angel, and said he would trust you to outsmart the devil himself. Only one night, near Gettysburg, you met your match, hero." He smiled, enjoying his own narrative. "And found yourself removed from the action, and rotting in a prisoner-of-war camp."

Quin's eyes narrowed and Cyrus knew his words had found their mark. "There's a rumor that you killed a guard in that camp, McAllister. Nobody could ever prove it. But I don't need proof. That guard was a friend of mine, and just for tonight we're going to pretend the war is still being fought. I'm going to enjoy killing a Reb tonight, McAllister.''

Quin relaxed a bit. When it came to his own life, it didn't matter. He'd been prepared to die a hundred times during the war. If only he could barter his own life for Cassie's, he would die a happy man. "All right. So you still want to kill Rebs. I'm your man. But you don't need to kill the women, Cyrus. With this vein of silver, you'll be the richest man in Montana. Just give Cassie enough money to take her family away, and you'll never hear from them again.''

"Cassie, is it? The lady has gone from Mrs. Montgomery to Cassie.'' Stoner's smile grew. "Know what I think, McAllister? I think you're sweet on her.''

He glanced from Cassie to Quin, saw the look that passed between them, then laughed. "Oh, this is too good. Now I know how to really hurt you, Reb.'' He shoved back his chair and stormed around his desk, grabbing Cassie roughly by the arm. "My men and I are going to have a little fun with the lady. And when we're through, guess who's going to be blamed for such...unspeakable crimes?'' His laughter grew. "You, Reb. You and those Crow. And after the rumors we've been spreading in Prospect, no one will doubt it.'' He turned to his men. "Tonight we're all going to celebrate my good fortune. We're going to drink, and pleasure ourselves with this pretty little thing, and—'' he threw back his head, enjoying his own joke "—for good measure, we'll let our gambler watch the festivities. And when we've had enough fun, we're going to kill him. And tomorrow, McAllister and his good friends the Crow are going to be hated and reviled by every good citizen of Prospect. Now what do you think about that?''

He hauled Cassie roughly into his arms, and with his knife, cut her bonds. While his men laughed and hooted, and Luella silently wept, he drew Cassie's head back sharply and covered her mouth with his.

Though he was forced to sit helplessly by and watch, Quin vowed that, with his last breath, he would see Cyrus Stoner pay dearly for this.

Chapter Twenty-One

With a sound of disgust, Cassie pushed free of Stoner's arms and stood rubbing the back of her hand across her mouth to erase the foul taste of him.

"Pour the whiskey," Cyrus shouted.

At once one of his men holstered his pistol and filled several tumblers from a decanter.

Cyrus accepted a glass, saying, "Help yourselves, boys."

When everyone had a glass, Cyrus lifted his aloft, saying, "Here's to my new fortune." He bowed grandly to Cassie. "By the time we finish with you, woman, you'll not only sign away your property, you'll beg to be put out of your misery."

He flashed a smug smile at his men. "From now on, I'll own the entire Montana Territory. Anyone who gets in my way will have to deal with the army I intend to form. And you boys will be my officers."

They let out a cheer before draining their glasses.

While they were distracted, Quin worked frantically at his bonds. The leather strips cut clear to the bone, and the pain was so severe he had to fight to remain conscious. Blood dripped from his wrists to pool on the floor, but still he struggled against his bonds.

Across the room, Luella watched him and knew, from the pain etched on his face, how desperately he was working to save them. Overcome with regret for all the unkind things she'd said to him, she moved her lips in silent prayer.

"Pour another round," Cyrus ordered.

The men relaxed, clearly relieved to be warm and snug and enjoying the friendship of this powerful man. Not one of them would trade places with the men riding shotgun on the far-flung boundaries of Stoner's empire on this bitterly cold night.

Cyrus knocked back a second drink, then turned to Cassie. "Come here, Miz Montgomery. Let's put on a show for your hero."

She stood her ground.

Quin studied her, head high, chin lifted in that haughty way he'd come to know, and felt a surge of pride. Even in defeat, she was magnificent.

"I said come here." Stoner's voice took on a dangerous tone.

Cassie refused to move.

Cyrus started across the room. "It's time you learned a lesson, Miz Montgomery. In this house—"

"Don't you touch her."

Everyone turned as the door was flung open. Becky and Jen stood framed in the doorway. Becky held Quin's rifle to her shoulder and took aim at Cyrus.

"I know you told us to go, Mr. McAllister." Becky's wavering voice revealed her nerves. "And we really tried to. But by the time we got to your horse, we both knew that we had to be here with Mama and Gram. I was sick and tired of being afraid all the time. Did we do right?"

"You did just fine," Quin said.

"Now Jen," Becky said to her little sister, who stood uncertainly beside her, "untie Mr. McAllister and Gram."

As the little girl darted across the room, Cyrus bellowed, "Are we going to be ordered around by a couple of kids?"

"She's got that rifle pointed straight at you," one of his men called.

"Yeah? Well, I say she's too scared to fire." Cyrus took a tentative step toward Becky.

"You stop right there," she cried. But though she tried to put up a brave front, she couldn't keep her hands from trembling.

Seeing it, Cyrus laughed. "I was right, boys. The kid is shaking in her boots."

He took several more steps. As he reached for the rifle, Quin, freed by Jen, leapt at Cyrus, knocking him to the floor.

Racing to her daughter's side, Cassie took the rifle from her trembling hands and aimed it at the circle of men.

"If any of you go for your guns, I'll be more than happy to shoot. And if you think, because we're outnumbered, we're easy prey, just remember this. At least some of you will die before you manage to kill all of us. I ask you, is Cyrus Stoner worth dying for?"

The men exchanged glances but remained motionless as their boss fought with Quin.

"Jennifer," Cassie said, "you may retrieve their guns."

The little girl scampered around collecting weapons, which she piled on Stoner's desk. Luella and Becky each shouldered a rifle and took up positions on either side of Cassie.

Quin and Cyrus, oblivious to everything except the fury that had been building, thrashed and rolled around the floor, exchanging blows.

"This is for Cassie," Quin said, sinking a fist in Stoner's midsection that had him doubling up.

Cyrus gasped, then pulled a knife from a sheath at his hip. In the firelight the blade glittered dangerously. "And this is for you, Reb."

The two men struggled and Quin, already wounded, could feel his strength ebbing. But the deep, simmering anger he felt renewed his determination. With his last ounce of willpower he wrestled the knife from Stoner's hand and gave him a blow that sent him sprawling.

Stumbling to his feet, Quin took several deep breaths, then glanced at Luella and Cassie, Becky and Jen, to reassure himself that they were all unharmed.

They looked up at the sound of approaching horses. Quin grabbed up his pistol and raced to the window.

Cyrus, looking supremely pleased with himself, listened to the sound of booted feet marching along the hallway and said, "You don't really believe you can hold off the rest of my men, do you, McAllister?"

Before Quin could respond, Stoner's voice thickened with anger. He dragged himself to his feet, holding firmly to the back of a chair for support. Indicating the document on his desk, he thundered, "Now, Miz Montgomery, this game is over. Your guns will be meaningless against all of ours. Sign away that property, or prepare to die."

The door was thrown open and Cyrus turned toward it with a triumphant smile. His smile faded when he caught sight of Sheriff Clayton Wilson, pistol in hand.

For a moment Cyrus looked puzzled. Then, finding his voice, he said in his most indignant tone, "Sheriff.

I'm glad to see you're looking out for me. This man attacked me in my own home."

"Then you'll want him arrested." The sheriff remained where he was.

"That won't be necessary. As you know, he's nothing but a two-bit gambler and drifter who insinuated himself into Miz Montgomery's life like an unwelcome pestilence. My men and I will look out for the lady and her family and see that he doesn't bother any of us anymore."

Sheriff Wilson peered at Cassie and the others, who held rifles in their hands. "Looks to me like these folks can look out for themselves."

He held out his hand to Cassie, who gripped her weapon so tightly her knuckles were white from the effort. "Would you care to hand over that rifle, ma'am?"

"No, Sheriff." She kept her eyes firmly on Cyrus while she spoke. "This man killed half a dozen Crow warriors and forced my family and me to accompany him to this place. We are here against our will."

"Now why would he do a thing like that, ma'am?" The sheriff flicked a glance at Luella and the children, then back to Cassie.

"Because he wants me to sign over my rights to my property."

"Are you trying to tell me that a wealthy man like Cyrus Stoner would go to all this trouble just to steal your property, Mrs. Montgomery?"

"Yes, Sheriff."

"Why?"

"Because we found a treasure."

"That so?" The sheriff's lips curved. "A treasure, you say. Gold?"

"No, sir. Silver."

The lawman arched a brow in surprise. "Silver? So that's what this is all about." He turned to Cyrus. "If what the lady tells me is true, it looks like I'm going to have to take you back to Prospect, Mr. Stoner."

"What are you saying?" Outraged, Stoner drew himself up to his full height. "Are you going to take the word of this woman over me? Have you forgotten who hired you?"

"No, sir. I sure haven't. And I was hoping, when I rode over here, that you'd have a logical explanation for all those dead bodies over at Mrs. Montgomery's cabin."

"You've been there?" Cassie asked.

"Jedediah brought me." He nodded toward the hallway with a sheepish smile. Jedediah poked his head around the doorway.

"I dropped by to bring the children some rock candy for Christmas," the grizzled old man said, "and discovered what looked like a bloody massacre. So I rode back to town to fetch the sheriff."

"But what brought you here to Stoner's?" Quin asked.

Jedediah shrugged, and behind those lively eyes, Quin could see just how much the old man had already figured out.

The sheriff answered. "Jedediah suggested that Mr. Stoner, being the closest neighbor, might know something about all this." His smile faded and his features hardened. He turned to Cyrus. "You and your men are under arrest, Mr. Stoner, for the murder of six Crow warriors, and for the abduction of these good people." He glanced over at Quin. "Would you mind giving Jedediah and me a hand with these men?"

"I'd be happy to." Quin picked up the bloodstained leather strips that had been cut away from his own wrists and tied them around Stoner's. Though he still seethed with anger, it helped to know that justice would be the sweetest revenge of all.

"Are you folks going to be all right now?" Sheriff Wilson asked.

Cassie gathered her mother and children close, and let out a long, steadying breath. "We're going to be just fine, Sheriff. Thank you."

Quin awoke with a start and glanced around. He was lying in the familiar nest of furs in the corner of the cabin. A fire blazed in the fireplace. Coffee bubbled, meat sizzled, biscuits gave off their wonderful fragrance.

Cassie and her mother barely looked up when Becky and Jen returned from the barn with a pail of milk and several eggs. They were busy preparing a breakfast fit for a celebration.

"Good morning, Mr. McAllister," Jen called out. "You'd better get up or you'll miss breakfast."

Moving slowly, stiffly, Quin pulled on his boots, then walked to the basin and washed. Cassie stared at his broad shoulders, his muscled back, with an affectionate smile.

Lifting his shirt from a peg by the door, he worked his arms into the sleeves. He glanced down at his wrists. Cassie had insisted on bandaging them before going off to her bed the night before. She had kissed him, a slow, leisurely kiss that had kindled a fire in his loins and had him wishing he had the strength to carry her off to the mine for another night of loving. Instead, he'd done nothing to hold her back when she walked away to her bedroom.

That was when he'd realized that he had some serious thinking to do. He'd stayed up half the night mulling things over in his mind. But before sleep overtook him, he'd come to a decision.

Luella filled a cup with coffee and handed it to him. "Good morning, Mr. McAllister. You'd better drink this. You look like you could use it."

"That bad?"

"I've seen you look better."

He drank deeply, then finished dressing and made his way to the barn.

Outside, a fresh snowfall obliterated all sign of the earlier carnage. The Crow had retrieved their dead and had been assured that their murderers would taste swift justice. The tribe, known for their love of the plains, had retreated to the mountains, where they would spend the rest of the winter seeking solace from their grief.

In the barn, Quin mucked the stalls, grateful for the release of such simple tasks. Now that the threat from Cyrus Stoner had been removed, he was forced to deal with an unpleasant fact.

His job here was over.

Cassie and her family were wealthy beyond their wildest dreams. With their fortune, they would no longer have to live out here in this wilderness. They could afford to hire a foreman and crew. That would free them to move to Prospect, or even to return to Atlanta if they chose. Hell, he thought with a frown, if the assayer's report was correct, they could afford to live any life-style they wanted, in any setting.

The barn door was thrown open on a swirl of snowflakes, and Jen rushed in. "Gram said—" Her glance took in Cutter, who was already saddled. The saddle-bags were packed, Quin's bedroll tied behind the saddle.

The little girl blanched. "What are you doing, Mr. McAllister? It looks like you're getting ready to leave us."

"That's right, Jen." Avoiding her eyes, Quin lifted Cutter's leg and examined the knee. The swelling was completely gone. The horse could easily handle a long journey. "I figured it was time I was on my way."

"But where will you go?"

"I haven't really thought about it. California, I guess."

"San Francisco?" Jen twisted her tongue around the big word.

"Maybe." Funny, Quin thought. There was a time when the very word fueled his imagination, conjuring images of high-stakes games that went on for days. Now all he could think of were the snow-covered miles that would separate him from this family, from this small cabin. He looked up. "You started to tell me something about your grandmother."

"Gram said to come and eat." The little girl's tone was flat.

Quin left Cutter in the barn and followed Jen to the cabin. Inside, he washed his hands and took a seat at the table.

"Mr. McAllister is leaving," Jen announced.

Everyone glanced up. At Cassie's surprised look, Quin ducked his head and busied himself buttering a biscuit.

"Why?" Cassie asked. The shock, the pain, were evident in that one word.

"You don't need me now, ma'am." The words were like ashes in his mouth. "It's time I was moving on."

"I see." Cassie's tone grew crisp to cover the ache. "We've stood in your way too long. You must miss the excitement of the life you left behind."

"I suppose there will still be plenty of poker games to be won," Luella remarked.

"I suppose." Quin found he wasn't hungry. Shoving aside his plate, he drained his cup. The coffee tasted bitter.

He glanced around the table. "Why all the sad faces? Don't you realize yet that you have everything you dreamed of? You're rich, you're free of Cyrus Stoner's threats, and you can leave this isolation and live among people again."

Nobody said a word.

He shoved back his chair and got to his feet. No sense dragging out his goodbyes. Besides, if he hung around too long, he might be persuaded to change his mind.

Walking to the door, he removed his duster from a peg and shrugged into it. From his pocket he removed a ragged, leather-bound book and handed it to Becky. "I think you'll enjoy Mr. Shakespeare's poetry. The words have a way of touching the heart."

"But I can't take it. You said it was special," she protested.

"It was my father's. That's why I want you to have it, Becky."

He withdrew a deck of cards and held them out to Jen. "These are for you. Don't forget to practice your card tricks."

The little girl refused to accept them. Placing them on the table, Quin turned away from her sad, accusing eyes.

"I'll say goodbye now, ma'am." Quin offered his hand to Luella, then to Cassie. As their fingers brushed, he steeled himself. When the jolt came, he showed no reaction.

"Goodbye, Quin." She would not cry, she told herself. She had always known that someday he would leave. Hadn't he warned them right from the start that he was a gambler, a drifter?

At least, for one special night, they had shared something truly wonderful. She would have to be content with that, and not selfishly hold him here when he yearned to be free. But the thought of all the lonely nights that stretched out before her had her lips quivering. To hide it, she bit the inside of her mouth until she tasted blood.

Luella wrapped meat and biscuits in a linen towel. "You'll need sustenance along the trail, Mr. McAllister." As he went to take it from her hands, she said, "I'll walk with you to the barn."

"Yes, ma'am." He pulled his wide-brimmed hat from a peg and held the door. Luella walked outside ahead of him. He gave a last look at Cassie and the children, then turned and walked out the door.

He and Luella strode in silence to the barn. Once inside, she handed him the parcel. While he stored it in his saddlebag, she said sternly, "I was wrong about you, Mr. McAllister. I once accused you of being a no-good drifter and gambler. I thought you to be a careless man. Careless with responsibility. Careless with other people's feelings." Her voice lowered with emotion. "I know why you are leaving, Mr. McAllister."

He looked up. "Ma'am?"

"You don't fool me. You are leaving because you think somehow this is best for my daughter."

When he said nothing in his own defense, she added, "But you are wrong to think that."

He secured the saddlebag, then looked up to meet her eyes. "No, ma'am. For once in my life I'm going to do something right. You once warned me that Cassie might confuse gratitude with love. And that's exactly what's happened. The best thing I can do is leave, so she can get on with her life."

"Oh, Mr. McAllister." Luella felt the sting of tears and turned away, embarrassed. "I feared you would break my daughter's heart, and you will, if you leave her now."

"You don't understand." He lowered a hand to her sleeve. His voice softened. "A long time ago I fell in love with my best friend's wife. And when I got his letter asking me to come here, I didn't hesitate. Do you know why? I wanted to see this wonderful, beautiful, paragon of virtue he had described to me in such glowing detail. Maybe I thought she wouldn't live up to all his claims. Or maybe I hoped she would."

"Did she?"

"Cassie was all that Ethan had said, and more. But you must see that there was nothing noble about my intentions. My motive was purely selfish. In fact, in my whole life, this is the first time my intentions have ever been noble. So, please, don't deny me this one chance to to something right. Your daughter, and her family, will be much better off without me. And when she puts her life together there will be all kinds of well-bred gentlemen vying for her attention."

Luella watched as he led his horse toward the door of the barn. Catching up with him, she whispered, "You are far too hard on yourself, Mr. McAllister. I do not know what you see when you look in your heart, but when I look at you I see a fine, noble man who changed our lives. I pray God will go with you on your journey.''

''Thank you, ma'am.'' He tipped his hat to her, then opened the barn door and pulled himself into the saddle.

Cassie and the children had gathered in the doorway. Seeing them, he felt a knife turn in his heart. He reined in his mount and took a last, lingering look at matching fiery hair, freckles and identical looks of concern in green eyes. The longing was so swift, so deep, he was stunned by it. If he had played his cards right, they could have all been his. His wife. His children.

He saluted them and rode smartly away.

Chapter Twenty-Two

The railway car was so lavishly appointed, Quin could almost convince himself that he was in the finest drawing room in San Francisco. The walls were wood paneled, the draperies lush red velvet. A poker table had been set up in the middle of the room, with chairs for six players. On a side table was a box of the finest Cuban cigars. A white-gloved waiter poured whiskey into a crystal tumbler and handed it to Quin. One taste proved it to be as smooth as silk.

"It doesn't get better than this," said the portly gentleman who stood beside him. "I've won and lost millions in my day. I've played in smoky saloons that reeked of stale whiskey and unwashed bodies. I've played in gentlemen's clubs in New York and Paris. But this..." He spread his hands to indicate their sumptuous surroundings. "This is how the game should be played." He took another long drink, then added, "The game, McAllister. It's always the game. That's what keeps men like us from getting trapped in dreary lives like ordinary people."

Men like us. Quin experienced a pain around his heart, remembering Luella's taunt. *A man like you.*

He finished his drink, then followed the others to the table. The cards were shuffled and dealt. A strikingly

beautiful young woman dressed in a red satin gown
from Paris, a mane of golden hair piled high on her
head, paused beside Quin and placed one soft hand on
his shoulder. Her French perfume was sweet, cloying.
He reached for a cigar and she struck a match and held
it to the tip, revealing perfectly manicured nails. She
retired to a gilt chair positioned a little to one side.

The men played in silence. Cards were tossed aside,
others dealt. The losers sat back, drinks in hand, to
witness the final outcome of the high-stakes game that
had been going on for more than twenty hours. It
seemed anticlimactic when Quin finally won. There
were hearty words of congratulations. A few slaps on
the back. The money was counted, a check issued. One
by one the players drifted away, back to their beautifully appointed sleeping cars, until only Quin remained.

The woman lingered, hoping the winner would take
notice of her. When he did, he sent her away with a dis-
missive wave of his hand.

The waiter refilled his glass, then took up a position beside the bar, yawning discreetly behind his gloved
hand.

Outside the railway car, the land was steeped in
darkness. The winter snow had melted. Except for an
occasional mountain peak or glassy body of water re-
flecting the stars there were no familiar landmarks.

Where had Cassie finally settled since he had left her
four months ago? he wondered. How was she doing?
She would wear her wealth, her success with quiet grace
and dignity. He tried to imagine her in an elegant gown,
gliding down a curving staircase, her every wish ful-
filled by a staff of well-trained servants. But the only
image that came to mind, the only one that ever came
to mind, was the way she had looked when she had

stepped out of her bedroom wearing his Christmas gift.
Cheeks flushed. Hands touching her hair nervously.
Lips curved in delight. Eyes alight with pleasure.

God, he was driving himself mad with the memo-
ries.

Whiskey sloshed over the rim of his glass and the
waiter was there at once, mopping the spill, seeing that
the glass was refilled.

"Sorry," Quin muttered. "I didn't realize you were
still here. Please, go to bed."

"No, sir. I don't mind, sir. I'll just stay here until—"

Quin turned on his heel and stalked away.

In the morning, when the train pulled into the station, a uniformed porter knocked on the door of Quin's
sleeping car. Along with his coffee, the porter delivered an envelope. Quin tore it open and read. His head
came up sharply.

"I have a horse on the last car of this train." He unfolded several bills and handed them to the man. "See
that he's saddled and ready."

"Yes, sir."

The coffee was forgotten in his haste to dress. By the
time the train pulled away from the station, Quin was
seated astride Cutter. From his position alongside the
tracks he watched as the gilded cars chugged past. Then
he and his horse blended into the line of trees, away
from the town, away from the lure of fast money. Away
from civilization. They were soon swallowed up in the
vast wilderness.

"How long will you be up at the mine?" Luella
asked.

She and Cassie were seated in Florence Claxton's
dining room, lingering over a last cup of coffee.

"Just overnight."

Cassie looked up as Jen and Oren raced down the stairs and snatched up their lunch baskets. Biscuit, who already stood as tall as the children, loped happily behind them. He was Jen's constant companion, even trailing her to school, and dozing in the schoolyard until she was ready to return home.

"Jennifer, you will mind your grandmother while I'm away."

"Yes, ma'am. I wish I could go with you."

"Another time. When school lets out. I promise we'll spend a whole week up at the old cabin this summer."

"Can Oren come, too?"

"I don't see why not, as long as his mother approves."

Jen gave her mother a quick kiss, then started toward the door after her friend. On a sudden impulse she retraced her steps and stopped beside her mother. In a solemn voice she said, "You won't have to be sad anymore, Mama."

Cassie stared at her little daughter in confusion.

"Pa talked to me last night," Jen said in that matter-of-fact tone they all recognized. "And said he was going to send Mr. McAllister back to us."

She gave her mother another quick kiss, then ran out the door, with Biscuit at her heels.

"I'm worried about that child," Luella muttered. "I intend to speak to Matthew about her."

"Ma—"

Becky entered the room, holding a fat envelope. "Gram, I wonder if you'd read this and tell me if it's good enough."

"Good enough for what?"

Becky stared at the toe of her shoe. "Good enough to get me into the Miss Atherton's Conservatory of Music."

Luella and Cassie exchanged looks.

"But I thought you had rejected the idea of going back to the South."

"I've said a lot of things. Mr. McAllister once told me that at my age his mouth used to work faster than his brain." Becky fiddled with her sash. "It's true that Savannah is a long way from here. But, like Mama pointed out to me, there are riverboats and stagecoaches. And soon, I think, the railroad will have to come to Montana."

"Didn't I hear you say you wanted to live in the fine, big house your mother is having built here in Prospect?"

"I do look forward to living in it. I still have a year before I would leave for the conservatory."

"What about Zack? You said you would never leave him."

At the mention of Zack's name, Becky smiled. "He is special. And he has said he'll wait for me. But this is something I need to do for myself. I think my music will become an important part of my life. I think I'd like to teach music here in Prospect."

"And when did you come to these momentous conclusions?" Luella asked with a gentle smile.

"I guess I've learned a few things from other people. Mr. McAllister said people have to be able to take risks for the things they believe in. And watching Mama, I realize that life must go on." She glanced shyly at her mother. "I'm proud of you, Mama, for taking charge of the mine, and hiring the men you'll need to run it. And for—" she looked away, suddenly embarrassed, but unable to stop the flow of words "—not giving up just because Mr. McAllister went away."

Blushing furiously, she kissed her mother's cheek, then her grandmother's. As she snatched up her lunch basket and slate, she called, "I wrote three pages, explaining to the director of the conservatory why I should be considered for enrollment. Gram, I'd like you to read it and tell me if you think it's good enough."

She was out the door in a rustle of petticoats.

"Three pages," Luella breathed. "I'm so proud of her." She closed a hand over Cassie's. "I'm proud of you, too, girl. I know it hasn't been easy."

"I had a good teacher, Ma."

The two women stared at each other in silence. They both looked up as the front door opened. Reverend Townsend hurried in, shaking snow from his hat.

At the sight of Luella, his face creased with smiles. "Here you are." He greeted her with a kiss to the cheek, and another kiss for Cassie. "I was hoping you could spare an hour or so to come to the church with me, Luella. I'd like you to hear the sermon I've prepared for Sunday's service and choose some hymns that are appropriate for it."

"I'd love to, Matthew. As long as we can be back by noon. I promised Florence that I'd help bake pies for supper tonight."

"Apple, I hope. They're my favorite. After lunch I'd like you to ride over to the new parsonage with me and see what you want done with the front parlor."

"I was thinking, Matthew. Even though it will be a public room, where you will counsel those who come to you, I also think it should reflect a cozy, comfortable feeling, so that those in need can relax and find solace. There are so many young people cut adrift since the war, frightened, lonely, in need of a loving, forgiving father...."

With a knowing smile, Cassie headed for the stairs, determined to give her mother and Matthew some privacy. "Jedediah will be along with the wagon," she called. "Tell him I'll be right down."

Even before she was gone, Matthew framed Luella's face between his hands and murmured, "God has truly blessed me. I count the days until we are wed."

She closed her hands over his. "Thank you for agreeing to wait until Cassie's house is completed. With the extra burden of both the mine and the new house, I couldn't desert her."

"I understand. And I agree. But soon, love, soon, we'll be husband and wife." He drew her close and kissed her.

Cassie took the stairs hurriedly, ashamed that she'd overheard. When she reached the bedroom she heard her mother's voice, alerting her to the approaching wagon. Minutes later, she handed a carpetbag to Jedediah, then climbed up onto the seat beside him. With a wave to her mother and Reverend Townsend, she was gone.

The mine bustled with activity. The area now resembled a small town, with dirt trails ringing the area, and wagon loads of ore and supplies sending up clouds of dust. Several large bunkhouses had been built to accommodate the workers. From a separate office, a mine foreman, hired from Virginia City, worked with three apprentices, one of whom was Zack Claxton. Several outbuildings stored explosives, tools and equipment.

A new mine shaft had been drilled directly over the cavern where the first vein of silver had been discovered, allowing easier access. Several new tunnels had been dug, revealing more veins of silver. The mine, which Cassie had named Speculation, contained the richest store of silver found in Montana.

After meeting with the foreman and his assistants, and going over the details of yet another mine shaft being planned, Cassie and Jedediah climbed into the wagon and drove to the cabin.

Smoke poured from the chimney and she knew that Zack had dispatched one of the workers to lay a fire in preparation for her arrival.

At the front door, the wagon came to a halt and Jedediah helped Cassie down, then carried her tapestry bag inside.

The cabin looked much the way it had when she and her family had lived here, blackened coffeepot on the warming ledge beside the fire, rocker and bench positioned in front of the fireplace, rough-hewn chairs placed around a battered kitchen table.

"I'll leave your bag here, Miss Cassie."

"Thank you, Jedediah."

He saw the way her gaze was drawn to the corner of the room. Turning in that direction, he strained but could see nothing. Clearing his throat, he said, "I'll be back for you tomorrow morning."

She nodded absently.

When he was gone, she forced herself into action, carrying her bag into her old bedroom, removing the faded quilt that served as a dustcover over her bed.

In the kitchen she made a pot of coffee and rolled biscuit dough. While stew bubbled in a kettle, she drew the rocker close to the fire and sat.

Becky's announcement at breakfast had been a pleasant surprise. Cassie felt a rush of gratitude that the once haunted, unhappy girl had been restored to an eager, hopeful young woman. She was grateful, too, that

Jen seemed to be blossoming in town, surrounded by friends, and that Luella's future happiness was assured.

She continued to rock, watching as late afternoon sunlight turned to evening shadows. The sounds of men and equipment began to fade as work slowed, then ended, and the men returned to their bunkhouse for supper. A strange feeling of peace descended upon her.

Strange, she thought, that this little cabin should become her refuge. It had felt like a prison until Quin had come into her life, setting her free. Free. She pondered the word. When she had been a girl, she had wanted, more than anything, the freedom to choose her own path, live her own life. It was not to be. Choices had been made for her that would forever alter the course of her life. Yet, as an adult, she had freely chosen to give her heart to a man. She had known, of course, that no promises were exchanged. She had gone into his arms with eyes open, asking for nothing more than a night of love. Still, his choice of freedom had left a void in her life that no one else would ever fill.

Her thoughts drifted to Jennifer. She was concerned that the child was becoming too fanciful. She'd hoped, with time, the little girl's conversations with her dead father would cease. And yet, how could she tell that sweet child to stop believing, when she had so many doubts of her own? So often since his death, she had felt Ethan's presence in her life, urging her to take courage and go on with her life. Even when she had given her heart to another, she had sensed somehow that Ethan understood and approved.

At the sound of an approaching horse, she roused herself from her musings and got to her feet. Though the men from the mine watched over her from a distance, they rarely intruded on her privacy here at the cabin, knowing how jealously she guarded it.

Through a crack in the door, she watched the shadowed figure of a horse and rider draw near. For a moment her heart forgot to beat, as she recalled another, wearing a wide-brimmed hat and a snow-covered duster. Then, scolding herself for becoming as imaginative as her daughter, she caught hold of her rifle and opened the door.

Light from the fireplace spilled into the darkness, illuminating the woman who stood in the doorway. For the space of several heartbeats Quin remained motionless, drinking in the vision. During the long ride here, he had feared the worst. For the first time since he'd left the train, he found himself relaxing. Then, reminding himself of the reason for this visit, he found his voice.

"Hello, Cassie. You look fine."

She lifted her chin a fraction. Even while her heart was doing somersaults, she was determined to be as calm, as cool as he. "Thank you. So do you, Quin."

He slid from the saddle. "I didn't really expect to find you here. I figured by now you'd have used your fortune to build your family a fine, big house somewhere far from here."

"Then why are you here?"

He took a step closer. "I had nowhere else to begin looking for you."

Up close he seemed taller, and if possible, even more handsome. Despite the fact that he needed a shave and his eyes were shadowed with fatigue, he still had the power to make her heart behave erratically.

"Why are you looking for me?"

"To help you with this latest trouble you've gotten yourself into."

She looked at him blankly. "Trouble?" When she stared into his eyes, the hand holding the rifle trembled violently.

Seeing it, he misunderstood. "Better get in out of this air, before you freeze to death."

When he reached out a hand, she turned away to avoid his touch. She placed the rifle beside the door, then strode to the fireplace, clutching her hands together tightly.

Quin remained just inside the door, staring around the little cabin. It pleased him to see that it was exactly as he'd remembered it. All the way here, he been afraid that nothing would be the same.

For several seconds Cassie watched him. Then, gathering her courage, she said, "I think you'd better explain yourself. Just why are you here?"

Quin reached into his breast pocket and retrieved an envelope. "I came because of the letter telling me that you were in trouble."

Her voice frosted over. "How could I possible write to you? If you'll recall, you left no forwarding address."

He heard the pain beneath the haughty words and winced. He deserved her contempt. But it was nothing compared with the contempt he felt for himself. Since the brief time he'd spent with her and her family, he realized just how useless his life was, and how empty his future.

His voice was gruff. "I don't know who wrote it. Frankly, I never even questioned it. When I heard that you were in trouble, I had to come."

"How very noble of you." She held out her hand. "I'm sure you won't mind if I see it?"

He crossed the room and handed it over. When their fingers brushed, they both felt the flare of heat, though both denied it.

As soon as Cassie began to read, her eyes filled with hot, furious tears. "How could you? Oh, how could you do such a cruel thing? I would have expected better of you."

Now it was Quin's turn to be puzzled. "What do you mean, Cassie? What are you talking about?"

"This letter." She clutched it in her fist, which she shook in his face. "I knew you did card tricks, Mr. McAllister, but I never expected something this foul, this hurtful."

His confusion turned to anger. Catching her hand to still it, he muttered, "I still don't know what you're talking about."

"This is Ethan's handwriting." The tears fell, not just from shock and pain, but also in frustration over the fact that, even now, with her heart breaking, this man had the power to arouse her with a simple touch. "Somehow, you have managed to copy his writing and pretend that this letter came from him."

His eyes narrowed, then widened in sudden comprehension. "Ethan's handwriting? Are you sure? Are you quite sure?"

She could read the shock, the look of horror, in his expression as he suddenly released her and took a step back, as though he'd been struck. This sort of stunned reaction was not something he could feign.

She took a long, deep breath. "Explain yourself, Mr. McAllister."

He shook his head. "I...can't explain. Until you said that, it never occurred to me to notice that the handwriting on this letter was the same as the first one I'd received. In both cases I was curious to know how these letters found me, when I had no permanent address. But the urgency of the situation kept me from questioning further, until now."

"Now?" She stood very still, watching his eyes.

"Now that you have confirmed that it is written in Ethan's hand, I am forced to believe what Jen told me. Her father is with the angels. And he continues to look out for those he loves."

"What are you saying?" Her heart had begun to beat wildly. And yet, at the same time, she felt strangely at peace. "Do you really believe that Ethan...?" She licked her lips and tried again. "That even from beyond the grave, he is working to bring us together?"

"I don't know what I believe anymore. I only know this." He struggled to keep from touching her, but the need was too great. Lifting a hand to her face, his fingertips grazed her cheek. He stared into her eyes and felt his throat go dry. "You are the very best thing that has ever happened in my life, Cassie. I tried to stay away, because I believed that I was the worst thing in yours."

"Oh, Quin." She blinked her eyes against the pain and allowed the tears to spill unchecked. "How could you think such a thing? Don't you understand what you did for us? Couldn't you see what a difference you made in all our lives?"

Her words seemed to melt the ice that had formed around his heart since the day he'd left this little cabin. Warmth flooded his veins. Love filled him, until the blood pounded in his temples and his body throbbed with need.

He took her face in his big hands and stared deeply into her eyes. "I have nothing to offer you, except my undying love. But know this. I love you, Cassie. I have loved you for so long."

His lips sought hers. And as the kiss deepened, she brought her arms around his neck.

"I love you, too, Quin. But this time, I want more. I want marriage, I want vows, I want my children to have a father."

"It's what I want, too. It's what I've always wanted. But until now, I never felt worthy of such a gift. Oh, God, Cassie. I can't believe you forgive me, and love me. I want to be with you and the girls forever." He kissed away her tears, then covered her mouth with his. Against her lips he whispered, "My life has been so empty, so lonely, so—"

"Stop talking," she said with a sigh, "and show me." On a moan he scooped her up and carried her to her bed.

The letter slipped from Cassie's nerveless fingers and dropped to the floor. Outside, the wind picked up and a breeze, stirring through the crack in the door, caught and lifted the slip of paper, carrying it into the fire. Despite the intense heat, it neither curled nor burned. As the flames grew hotter and leapt higher, it suddenly disappeared, leaving behind nothing but fine white ash.

In a little schoolhouse in Prospect, six-year-old Jennifer Montgomery was dreaming of summer, when she and her mother would go back to the little cabin in the plains. In her mind's eye Quin was there, too. She glanced out the window and caught sight of a strange golden-tipped cloud. For some reason it reminded her of her father's face. She smiled, remembering what Quin had once told her. Though her memory of her pa might fade in time, she would never forget his love. It was etched forever in her heart.

*   *   *   *   *

COMING NEXT MONTH

#247 DESIRE MY LOVE—Miranda Jarrett
In the continuation of the Sparhawk series, Desire Sparhawk enlists
Captain John Herendon to rescue her brother, but finds the captain's
motivation far different from her own.

#248 VOWS—Margaret Moore
The seventh book in the Weddings, Inc. promotion, *Vows* is the story
behind the legend of Eternity, Massachusetts, the town where love lasts
forever.

#249 BETRAYED—Judith McWilliams
Coerced into spying on her British relatives, American heiress Eleanor
Wallace finds herself in a trap that could cost her the man she loves.

#250 ROARKE'S FOLLY—Claire Delacroix
When obligations force a landless knight to become a weaver's
apprentice, he discovers he has an affinity for trade, as well as for the
man's fiery daughter.

AVAILABLE NOW:

#243 FIRE AND SWORD
Theresa Michaels

#245 ANGEL
Ruth Langan

#244 THE TEMPTING OF JULIA
Maura Seger

#246 TAPESTRY OF FATE
Nina Beaumont

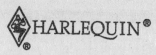

VOWS
Margaret Moore

Legend has it that couples who marry in the Eternity chapel are destined for happiness. Yet the couple who started it all almost never made it to the altar!

It all began in Eternity, Massachusetts, 1855.... Bronwyn Davies started life afresh in America and found refuge with William Powell. But beneath William's respectability was a secret that, once uncovered, could keep Bronwyn bound to him forever.

Don't miss **VOWS**, the exciting prequel to Harlequin's cross-line series, **WEDDINGS, INC.,** available in December from Harlequin Historicals. And look for the next **WEDDINGS, INC.** book, *Bronwyn's Story,* by Marisa Carroll (Harlequin Superromance #635), coming in March 1995.

If you are looking for more titles by

RUTH LANGAN

Don't miss these fabulous stories by one of
Harlequin's great authors:

Harlequin Historical®

#28796	DECEPTION	$3.99	☐
#28828	THE HIGHLANDER	$3.99 U.S.	☐
		$4.50 CAN.	☐

(limited quantities available on certain titles)

TOTAL AMOUNT	$
POSTAGE & HANDLING	$
($1.00 for one book, 50¢ for each additional)	
APPLICABLE TAXES*	$_____
TOTAL PAYABLE	$_____
(check or money order—please do not send cash)	

To order, complete this form and send it, along with a check or money order
for the total above, payable to Harlequin Books, to: **In the U.S.:** 3010 Walden
Avenue, P.O. Box 9047, Buffalo, NY 14269-9047; **In Canada:** P.O. Box 613,
Fort Erie, Ontario, L2A 5X3.

Name: _____

Address: _____ City: _____

State/Prov.: _____ Zip/Postal Code: _____

*New York residents remit applicable sales taxes.   HRLBACK2
 Canadian residents remit applicable GST and provincial taxes.

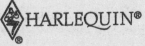

HARLEQUIN®

"HOORAY FOR HOLLYWOOD" SWEEPSTAKES

HERE'S HOW THE SWEEPSTAKES WORKS

OFFICIAL RULES — NO PURCHASE NECESSARY

To enter, complete an Official Entry Form or hand print on a 3" x 5" card the words "HOORAY FOR HOLLYWOOD", your name and address and mail your entry in the pre-addressed envelope (if provided) or to: "Hooray for Hollywood" Sweepstakes, P.O. Box 9076, Buffalo, NY 14269-9076 or "Hooray for Hollywood" Sweepstakes, P.O. Box 637, Fort Erie, Ontario L2A 5X3. Entries must be sent via First Class Mail and be received no later than 12/31/94. No liability is assumed for lost, late or misdirected mail.

Winners will be selected in random drawings to be conducted no later than January 31, 1995 from all eligible entries received.

Grand Prize: A 7-day/6-night trip for 2 to Los Angeles, CA including round trip air transportation from commercial airport nearest winner's residence, accommodations at the Regent Beverly Wilshire Hotel, free rental car, and $1,000 spending money. (Approximate prize value which will vary dependent upon winner's residence: $5,400.00 U.S.); 500 Second Prizes: A pair of "Hollywood Star" sunglasses (prize value: $9.95 U.S. each). Winner selection is under the supervision of D.L. Blair, Inc., an independent judging organization, whose decisions are final. Grand Prize travelers must sign and return a release of liability prior to traveling. Trip must be taken by 2/1/96 and is subject to airline schedules and accommodations availability.

Sweepstakes offer is open to residents of the U.S. (except Puerto Rico) and Canada who are 18 years of age or older, except employees and immediate family members of Harlequin Enterprises, Ltd., its affiliates, subsidiaries, and all agencies, entities or persons connected with the use, marketing or conduct of this sweepstakes. All federal, state, provincial, municipal and local laws apply. Offer void wherever prohibited by law. Taxes and/or duties are the sole responsibility of the winners. Any litigation within the province of Quebec respecting the conduct and awarding of prizes may be submitted to the Regie des loteries et courses du Quebec. All prizes will be awarded; winners will be notified by mail. No substitution of prizes are permitted. Odds of winning are dependent upon the number of eligible entries received.

Potential grand prize winner must sign and return an Affidavit of Eligibility within 30 days of notification. In the event of non-compliance within this time period, prize may be awarded to an alternate winner. Prize notification returned as undeliverable may result in the awarding of prize to an alternate winner. By acceptance of their prize, winners consent to use of their names, photographs, or likenesses for purpose of advertising, trade and promotion on behalf of Harlequin Enterprises, Ltd., without further compensation unless prohibited by law. A Canadian winner must correctly answer an arithmetical skill-testing question in order to be awarded the prize.

For a list of winners (available after 2/28/95), send a separate stamped, self-addressed envelope to: Hooray for Hollywood Sweepstakes 3252 Winners, P.O. Box 4200, Blair, NE 68009.

CBSRLS

OFFICIAL ENTRY COUPON

"Hooray for Hollywood"
SWEEPSTAKES!

Yes, I'd love to win the Grand Prize — a vacation in Hollywood — or one of 500 pairs of "sunglasses of the stars"! Please enter me in the sweepstakes!

This entry must be received by December 31, 1994.
Winners will be notified by January 31, 1995.

Name _____

Address _____ Apt. _____

City _____

State/Prov. _____ Zip/Postal Code _____

Daytime phone number _____
                              (area code)

Account # _____

Return entries with invoice in envelope provided. Each book in this shipment has two entry coupons — and the more coupons you enter, the better your chances of winning!

DIRCBS

- -

OFFICIAL ENTRY COUPON

"Hooray for Hollywood"
SWEEPSTAKES!

Yes, I'd love to win the Grand Prize — a vacation in Hollywood — or one of 500 pairs of "sunglasses of the stars"! Please enter me in the sweepstakes!

This entry must be received by December 31, 1994.
Winners will be notified by January 31, 1995.

Name _____

Address _____ Apt. _____

City _____

State/Prov. _____ Zip/Postal Code _____

Daytime phone number _____
                              (area code)

Account # _____

Return entries with invoice in envelope provided. Each book in this shipment has two entry coupons — and the more coupons you enter, the better your chances of winning!

DIRCBS